REMEMBER Texas

LAURA CONNER KESTNER

Printed in the United States of America

First Printing, 2018

ISBN 978-1-7327562-0-5

Sycamore House Publishing
P.O. Box 344
De Leon, Texas 76444
www.lauraconnerkestner.com

ACKNOWLEDGMENTS

Thank you to Mary Yantis, Coby Sauce, Jordan Atkins, Audrey Gibson, Emily Atkins, Sue Keith, Rachel Spencer, Bob and Kathy Tarpley, Madalene Spencer, Katie Keith, Kathy and David Prickett, Charlotte Jacks, Bette House, Anna Horton and Tina Conner for reading my work and offering feedback. Your prayers, support and encouragement meant more than you will ever know.

Thank you to Burt Atkins, my pastor and son-in-law, for answering my questions on everything from scripture to horses, from Gunsmoke to Andy Griffith, to the water level in the baptistery.

Thank you to Jay Sauce, my son-in-law, computer expert and all-around nice guy who patiently answers each and every one of my tech-related questions.

I also appreciate the advice and encouragement I've received from my Mentor Sisters Writing Group, the RWA GOLDEN HEART® Rebelles and Persisters, and the ladies of Seekerville.

A huge thank you to Karen Wright, editor extraordinaire, for her friendship, support, encouragement and unparalleled ability with a red pen. Any grammatical or punctuation errors you discover inside are my own (in other words, I dug in my heels on a few things) and do not reflect Karen's expertise.

Finally, my deepest appreciation to author Tina Radcliffe for reaching out to beginning fiction writers with support and encouragement, for sharing information, advice, constructive criticism and even a kick in the seat of the pants as needed. I'm especially grateful that she encourages new writers to enter contests and join writing organizations—both of which played a huge part in the completion of this book. Thank you, Tina, for everything.

*For my husband John Kestner, who always
believed in my dream, even when I didn't.*

*For our children and grandchildren: Jordie and Burt, Coby
and Jay, Audrey and Ryan, Emily, Cole, Mallie and Charlie.*

*For my friends, coworkers and extended family who
listened patiently as I babbled on about imaginary people
and places, for years. Your love, support, prayers and
genuine interest in my work made this journey easier.*

*And for all the preachers (young and old alike)
who've touched my life through the years.*

Chapter One

Moccasin Rock, Texas
July 1891

ABIGAIL HORTON SIGHED as her younger brother Robby eased the sleeve of his best shirt up over his wrist and deliberately scratched at a scabbed-over chigger bite until it bled.

"That's not going to help you at all," she whispered.

He glanced at her, shrugged, then let his arm drop and waited for the blood to run down onto his hand.

Abby understood her brother's frustration. She wasn't desperate enough to start clawing at her own skin yet, but she was more than ready to go home. They'd been sitting in this tabernacle for almost two hours now, and Reverend Wainright was still going strong.

Robby gave her a smug little grin when the trickle of blood finally touched his fingers. He replaced the grin with a frown, then reached around Abby and tugged their mother's arm.

Mama, who'd started the evening freshly starched, was now wilting in the heat and not in the best of humor. She glanced his way, narrowed her eyes, and returned her attention to the pulpit.

Abby bit back a smile, then withdrew a linen handkerchief

from the pocket of her calico dress and passed it to her brother. His shoulders sagged and his lower lip thrust out in a pout as he made a half-hearted swipe at his hand. Even though Abby was twenty-two and Robby only eleven, he resented her attempts at mothering. But Mama had more than enough to deal with. Abby tried to help as much as she could, whether her brother liked it or not.

Robby offered her the hanky when done. Abby waved it away. He shoved it into his own pocket and laid his head back against the pew with a sigh loud enough to earn him a sharp look of rebuke from Mama. No one else in the congregation seemed to notice. All eyes were on Hamilton Wainright, the legendary traveling evangelist.

Reverend Wainright was shouting now, punctuating each word with a thud of his fist on the pulpit. His thick, white eyebrows were drawn together over deep-set eyes and a nose that resembled an eagle's beak.

The man had dashed back and forth across the Bible several times tonight—from Genesis to Revelation, from New Jerusalem back to the Garden of Eden—and should have been tired.

Strangely, he seemed to grow stronger with each word. His deep voice reverberated now throughout the open-air structure.

A baby, one of several stretched out on a pallet next to the tabernacle, began to fuss. The child's older sister scooped her up and carried her to one of the many wagons nearby. Folks had come from miles around for this service; no one wanted to miss the last night of a week-long revival.

The pews were packed with people of all ages and all denominations—some nodding or shaking their heads, others murmuring "amen" or "Lord knows." Most were waving cardboard fans supplied by the Moccasin Rock Funeral Parlor, and the faster the evangelist spoke, the faster the fans moved.

Abby closed her eyes. She was trying to pay attention, but it was a losing battle. She'd been up at dawn to help Mama prepare breakfast for their boarders and was exhausted through and through.

There couldn't possibly be a potato left in the whole state of Texas. Surely she'd peeled them all by now.

Reverend Wainright's voice started to slow and soften. He was beseeching the brethren; it would be invitation time soon. The fast-paced whir of the fans slowed. The entire congregation quieted. The chirp of crickets and the hiss of lanterns were the prominent sounds now.

The splash of a dipper dropping into the water barrel drew her attention. The barrel was set up just beyond the seating area and Robby had already slipped out once tonight for a drink. She opened her eyes, ready to silently scold him. Her brother hadn't moved.

It was Henry Barnett at the barrel. He was wearing his best clothes, too—white cotton shirt, black trousers and new black suspenders. She couldn't see them, but she suspected his shoes were polished to a high shine. As usual, he'd not been able to completely tame his wavy blond hair, though it appeared as if he'd tried.

Henry looked directly at her as he took a drink, and then wiped his mouth with a swipe of a hand. He deftly hooked the dipper back onto the side of the barrel without breaking eye contact, his expression unreadable.

Abby had hurt his feelings earlier, but she hadn't been able to avoid it. How dare he say they'd be married by Christmas. He hadn't asked her this time, he'd marched right up and told her so. They were friends. Why couldn't he leave well enough alone?

She glared at him now. He smiled and winked before turning away. Infuriating man.

Reverend Wainright's voice had taken on a rhythmic cadence and a persuasive tone. "None of us know when we'll be called from this world," he said. "You could leave here tonight and step out to meet eternity. Is your soul prepared? If not, He's waiting."

With a wave of his hand, the reverend motioned for all to rise.

Miss Hattie moved forward to the piano and began to play the hymn *Softly and Tenderly*. The melody was one of the prettiest Abby had ever heard, and the lyrics went hand-in-hand with Reverend Wainright's sermon. Had they planned that in advance?

"Softly and tenderly Jesus is calling,

Calling for you and for me;

See, on the portals He's waiting and watching,

Watching for you and for me."

Miss Hattie continued to play as several people stood and made their way to the front. Abby had reached out to pull Robby to his feet when Hattie hit a faltering note and then crashed to a stop.

The elderly pianist now stared, wide-eyed and open-mouthed, at the back of the tabernacle. Others began to turn, so Abby glanced behind her. Two men stood in the aisle.

One was dressed in black from his hat to his boots. He had dark hair, and a steely expression. He was breathtakingly handsome.

Abby was so spellbound that it took her a moment to notice the stranger was wearing a badge and a gun—and was handcuffed to her father.

Daddy? How could he be standing here when he'd died months ago? The blood rushed to her head and the ground tipped beneath her feet as she tried to make sense of what she was seeing.

She reached out for her mother in an attempt to steady herself, but Mama had dropped to the pew, and faced the opposite direction. "Mama, Daddy's here." *How?* She glanced at her mother, still sitting there as if in a trance, then turned her attention back to the men. Her gaze connected with her father's. He looked sad, sick... and scared.

***

Caleb Calhoun glanced around the big kitchen that spanned the back of the Horton Boarding House. A huge wooden harvest table stood in the center of the room, lined by simple ladder-back, cane-bottomed chairs. One whole wall was anchored by pine shelves, a dry sink and an iron cook stove. There were four windows—two on each side—with white cotton fabric draped across the bottom half. The smell of fresh-baked bread wafted through the room.

The place had a simple, scrubbed-clean look that appealed to him, but he was more interested in the fact that there were only two doors. The one he and his prisoner had passed through from the hallway of the long shotgun style structure, and the outer door on the back wall. A sheriff's deputy was posted outside so he wasn't worried about his prisoner escaping. But getting the layout of a place as soon as he entered had become second nature.

Caleb leveled a hard look at the man standing next to him. "Don't try anything," he said as he unlocked and removed the handcuffs from Bob Horton's wrist. "I'll be back in about ten minutes to take you to the jail."

Caleb pocketed the cuffs and key, and then turned and pinned Mrs. Horton with a stern stare. "I'd appreciate your cooperation, too, ma'am. I'm giving you a few minutes of privacy. Don't make me regret my decision."

"I'm not going anywhere," Bob said before his wife could respond. "Even if I wanted to, I don't have the strength to run." Caleb knew Bob Horton was only in his early fifties, yet as the man slowly sank into one of the kitchen chairs he seemed downright old.

Bob motioned for his wife to take the seat next to him. "Come on, Irene. We've got a lot to talk about, and only a little time to get it all said."

Mrs. Horton glared at him, her lips a thin line, brows drawn together over faded blue eyes. She didn't move. Caleb suspected she'd once been a beautiful woman. Now she looked washed out, weary and mad as all get-out.

She stopped glaring at her husband long enough to address Caleb. "Please forgive my poor manners, Ranger. May I get you something to eat?"

Caleb shook his head, surprised by her friendliness. "No thank you, ma'am."

"How about a piece of chocolate cake when you return?"

He smiled at that. "Sounds too tempting to pass up. Much obliged."

Mrs. Horton still stood, arms folded, when Caleb left the kitchen. From the looks of it, Bob wasn't in for the happy reunion he'd been hoping for. Irene Horton wasn't merely unhappy, though—at the church she'd acted as if he had shown up with a ghost instead of a prisoner.

Caleb wasn't sure what was going on, but it was really none of his concern. He'd paid for a room for the night, and was eager to check out his sleeping quarters. Thanks to the local sheriff, his prisoner would be spending the night in the Moccasin Rock jail, and Caleb would have a good night's rest for the first time in a long time.

The hall leading to the front of the house was long, with two doors on each side, all closed as he passed through. Mrs. Horton had told him earlier that his room was upstairs.

As he entered the parlor and headed for the stairs, Bob's daughter, Abigail, approached. Caleb's steps slowed. The girl had been the first to reach them at the tabernacle, throwing herself at her father and crying softly as she wrapped her arms around him. Bob had tried to return the hug with his free arm, but it had been an awkward, unwieldy embrace.

Caleb wasn't comfortable with a crying female, and even less comfortable in a church setting, so he'd turned his head and tried to establish some semblance of distance. That was impossible when he was shackled to one of the two emotional relatives.

When others had begun to rush toward them, Abigail Horton had stepped back and rubbed her fingers over her face to dry her tears. She'd then turned her attention to Caleb and smiled. Her expression had sent a shiver up his spine. She was looking at him as if it was Christmas morning and she'd spied a gift with her name on it under the tree.

Caleb had made a point of ignoring her as he escorted Bob the few blocks to the boarding house. There was no escape now.

Normally, he wouldn't have minded at all. She was a beautiful young woman, tall and slender with reddish-brown hair. She'd had it pulled back with a ribbon at the revival. Now it was loose and tumbled down in waves around her shoulders. He was willing to bet it was every bit as soft as it looked, though he didn't plan on being around long enough to find out.

"May I talk to my father?" she asked as he neared.

"That's up to him and your mother," Caleb said. "They're in the kitchen."

She nodded, a smile curving her full lips. "I hope you find the room to your liking. I've made sure the bed linens are clean. You'll be in number five. I've filled the water pitcher, and I'll bring you a towel as soon as I gather them in from the line. I meant to bring them in before the revival service, but time slipped away from me."

She seemed breathless, eager to please, and was staring at him with that look again. Caleb decided to put a stop to it before she showed up in his room later with the towel. He was travel-weary, pressed for time and duty-bound to get her father to the jail in Austin. Abigail Horton was young, probably as innocent as she seemed, and a complication he didn't need.

"Look, darlin', although I appreciate your thoughtfulness, I want to make one thing clear. I'm not interested."

Her brow furrowed as she peered up at him with big blue eyes. "You're not interested in a clean towel?"

"I'm not interested in you," Caleb said softly. He cringed as her face lost all color. But better this way than for her to take a serious liking to a man like him.

He turned toward the stairs and had cleared the first couple of steps when he heard somebody snicker. Abigail must have heard it, too, because when he glanced back, her face had regained the lost

color…and then some. He spotted the culprit, a young man loung-
ing in a chair tucked away in the darkest corner of the room.

Caleb was impressed by the girl's reaction. She didn't run, or cry.
She lifted her chin and spoke calmly when she faced the man. "I didn't
hear you come in, Henry. How long have you been sitting there?"

The young man stood and sauntered closer to her. Though he
wasn't laughing now, there was a smirk on his face. "Long enough."

Abigail lowered her head, and Caleb suspected she was hanging
on to her pride by a thread. He couldn't stand it. Telling himself it
was a mistake even as he did it, he stepped back down the stairs,
strode across the room, took her by the shoulders and kissed her.

She stared up at him, blinking rapidly, and swayed a little on
her feet. Caleb steadied her, while his mind raced. He couldn't tell
her he'd done it because he felt sorry for her. So he told her the partial truth.

"My apologies," he said. "I know I shouldn't have done that,
but I couldn't seem to help myself."

He turned toward the stairs, aware of the young man glaring
at him—looking fit-to-kill—and the girl's wide-eyed amazement.
It wasn't their reactions to the kiss that concerned him, though. It
was his. As kisses went, it was brief, chaste and most certainly ill-
advised…and it had rattled him clear down to his boots.

Caleb forced that thought away as he reached the top of the
stairs and started down the hallway in search of room number five.
A couple of wall lanterns with tin reflectors created a warm glow
against the faded rose-patterned wallpaper. The wide plank floor-
ing—worn from time and traffic—was spotless. He found his room
at the far end of the hall, directly over the kitchen. It was as simple
and clean as the rooms downstairs, with an iron bedstead, a single
chair, a small chest of drawers and a rag rug beside the bed. A pitcher
and bowl, again nothing fancy, sat atop the chest.

After living in a house filled with lace, tapestries, costly rugs,
and furnishings that were more artwork than furniture, this room

appealed to him. The whole place smelled like soap and wood polish. He longed to fall into the bed, draw the cotton sheet up over his eyes and sleep for hours, but there'd be time enough for that later.

He pulled out his pocket watch. Bob and Irene's time was almost up. Voices drifted up to him as he started down. Abigail and the man she'd called Henry, he supposed. He couldn't really hear what they were saying. And then he did.

"I don't want to marry you, Henry."

"I suppose you've had your head turned by that ranger…"

No! What had he done? Caleb took the rest of the stairs at a brisker pace, and passed through the parlor even faster. He didn't even glance in the couple's direction. He was getting out now, and wouldn't return until everyone else was in bed. He'd be gone for good at first light. Hopefully the young woman would forget all about him.

Pushing open the kitchen door, he skidded to a stop. Irene Horton sat at the table, tears on her face. Bob Horton was nowhere to be seen.

Caleb slammed his hand down on the table. "Where is he?"

Mrs. Horton flinched. "At the jail, I suppose." She gestured toward the back door. "I thought it was your doing."

He bolted outside. There was no one in the alley. He returned to the kitchen. *Would he be forced to arrest Mrs. Horton, too?* "Tell me exactly what happened."

"Right after you left a man knocked at the back door, showed us his badge and said he was supposed to move Bob to the jail. I thought you'd changed your mind about letting us visit."

Caleb groaned. "Did you recognize the man?"

She shook her head. "No."

"I certainly hope it was somebody from the local jail, Mrs. Horton. If not, it doesn't bode well for your husband at all."

She was wringing her hands now. "Why?"

"Because there are a lot of people looking for him—people who aim to do a lot worse to him than put him in prison."

"Why, what did he do?"

Caleb shook his head in amazement. *Did she not know?* "Your husband is one of the most notorious outlaws in all of Texas, ma'am. He's made a lot of enemies...bankers, railroad companies, lawmen, even members of his own gang. He's going on trial in Austin. He'll probably be sentenced to life in prison." *Unless one of the people he's wronged lynches him first.*

"Gang?" Mrs. Horton's voice was barely a whisper.

The word was repeated in a strangled cry from somewhere behind him. He turned to see Abigail Horton standing there, staring at him with wide, frightened eyes. She crumpled to the floor.

Chapter Two

ABBY OPENED HER eyes when she heard her mother's worried voice, yet Henry Barnett was the first person she saw. He was waving one of the funeral home fans in her face, begging her not to die. She pushed at his arm. "Henry, please. I'm fine."

She spotted her mother hovering nearby. Mrs. Horton managed a smile, but lines of concern etched her face. "Abby, are you okay?"

Abby pushed herself to a sitting position, evading Henry's attempts at assistance, anxious to ease her mother's worries. Still a little light-headed, she leaned back against the sofa before she spoke.

"I'm all right, Mama. Please don't worry. The whole evening was a bit of a strain. Finding out that Daddy isn't dead, being so glad to see him." Her voice broke, but she forced the rest of the words out. "I don't understand what's happening."

Her mother glanced away. "Me either. Hopefully we'll know more soon."

Abby knew instantly that her mother was holding something back. *Why?* She wanted answers, but not in front of Henry. And she had some things to discuss with that young man first.

She stood, grateful for his assistance this time. "Where did that ranger go?"

"He's searching for your father," her mother said.

It was the answer that Abby had expected, but the words still hit her like a blow. *This has to be a mistake.*

"Why don't you go on to bed, Mama? I want to visit with Henry for a minute. I'll come up and check on you later. I'll take care of everything down here."

Her mother hesitated, yet it was obvious the idea appealed to her. "If you're sure. You'll need to wait up until everyone is in for the night, and then lock up. And turn the lamps down. I don't think Reverend Wainright has made it in yet. He's paid up for one more night. And Robby…" She grabbed at Abby's arm, eyes wide. "Good heavens, where's Robby?"

"The Wilsons took Robby home with their boys for the night, remember? Since…so much was going on here."

Her mother sagged with relief. "Oh, how sweet of them." She turned and started toward the kitchen, muttering something about baking a cake for the Wilsons. Abby followed, gently turning her around. "Go on up, Mama. I'll take care of everything."

"Are you sure?"

"I've done this dozens of times. I can handle things. Now please get some rest."

Mrs. Horton's footsteps were slow and heavy as she started up the stairs. She stopped midway and shot a stern look at Henry over the banister. "You shouldn't stay long. It's a little late to be sitting in the parlor alone with a respectable girl."

Abby suppressed a chuckle as Henry sputtered, "Yes, ma'am." Her mother wasn't as confused as she'd seemed.

As soon as they heard the door shut upstairs, Henry pulled Abby back to the sofa.

He settled in beside her. "Look, I'm willing to forgive you for kissing that man earlier. We can still be married."

Abby sighed. "I don't want to marry you. And I didn't kiss him, he kissed me. Before you ask again, I don't know why he did it." *But*

I intend to find out. He'd said he couldn't help himself. Had he been overcome by...passion? Oh, my. "While we're on that subject, Henry, why did you laugh at me?"

As always, Henry's words were honest, heartfelt and straight to the point. "I was jealous."

"Well, you were being about as mature as Robby," Abby said. She turned sideways on the sofa to face him. "Tell me what happened after we left the revival. I was so shocked to see my father that I didn't think about what a disruption it must've been to the service."

Henry nodded. "Yes, things were in an uproar for sure"—his lips twitched for a moment before tipping up into a smile—"mostly because Josiah Smithfield wanted to rededicate his life to the Lord and give up alcohol."

"Why?"

"Because he was sure he'd seen a ghost."

Abby shook her head. She didn't know whether to laugh or cry.

"Pastor Brown and Reverend Wainright got everything back under control though, and resumed the invitation. Several people were saved."

"That's wonderful," Abby said.

"Now you tell me something; what's going on with your father?"

Abby shrugged. "You heard what I said to my mother. I honestly don't know. I'm thrilled that he's alive, but I have so many questions. Where has he been? What was he doing? Where is he now?"

He squeezed her arm. "I'm sorry, Abby. Hopefully, you'll get those answers soon."

"Thank you." She pushed to her feet. "I guess I'd better go straighten things up in the kitchen. It'll be breakfast time all too soon."

Henry cleared his throat. "First, I've got something I want to say."

Abby sat down again as he began his usual proposal speech. She knew each of the highlights by heart. She could almost recite it with him.

"You're not getting any younger, Abby, and neither am I. We're twenty-two now. Most people our age, even younger, already have children. I'm tired of waiting. We've known each other all our lives. We'll make a good match."

She stopped listening and studied his face, his dear sweet face, and wished fervently that it stirred something in her. But it didn't. Would it in time? He was honest and dependable, and, except for the episode earlier in the evening, he'd always treated her with kindness. His brown eyes were bright as he listed his plans for their future.

Abby was brought abruptly out of her reverie when she heard him say, "So, it's settled then. A Christmas wedding. We'll have to live with my folks for awhile. Hopefully I can begin building us a house of our own next year."

She shook her head. "Henry, no."

"You won't live with my parents? Even for a little while? They think highly of you. It'll be okay."

"I adore your parents, and you know that. I mean no, I won't marry you."

He groaned. "But why?"

"I've told you before, I don't love you...not like a wife should."

"I have enough love for the both of us. It will work." He said it with such conviction that it broke her heart.

Tears stung her eyes but she refused to let them fall. This needed to end, once and for all. For both their sakes. "Henry, you are one of the dearest people I've ever known. And maybe the best friend I'll ever have. But I want...more."

"More what? If you're talking about children, I'm willing. I think we should have four. Two boys and two girls would be nice."

Abby swallowed hard. "I don't know how to explain. Only that I want more out of life. There has to be more. More than Moccasin Rock, more than this boarding house...more than potatoes."

"Potatoes?" Henry took her face in his hands. "You're making me crazy, you know that? What exactly do you want?"

I don't want to end up like my mother. She couldn't bring herself to say it aloud. It seemed like a betrayal. Henry wouldn't understand anyway. "I just want more," she said.

Henry pressed his forehead to hers. "Can I kiss you?"

"No, I think it'd be better if you didn't."

He gently brushed his lips against her temple. "I think I'm beginning to understand. You want more than me."

When Abby didn't respond, he stood and walked away. At the door he gave her a small smile. "You're confused right now—"

"Henry…" The lump in her throat wouldn't let her continue.

He held up his hands. "Don't worry, I'm leaving. But I'll be waiting if you ever change your mind."

When he was gone, she sank back into the sofa and let the tears fall, wondering how she could mourn the loss of something she'd never had, and never wanted. *Lord, please let him find a sweet girl for his wife.*

***

"Excuse me, are you the sheriff?" Caleb repeated the question three times before the sleeping, stoop-shouldered old man with his feet propped up on the desk answered him. Even then he was yawning when he spoke.

"Nope. I'm the deputy."

Good. Caleb would hate to have to rely on this old-timer's help.

"What can I do for you?" the deputy asked, dropping his feet to the floor with a considerable amount of moaning and groaning. He glanced up, and then did a double-take.

Caleb had been mistaken for a gunslinger on more than one occasion so he pointed to his badge and hastened to reassure the man. "I'm a Texas Ranger. I'm looking for the sheriff. Hoping he's got a prisoner of mine here."

The old man shook his head, still peering at Caleb with a strange look in his eye. "No prisoners."

Caleb cursed under his breath.

The deputy blinked a couple of times. "What'd you say your name was?"

"I didn't. But it's Calhoun. Caleb Calhoun."

The old man's mouth dropped open.

Caleb wasn't sure why that was such startling news. He'd only been a Ranger for about a year—it wasn't like he was a legendary lawman or anything. And if word got out he'd lost a prisoner, he might not be any kind of lawman at all.

"I'd best fetch Eli," the man said. He motioned toward several chairs grouped around a cold pot-bellied stove as he ambled away. "Sit a spell and make yourself at home."

Caleb bit back a growl. He didn't have time for that. "Is this Eli person the sheriff here?"

The old man gave him a nod, and one more bewildered look before pushing through the door.

Caleb was pacing back and forth in front of the empty cells, wondering if the whole town was crazy, when the door opened. He turned to greet the big man who'd entered, and then stopped.

The sheriff stood there, eyes narrowed, jaw tight, fists clinched. Caleb couldn't imagine what he'd done to garner this man's ire. He looked familiar, yet Caleb was certain they'd never crossed paths.

The man was broad shouldered and appeared to be a good two inches taller than his own six-foot-one. The tin star pinned to his vest was much like any other, but the Colt .45 Peacemaker on his right hip was enough to gain him instant respect. He sure would hate to tangle with this fellow.

Caleb was being studied every bit as closely. The sheriff hadn't moved or said a word since he'd walked through the door, but the man's gaze sharpened when Caleb's fingers drifted a little too close to the Remington 44-40 he wore. Caleb slowly let his hand drop. He didn't need any additional trouble.

The old deputy had followed the sheriff in, and now made his way to one of the chairs and settled back. Caleb could tell he didn't plan on missing a moment of what happened next. *Whatever that might be.*

The sheriff was the first to blink and speak. His voice was a harsh rasp, his words completely unexpected. "What's your father's name? Where is he?"

Caleb bristled at the tone and the question. "I don't see what that's got to do with anything, but his name was Amos Calhoun. He's dead. Now, if you don't mind answering a question for me, I'd like to know where my prisoner is. I'm the Texas Ranger you were expecting. I stopped here in Moccasin Rock a little earlier this evening to let Bob Horton visit with his family. I was told there'd be a deputy outside, and that you'd keep him here overnight. He wasn't outta my sight for ten minutes before someone showed up at the Horton place and escorted him out. The fellow who took him supposedly had a badge. Does he work for you?"

The man finally stepped closer. "I don't know anything about your prisoner, but I do know your father was a low-down, sorry…"

He didn't get any further with his list of Amos Calhoun's shortcomings. Caleb punched out at him in a blind rage, one fist connecting with the man's right eye with a satisfying thud, his other landing a solid punch to the nose. Before he had a chance to inflict any further damage, he heard the unmistakable sound of a gun being cocked.

Caleb froze. The Peacemaker was now aimed at his chest. Despite the blood dripping from the other man's nose, his hard gaze never wavered. Neither did the gun.

Anger surged through Caleb, most of it directed at himself. He'd let some backwoods lawman get the better of him.

The sheriff suddenly shoved him, hard, with his left hand, holstering his gun only after Caleb lay sprawled at his feet.

Caleb's blood boiled as he started to stand. A big boot pressing firmly against one shoulder stopped him. He grabbed for the boot, determined to flip its owner head over heels, but the man stepped back. "Stay where you are. I don't mind letting you have a couple of free punches, but I'd hate to have to shoot you."

Caleb sat up, but didn't stand. "You're lucky I didn't shoot you first, you crazy fool. What's wrong with you?"

The other man laughed, making the blood flow from his nose faster. "You didn't even think about going for your gun, and you know it. You just started throwing your fists like a little kid." He reached into his back pocket, pulled a handkerchief out and pressed it to his nose. "I'm glad. I would've hated to shoot my own brother."

The cloth had muffled the words. Caleb wasn't certain he'd heard the sheriff correctly. Surely he hadn't.

"Br...brother?"

All he got was a nod of confirmation.

Shock shot through Caleb with a jolt. He looked closer at the man towering over him, wanting to shout out a denial. He couldn't. No wonder he'd seemed so familiar. That was the face he saw in the mirror. A little older. A lot harder. Brown eyes instead of green. But it was his face. His father's face.

The sheriff reached out a hand and pulled him to his feet. "I'm Elijah, the first-born son of Amos Calhoun."

The deputy must have decided the introductions signaled the end of the excitement because he rose slowly from the chair, and stepped over to his boss. "I'm going to fetch Nathaniel to look at your injury, Eli."

The sheriff nodded. "Yeah, best get him. I'm fine, but he might want to meet Ranger Calhoun here. It's gonna be like a regular family reunion."

Caleb opened his mouth and then closed it again, finally managing one word. "Family?"

"Yep. Dust yourself off. You got one more brother to meet."

"One more..." Caleb's words trailed off.

"Didn't you know about us?"

Caleb shook his head.

"Well, if it makes you feel any better, you're a surprise to me, too. How old are you?"

"Twenty-five."

Eli's expression tightened. "The old man sure didn't waste any time replacing us. Where were you born? Any other siblings?"

"Colorado. And no, I'm an only child. Or at least I was. How old are you?"

"Thirty-one. Nathaniel's thirty. Reckon that makes you the baby." It was said in jest, yet it still rankled some. Caleb didn't say anything, though. He wasn't sure there were words to express all he was feeling.

Then he remembered. "I'll have to deal with this later." Picking up his hat, he slapped it on his head. "I've got to find my prisoner."

Eli dipped his handkerchief in a bucket of water by the door, and cleaned the blood from his face. "You might as well stick around a little longer. Doubt if you'll find him tonight. It seems to me you've been hornswoggled. I didn't know anything about you or your prisoner. I'll be glad to help you track Bob down, though."

He smiled, causing the swollen right eye to close completely. Caleb got the feeling that the smile was a rare one. "It'll be a good chance for us to become better acquainted and all," Eli said.

Caleb stared at him, feeling helpless. *Was any of this real?*

Chapter Three

TWENTY MINUTES LATER, Caleb was settled in to one of the chairs at the jail, sipping lukewarm coffee from a battered tin cup, and staring at yet another version of a Calhoun. This one, Dr. Nathaniel Calhoun, was younger than Elijah, not quite as big, and not as hard looking. His hair was a lighter brown, as were his eyes. But it was the same face.

Caleb shook his head. "I don't understand this."

"It's really pretty simple," Eli said, rising to pour himself a second cup of coffee. "Our father walked out the door and hit the road one day, leaving everything behind—including his wife and kids."

"He said he had something important to do," Nathaniel said, his tone quiet but bitter.

Eli grunted. "Since he never returned, I'm assuming that whatever he was tending to was more important than us."

"I'm sorry." Caleb didn't know what else to say. Part of him wanted to deny the accusations, to defend the father he'd known. But the evidence was overwhelming.

"So he never talked about us?" Eli asked.

He sounded so wistful that Caleb's throat tightened. He suspected that not many people ever got a glimpse of vulnerability from this man. Nathaniel was waiting for the answer, too, a mixture of sadness and confusion on his face. Caleb wanted to lie to them, but he couldn't.

"No. He never told me he had other sons. He used to talk about happier times though. And Texas. He spoke of it so often I felt as if I'd grown up here myself. He died when I was in military school. At the first opportunity I headed straight for this part of the world. I served in the Army at Fort McIntosh and joined the Texas Rangers over a year ago."

"Military school, huh? I guess the old man was proud of you." Eli's words were softly spoken, but they were laced with bitterness.

"I'm sure he'd be proud of you two, as well," Caleb said, trying to ease a pain he couldn't even comprehend. "A doctor and a sheriff, that's pretty impressive."

Nathaniel and Eli glanced at each other. There was a lifetime of shared memories in that look.

"We've only recently arrived at respectability," Eli admitted. "Our mother died not long after Daddy left. Our young years were rough ones. It's not something I want to talk about."

Caleb nodded. "Okay." He took a sip of coffee, trying to sort the scattered thoughts bouncing around his mind. "Now that I think about it, some of the things my fath—our father—said make a little more sense now."

"How's that?" Eli said.

"As he got sicker, he'd often talk to me about things we'd done together—like working on some sort of little wood carvings—and I couldn't recall doing those things. I thought at the time that he'd drifted back to his own childhood. I think now maybe he was talking about you two."

Both men lowered their eyes, Eli staring into his coffee cup, and Nathaniel at his clasped hands.

Caleb continued. "On his deathbed, he kept saying the same thing over and over again, 'Remember Texas.'" Caleb took a deep breath. "I thought he wanted me to visit here. Then, on the last day, he said, 'Remember Texas, son. Find them.' He was delirious and I had no idea who, or what, he was talking about at the time. I guess I do now."

Nathaniel got up and turned away without saying a word. "Thank you for telling us," Eli said. "Someday that might bring us comfort. Not yet, though."

Caleb understood that. "I don't know what to say about all this. I'm sorry for what y'all went through, but I didn't grow up hating my father. I loved him. Right now I'm as bitter and confused as you two. I feel as if my whole life has been a lie. I'm not sure what I'm supposed to do now."

Eli cleared his throat and then stood. "Me either. But I suppose the first thing should be to find the ghost of Bob Horton and get him back in custody. We can start in the morning. You got a place to sleep?"

"Yes, I'm staying at the boarding house."

Eli nodded and walked over and gently shook the deputy awake. "Bliss, go on and get some shut-eye."

"Whadda you think I was doing?" the old man grumbled.

"Well, get it at home," Eli said. "Be here bright and early in the morning. We've got us a prisoner to track."

The old man slowly rose, stretched, yawned and nodded.

Nathaniel stood, too. "If I don't have any patients tomorrow, I'll be glad to help."

Caleb was still seated. "Wait," he called, as everyone else headed for the door.

They all looked back at him.

"I have two questions. Why does everybody keep calling Bob Horton a ghost? And"—he pointed at the deputy—"is his name really Bliss?"

All three of the other men laughed. The old man answered the second question first. "Yes, sir. Bliss Walker is my real name. When I was born, my mama took one look at me and declared that I'd brought pure bliss into her life. The name sorta stuck."

Caleb shook his head, still not convinced, yet he couldn't help but grin. "What about Bob Horton? I heard the word ghost several times when we stopped by the tabernacle tonight. Even his family was acting odd. Why?"

Eli shook his head. "I'm sorry I missed that. It's got the whole town in an uproar."

"We'll leave you to explain," Nathaniel said. He and Bliss wandered out.

Caleb was grateful for the privacy. "I hate that we got off to such a rocky start," he said to Eli, "and I appreciate you not shooting me."

Eli nodded. "When Bliss found me and told me a man named Calhoun was here, and he looked like me, I thought that after all these years Daddy had finally found us. I was still mad at him, but I was willing to listen to what he had to say. When I walked in here and saw you, and realized what it meant, I lost my mind. Sorry about that."

"All forgiven and forgotten. I'm sorry for punching you. Twice," he added, hoping to lighten the mood.

Eli flashed him a grin. "Remember, that's the only two you ever get."

Caleb smiled in return. "I know. So, tell me about Bob Horton."

"Now there's an interesting story. The reason people were referring to Bob's ghost is because most of them attended Bob's funeral a few months ago."

"I'm about to voice something I've thought a hundred times since landing in this town," Caleb grumbled. "I don't understand."

Eli shrugged. "It is a puzzler," he agreed. "Supposedly Bob was killed in an accident while on a trip up north, and his body was shipped back here in a casket. I've only lived here a little over a year, so I haven't attended many funerals, but I've been told that Bob Horton's service was the biggest they've ever held in Moccasin Rock."

Caleb shook his head. "The man's not dead. Who did they bury?"

Eli slapped him on the back as they headed for the door. "That'll be the first question I ask Bob. Right after we find him. Right now I'm going to drop by and see Walter Moore, the telegraph operator. Hoping he'll send some messages tonight. Even though we're heading out in the morning, I want to alert every lawman in every direction as soon as possible."

Caleb rubbed a hand across his eyes. "Thanks for your help. Do you mind if I tag along?"

At Eli's questioning look Caleb added, "I'd rather take a beating than do it, but I'd better send a message to my captain. No sense putting it off."

"You're right," Eli said. "Best get it over with, Ranger Calhoun."

"Hopefully you can still call me that tomorrow," Caleb muttered.

***

The Horton house was quiet when Caleb let himself in the front door. He crept along, intent on getting upstairs undetected, when a movement in the shadows drew his attention. He automatically went for his gun, then let his hand drop when he realized it was Abigail Horton.

She stood from the sofa. "Did you find my father?"

The words were softly spoken, but the quiver in her voice told him she was struggling more than she let on, and even in the dim lamplight the despair in her eyes was easy to read.

Caleb shook his head. "No. We're taking out after him in the morning."

She swallowed several times before speaking again. "I never got an opportunity to talk to him. Could you please tell me what happened? Exactly why was he arrested?"

"You didn't know about the Latham gang?"

Abigail closed her eyes, and crossed her arms at her waist as if to shield herself. "I've heard of the gang," she said, "but I didn't know my father was associated with them."

"It appears that your father has been the leader of that gang for a good long while. We believe he *is* Webb Latham."

Her eyes popped open, and this time there was a spark of anger in them. "He's lived here for years. That doesn't make sense."

"Maybe not, but it's true," Caleb said. "I guess he was living a double life." *His own father sure had been.* "Whatever he calls himself, Bob or Webb, he's been a wanted man for a while now. Somehow, he's always managed to stay one step ahead of the law."

"Where did y'all find him?" she asked.

Caleb gave her the rest of the details in a straight-forward recitation, just as he would for trial. "About a week ago one of the deputies from Palo Pinto County happened to stumble across a little shack down in a gap. The fellow wasn't even looking for the gang. He'd only stopped to water his horse. But a rattlesnake spooked it so he was wandering around on foot when he spotted the place. He was about to go up and ask if anyone had seen his horse. Before he got near, the door opened. A couple of men emerged, and they were arguing. The deputy stepped back out of sight, and heard them talking about a robbery. He waited until they went back inside before sneaking away. At some point he found his horse and high-tailed it out of there to spread the news."

Abigail straightened her shoulders, as if bracing for the rest. "What happened then?"

Caleb hesitated, unsure of how much to tell her. "It wasn't pretty. Every lawman in the area followed the deputy back to the hideout. We surrounded the place and called for them to come out. Within seconds there were guns poking through the door and windows."

She swallowed hard. "Did you actually see my father do anything wrong?"

He shook his head. "No. There was too much going on to see faces in detail once the lead started flying."

"And afterwards?"

"When the smoke cleared one of the gang members had escaped, three were dead and one was dying. The last one had his hands up."

"My father?"

Caleb nodded. "Yep. And right before the dying outlaw breathed his last, he looked at your father, smiled and said, 'Well boss, I guess we've come to the end of the line.'"

Abigail shook her head, obviously bewildered. "I've read stories in the newspaper about that gang. Don't they wear bandanas over their faces? Maybe he'd mistaken my father for someone else."

The hope in her voice tugged at Caleb's heart, but it was false hope, and in the end that could be more painful.

"I guess anything's possible, but I don't believe there was a mistake," Caleb said. "For one thing, they didn't have their faces covered right then. They hadn't known we were coming. And that man was looking right at your father. He knew who he was talking to."

She stood there, staring past him for several moments. "I don't understand any of this," she finally admitted. "Daddy being an outlaw is bad enough, but why would he want us to believe he died?"

At least now he understood what she was referring to. "That I don't know. He told us immediately that his name was Bob Horton, and that he ran a boarding house in Moccasin Rock."

"He does," Abby said. "He's run this place for years. He's a good man. I can't believe otherwise. Something's not adding up here."

"All I know is that he wasn't running a boarding house when we found him," Caleb said. "And obviously, he's known as the leader of the Latham gang to some folks. Can you honestly say you know exactly where he's been and what he's been doing for every minute of every day?"

She shook her head and swiped at her eyes, and he felt a pang of remorse. First her father had blindsided her, and then Caleb himself had caused problems with her beau.

"I truly regret the trouble I caused earlier," he said softly.

She gave him a distracted little shrug. "You were only doing your job, I suppose."

"No, I mean with that young man, Henry."

Her brows drew together. "I don't understand."

Just let it go. "I heard you tell Henry that you wouldn't marry him"—he cleared his throat—"after I kissed you. I sure didn't mean to come between you two."

Her puzzled look cleared. "Oh. That's not what happened."

"It's not?"

"No, I've turned Henry down every single time he's asked. It had nothing to do with…" Her words trailed off and Caleb felt a stab of something he couldn't quite identify.

What was happening to him? Since he'd arrived in Moccasin Rock he'd lost a prisoner, been outgunned by a small-town sheriff, made an enemy of a young man who hadn't done a thing to him, and kissed an innocent young girl. And now he was annoyed that she hadn't been devastated by it.

The girl was talking again, yet Caleb couldn't hear a thing she was saying. Her long lashes fluttered, her lips curved in a half smile. He hadn't spent much time around a girl like this. Was she flirting with him? Baiting him? No, she was saying something about cake. *Cake?*

You've been given a reprieve. Get out while you can. He spun on his heel, took a step and then stopped. Turning back, he reached out, hooked an arm around her waist and pulled her close. She gave a startled little squeak but didn't say anything.

Caleb cupped his hand behind her head, confirming that her hair was as soft as he'd imagined it. Her eyes were the deepest blue he'd ever seen. He studied her upturned face. What was he seeing there? Curiosity. Concern. The first he could live with, but any doubt and he was out. He let her go as if she burned him.

"Night, Miss Horton."

She sounded breathless again. "Goodnight."

Caleb had reached the top of the stairs and stepped into the hallway when he heard footsteps. Was she following him?

He turned around to tell her to get on to bed before he did something they'd both regret, only to encounter a tall, thin man dressed in a long, black coat, gray trousers, and worn, knee-high black boots. The preacher from the revival.

Had the old man seen what happened downstairs? Regret slammed through Caleb. He didn't want to cause the girl any trouble. He'd seen people de-churched for less. Ostracized by their families. Disciplined to the point of abuse. In some parts of the country, in some families, a young girl had a certain amount of freedom. In other areas, being seen with a man, alone, after dark, was enough to cause a whole world of trouble.

He wouldn't let Abigail Horton pay for something that was his fault. Caleb assumed his sternest expression and fixed his gaze on the preacher. The old man drew himself up straighter, not seeming the least bit intimidated.

Caleb drew in a breath and said what was on his mind. "Look, I don't want any trouble."

The preacher stared at him, his dark brown eyes solemn and unblinking. "I don't recall offering any."

"I'm saying that I don't want anything bad happening to that girl." Caleb started to apologize specifically for touching her, and then stopped. What if the old man hadn't seen anything? He could be making things worse. He gentled his voice. "It's only that I've seen people do some terrible things in the name of God."

The old man didn't seem offended by his blunt statement. He nodded in agreement. "Can't argue with you. But I've also seen people do some disturbing things in the name of the law."

Caleb's interest in the man shot up a notch. "And I can't argue with that."

They stood there, each sizing the other up. "How long do you figure on staying in town?" the older man asked.

"I had planned on leaving tomorrow morning, but some complications have arisen," Caleb admitted. "I can't leave until I find a missing prisoner. My captain wouldn't be happy about me showing up at the jail empty-handed. When are you leaving?"

"I'd also planned on departing tomorrow." The preacher raised a long, bony finger and pointed upwards. "But I think maybe my captain wants me to stay."

Caleb's stomach sank. "In that case, I guess I'll see you in the morning."

The man nodded and then walked away, giving Caleb one more look before opening the door to room number six.

Once inside his own room, Caleb removed his gun belt and looped it over a bedpost. He then pitched his hat on a hook, and sat down on the chair to tug off his boots. Nudging them to the side with his toes, he undressed and made his way to the water pitcher.

As the girl had mentioned earlier in the evening, there was water, soap and a fresh towel. He washed up as best he could, yet he longed for a full bath. Most hotels had a tub that could be placed in the room for an extra fee. Maybe the Hortons had a similar set-up. As hot as it was, they wouldn't need to heat the water.

Caleb stretched out on the bed. If he was here more than a few days—although he hoped that wouldn't be the case—he'd need to find somebody to do his laundry. Maybe the Hortons offered that service. If not, he could always see if the local store had any ready-made clothing he could purchase. And he'd need to buy a horse. Neither would be a problem. Although the opulent lifestyle he'd grown up with was gone, he still had money. Lots of it. More than he'd ever use in a lifetime.

According to his great-aunt Victoria's latest letter, it was all stored away in a bank, waiting, in her words, for him to come to his senses and "quit fighting with outlaws and Indians."

Caleb had grown tired of trying to explain to her that he'd only encountered a handful of Indians, none of them dangerous, but that outlaws still posed a serious threat to law-abiding citizens. His work mattered to him. He liked to think it mattered to others, that it made a difference.

Blast Bob Horton anyway. Several choice colorful names ran through Caleb's mind, and he couldn't wait to catch up with the missing outlaw and call him each one of them. Sighing, he realized that he'd have to watch his mouth for a while. Not only was he staying in close proximity to a family, but that preacher would be hanging around. How in the world had he let this happen?

Shifting to his side, Caleb punched the pillow into the shape he preferred, but the sleep he'd wanted so desperately eluded him. He couldn't quit thinking about his brothers. *Brothers.* "Daddy, what did you do?" he whispered.

How could his father, one of the kindest men he'd ever known, have abandoned his own children? Caleb had so many questions. And there was no one left to ask. His mother had died even before his father. Victoria, his mother's elderly aunt, was his last living relative—well, that wasn't true anymore.

His stomach growled and that drew his thoughts to the cake he'd been offered, and that brought him straight back to Abigail Horton. Clearly, considering that preacher's watchful eye and Caleb's own lapse into impulsive, reckless behavior—the very thing that had gotten him sent to military school—he had to steer clear of that girl.

Acting before thinking had always been a problem for him. As a young boy, all it had taken was someone saying "I bet you can't" and he would, or nearly die trying. Those boyhood stunts were one thing, but this was another. If he messed up this time, it might be someone else who got hurt.

So hands off the girl.

Chapter Four

ABBY PULLED A pan of biscuits from the stove, let them cool a moment, and then gingerly tossed them into a napkin-lined basket.

Potatoes—peeled and diced into small pieces—were sizzling in a huge cast iron skillet behind her, while her mother stood near the counter, cracking eggs into a heavy glass bowl and stirring them briskly.

The two women worked side-by-side, as they had every day for years. Yet today something was different. The silence was strained. Abby wanted to know everything there was to know about her father's disappearance, including whether her mother had known that he was alive. Why would she keep something like that from her children?

By the time Abby had gone upstairs the night before to ask those questions, Mama was asleep. Or pretending to be. This morning, Reverend Wainright was already sitting at the table when she'd entered the kitchen. He was an early riser. Abby herself had slept later than she'd intended. She had nodded in the preacher's general direction, but had yet to make eye-contact with him.

"Reverend, where are you headed from here?" her mother asked.

Taking a long sip of his coffee, Reverend Wainright answered in a much softer voice than he used in the pulpit. "I'm not entirely certain. I was thinking I'd stay on here a little while. Unless you have the room promised to someone else."

Mrs. Horton hesitated, for only a second. "No, it's available. We'd be honored to have you stay."

Abby stifled a groan. The revival was over. Why did he want to stay? Had he seen her with the ranger? She had still been standing there, trying to figure out what in the world had happened, when the reverend had entered the parlor through the hall the night before.

She hadn't been able to tell from his expression whether he'd witnessed anything. But she'd been embarrassed and scared, nonetheless. Did he plan on seeing to it that she was punished? Her mother wasn't the type to go along with that, after all she was a grown woman. Yet it could cause problems. After all the talk that was probably swirling around town about her father, additional trouble was something they didn't need.

Abby looked directly at the old man finally, bracing herself for his remarks—however damaging they might be—but Reverend Wainright said simply, "Morning, Miss Horton."

"Good morning, sir." She offered him a hesitant smile, and breathed easier when he returned it. "Can I get you more coffee?"

"Maybe a drop or two," he said.

Abby had topped off the cup when Caleb Calhoun entered the kitchen with his hat in hand. His thick brown hair was combed neatly, but still damp. He was freshly shaved. Even in the light of day he was so handsome he took her breath away. Yet he didn't seem quite as sure of himself as he had the day before.

Abby, thoughts in a whirl, couldn't bring herself to speak. Her mother greeted him.

"Sit down, Ranger, and I'll bring you a cup of coffee. We'll have food ready for you here in a few minutes."

"Thanks," he said, with a darting glance in Abby's direction. "And please, call me Caleb." He rubbed his jaw. "I sure appreciate the hot water this morning."

"It was no trouble at all," her mother said. "Make yourself comfortable. I'll show you the bathing room with the tub in a bit. It's not fancy, but it is private. There's no extra charge, although we do need advance notice if you want hot water."

"Heated is good for shaving, but I don't need it for bathing," Caleb said.

Abby turned back to the potatoes.

Her mother continued to talk as she set another place at the table. "Due to the varied schedules of our guests, breakfast is a come-and-go arrangement," she told the ranger. "If you arrive late, you can still get something to eat, even if it's cold meat and bread. Dinner and supper, however, are served at specific times, so when it's possible, let us know when you'll be joining us for meals."

"I can tell you for sure that I won't be here today. I've…" Caleb's voice trailed off, and Abby realized he was hesitant to say that he'd be out tracking her father.

"All right, we won't plan on you being here," Irene Horton said. "Let us know about tomorrow when you can." She maintained the bright chirp to her voice, yet Abby suspected they were thinking the same thing. *If he finds Daddy today, he won't be here tomorrow.*

From the corner of her eye, Abby saw Caleb nod at the preacher as he sat down at the table.

"Good morning… sir," Caleb said. "Sorry, I don't know your name."

Abby tensed. Why was he engaging the man in conversation? She wanted them both to eat and move on.

"My name is Hamilton Wainright, but I'm fine with being called Preacher."

A tap sounded at the back door just as the whiny spinster that had boarded with them for the past few months wandered in from the front hall.

"I'll get the door," Abby volunteered. She'd do anything to avoid

Agatha Culpepper. Although Abby sympathized with the woman, she found her constant health complaints annoying.

At first glance the gray-haired woman seemed sturdy, robust even, yet she carried on constantly about one ailment or another. Sometimes her assorted aches and pains gave Abby a specific pain in the neck. But the Hortons needed the money, so she did her best to get along with the woman.

Abby headed for the back door, glad to be able to avoid the older woman's daily "summing up." Whenever she was asked as to her well-being, Miss Culpepper would clear her throat and say, "Well, to sum it up, I'm hurting from head to toe." The only problem was she didn't leave it summed up. She would start by describing the pain in her head, and continue on down. Other times, she complained from the feet up.

Abby opened the door just as her mother cut the older woman off at the throat...or at least the pain in her throat.

"I'm so sorry to hear that you're having trouble swallowing," Mrs. Horton said. "Would you care for a cup of peppermint tea?"

Miss Culpepper settled down into a chair before answering. "Yes, that would be wonderful. And some eggs. And potatoes and ham. Maybe I'll feel better if I'm able to force a few bites down."

"Perhaps you're right," Mrs. Horton said. "You sit and visit with the gentlemen, and I'll have it ready in a moment."

Abby turned away from the sight of Miss Culpepper pulling the jelly jar closer, and smiled at the gangly young boy standing on the steps, holding a wooden crate.

"I've got your order from Martin's Mercantile," he said.

Abby motioned him inside. "Thank you, Jamie."

"You're welcome, ma'am."

Once the box was on the counter Abby began removing the items, including vinegar, baking powder, corn meal, coffee beans, a jar of honey, and a large spool of white sewing thread.

She turned to Jamie. "When you're done running errands for

Silas Martin today, will you tell your mother how much we appreciate her letting Robby spend the night at your house?"

"I will," the boy said. "But it weren't no trouble. Mama always says, 'what's one more,' and I reckon she's right. It seemed like any old night at home. Robby's playing with my little brothers right now. He should be home soon."

Abby suppressed a chuckle. Adger and Betty Wilson had eight children. She couldn't even imagine what "any old night at home" was like for them.

Jamie adjusted a suspender strap and then waved at Mrs. Horton and those seated at the table. Turning back to Abby, he said, "Silas said to tell you that when he brings the flour and sugar, he'll bring you more taters."

Abby cringed at the thought of more potatoes, but they were running low. They ordered their flour twenty-five pounds at a time, and the sugar came in a large barrel that they stored in the pantry. Both needed replenishing. "That sounds fine, Jamie. Carrying that many potatoes would've been a bit of a haul for you."

She turned her attention back to the crate, as her mother handed Jamie a biscuit with a slice of ham tucked inside. Abby smiled at the boy's gasp of pleasure.

Reaching into the box for the last item, her hand stilled. At the bottom was a thin book. A dime novel. It was definitely not something they'd ordered. Her mother didn't allow such books—with their often lurid covers—in the house. Mama didn't think it was a mortal sin, like some people did, however, she did believe them to be a waste of time and mind. She didn't want Robby tempted by them. Yet they'd always fascinated Abby.

A glance over her shoulder assured her that no one was watching. Abby wasn't sure how this book had ended up in their grocery order, but she planned on reading it before returning it.

As she slipped it into her apron pocket she got a glimpse of the title, "Abigail, the Wolf Girl." She barely suppressed a gasp. She knew this story. Hands shaking, she studied the cover. Her gaze flew to the author's name. H.D. Roberts. Who was that?

Abby looked up to see the door close behind Jamie. She turned to her mother. "I'm going to send this box back to the store now so we don't have to send Robby with it later."

Her mother nodded, but continued talking to their whiny boarder. "Well, of course you can have a second helping of potatoes, Miss Culpepper. How marvelous that your ability to swallow has returned."

Abby reached the alley as the boy rounded the corner toward Main Street. "Jamie," she called out, "can you take this back to Silas for me?"

"Sure," he said around a mouth full of biscuit. He retraced his steps as he swallowed.

Abby drew the book from her pocket. "This was in the box. Do you know why Silas sent it to us?"

The boy shook his head. "Weren't Silas. Some man was standing out behind the store as I left, and he asked me where I was going. I told him I was making a delivery to the boarding house. He jammed that book down into the box and said, 'Make sure Miss Abby gets this.' So I did."

"Did you know this man?"

He shook his head.

"What did he look like?"

Jamie scrunched up his thin face in concentration. "I really wasn't paying him no mind, but it seems now that his hat was pulled low, plum nearly to his eyes. Seemed kinda hunched in." He demonstrated by lifting his shoulders and lowering his head. "I didn't really get a good look at him."

Abby's thoughts were still whirling when Jamie grabbed the empty box from her and trotted off in the direction of the store. "I gotta go. Silas said I'd better not be lollygaggin."

"Bye, Jamie." After he was gone, Abby pivoted on her heel,

searching each of the neighboring houses and yards. Could the man be nearby?

Since the boarding house was only two streets over from Main, it wasn't unusual for people to wander in and out of the alley at all hours of the day and night. It was deserted now, except for their next-door neighbor, Mrs. Henderson, who was hurrying back inside after a visit to one of the privies that lined the alley. The woman glanced up and waved, and Abby returned the greeting while surveying the rest of the area.

An orange and white tabby cat stalked back and forth on another neighbor's porch, meowing loudly, tail twitching. Anxious for breakfast, no doubt. Windows were raised on most of the homes, and several back doors were open. There were dogs barking, a baby crying, the smell of bacon frying, the clink and rattle of kitchen cookware—the usual sights and sounds of a small town coming awake by degrees. No sign of a mysterious man with his hat pulled low.

Abby turned her attention to her own yard. The Hortons owned two large lots—one occupied by the house, the other with a garden and a chicken pen. They traded eggs and vegetables for fresh milk and butter from a neighbor who kept a cow. Everything else they purchased by mail-order, or bought from Silas—they could never grow all the potatoes they needed. All-in-all it was a good arrangement.

She took a quick walk through the garden, and then checked behind the chicken house. The hens squawked as she walked by, and the rooster began crowing loud enough to wake the dead. *How had she managed to sleep through that noise?* Seeing nothing unusual she turned toward the house. Whoever left the book was long-gone now.

She halted when the back door opened and the ranger stepped out onto the porch, a biscuit in one hand and his hat in the other.

Abby reached into her pocket, grasping the book like a lifeline as Caleb put the Stetson on and descended the steps to join her.

"Everything okay, Miss Horton? You look a little pale."

"I'm fine," she said. "And please, call me Abby."

He nodded, then glanced toward the house and lowered his voice. "I'm sorry about last night."

"So you said." Abby hesitated, but curiosity made her fumble on. "Y..you never did say why you kissed me in the first place?"

He looked at her, regret in his eyes. "I heard that young man laughing when I said I wasn't interested in you, and I just couldn't stand it."

Heat warmed Abby's face. So he hadn't been overcome with any strong feelings for her...except pity.

She lifted her chin and straightened her shoulders. "Henry's not a bad fellow. As I mentioned, he was out of sorts because I'd rejected his proposal again right before the revival service. He's actually one of my dearest friends."

"Oh." Caleb ducked his head and ran his free hand across the back of his neck. "So I made more of a mess of things. I really am sorry about all this."

Abby knew she was setting herself up for more humiliation, yet she had to ask. "So why did you start to kiss me the second time?"

He studied the toe of his boot as if it held the answer. Finally, he looked up and shrugged. "I honestly don't know, but I think that preacher saw us. I'm sorry about that, too."

She winced. "Yes, I was afraid of that. It's embarrassing, although there wasn't much to see." She studied him for a moment. "I don't feel ruined for life or anything, but I would like you to understand that I don't make a habit of letting strange men kiss me."

He nodded. "Understood. And for the record, I'm not all that strange."

Startled, she stared at him. *Was he teasing her?* He certainly didn't seem the type. Caleb smiled then, eyes crinkling at the corners. He was teasing, and it was as unexpected as the kiss. *And nearly as unnerving.*

"Well, you're certainly different than anyone else in this town." The words had barely cleared her lips when she realized why he'd seemed familiar. "Except maybe Sheriff Calhoun. Are you related to him and Dr. Nathaniel Calhoun? Y'all look enough alike to be brothers."

The ranger's expression changed. It wasn't the stern, steely look he'd worn the day before, or even the slightly unsure one he'd worn when he entered the kitchen. It was almost a lost look.

"We are brothers," he said softly.

She'd made the comment casually, and now didn't know how to respond. "I'm sorry if I spoke out of turn. I didn't know they had another sibling."

"Neither did they," he said, before abruptly turning away and heading down the alley.

That was certainly an intriguing statement. But Abby had her own problems to worry about. She hurried back inside, aware of the preacher's eagle eyes on her as she closed the screen.

Placing a spoonful of scrambled eggs on her own plate, Abby joined the others at the table, but she wasn't interested in food, or the congenial conversation flowing around her. Everyone else was talking about the weather now, and the excessively rainy spring and summer. How could her mother be so calm after everything that had happened. Wasn't she worried about her husband at all?

Though the others continued to chat, as soon as it appeared seemly to do so, Abby gathered the dishes and began washing them. She should have a little time to herself after the morning meal was over, before it was time to clean the rest of the house and start preparing for the next meal. She waited, not so patiently, as the conversation continued to hum around her. Eventually though, the first meal of the day was done and the clean-up was complete.

Abby rushed to her room, pulled a box from under the bed and began sorting through her mementoes—including a medal she'd won in a geography competition at school, a program from the Christmas play at church, a rock shaped like a heart, a string of buttons that had belonged to her Grandmother Horton, and a small piece of wood on which Henry Barnett had carved their initials.

Finally, she found what she was looking for—a roll of papers tied with a red ribbon. She tore the ribbon loose and let the pages fall across the bed, sifting through them until she found the one she wanted—a sketch of a little girl, her hand resting atop a great shaggy wolf, both with their heads tilted up, howling at the moon. Like the cover of the dime novel.

The sketch she was holding had been hastily drawn. She'd been a young child the first time her father told her the story. The Hortons had only recently moved to Moccasin Rock, and the town was sparsely settled. At night the sound of nearby animals terrified Abby. Especially the wolves howling. Her mother hadn't been able to comfort her at all. One night her father had picked her up and rocked her as he explained about the wolves, how they were simply talking to each other.

Over time, the stories had grown more detailed and elaborate— often involving other animals, and even Indians—until she was spellbound, and looking forward to bedtime each night. Especially when he told her about the girl who lived with the wolves. A girl named Abigail—a fearless little girl who howled at the moon right alongside her nocturnal friends. Eventually he'd written the stories down, and illustrated them for her.

Abby rolled the papers up and retied the ribbon before tossing everything back into the box. She had no idea who H.D. Roberts was, but the story of the little girl and the wolves had come from her father. Did this Roberts person know him? Was he trying to tell her something? She thumbed through the pages of the dime novel, clumsy in her haste. It wasn't until the last page that she noticed something penciled inside the back cover. One word in tiny letters. Cave. *Yes.* Heart pounding, Abby grabbed her sunbonnet, slipped it on, switched from her house slippers to her walking boots, and headed for the door. She knew where to look for her father.

Years ago, the two of them had stumbled across a cave at the base of a bluff that overlooked the Brazos River. They'd been picking berries for Mama to make jelly at the time, and had found blackberry bushes along with wild plum thickets nearby. But it was the cave that had captured their attention and imagination. Her father had wriggled through the narrow mouth of the black hole, and then led her inside. They had ventured no further.

"The wolves could be sleeping back there," her father had said to discourage any further exploration on her part. "They need their rest if they're going to be up howling and prowling tonight."

They'd gone back to the cave several times after that. Each time, little shivers ran up Abby's spine at the thought that wolves, and maybe other wild animals, could be sleeping inside.

Eventually she'd outgrown the stories, and she hadn't thought about the cave in years. Could her father be waiting for her there?

Chapter Five

CALEB POLISHED OFF the last of the biscuit before entering the jail, but his mind really wasn't on food. Even though he'd decided not to trifle with Abigail Horton, it might turn out to be more difficult than he'd first thought.

If there was anything cuter than Abby blushing when he teased her, he wasn't quite sure what it was. She might not have broken up with her beau because of him, but clearly she was more than a little interested.

He shook his head. Better get that girl out of his mind. There was work to do.

Bliss and Eli were waiting for him when he stepped through the door. Caleb cringed at the sight of his newly discovered sibling's black eye. He started to apologize again, but Eli waved it off, then handed him a cup of coffee.

"Nathaniel can't join us," he said as Caleb took the cup. "The local midwife has a patient who's run into a bit of trouble so he's helping out."

Caleb nodded his understanding, then got straight to business. "First thing this morning I checked at the train station. They hadn't seen anyone matching Bob's description. I'll stop by again when we get back."

"I checked at the telegraph office," Eli said. "So far no responses to the wires. I believe our search should probably start a little closer to home than I'd intended, anyway. According to the barkeep at Finley's Saloon, there was a man mumbling into his drink last night, talking about specters."

Caleb raised his brows. "And?"

"He was all shook up because he saw some sort of apparition down by the river," Eli said. "Unless he truly did see a ghost, which I find doubtful, I'm guessing he got a glimpse of your missing prisoner. I figured Bob would take outta here faster than greased lightning, but he may have decided to stick closer to home."

Caleb's interest quickened. "Did the man say what part of the river?"

"Yep, and it's not far from here. I'm ready to move out when you are."

Caleb swallowed his first and last gulp of coffee, placed the cup on Eli's desk, and headed for the door. He stopped short once he'd opened it. "I brought Bob in on the train. I need a horse."

Bliss ambled over carrying a short-barreled shotgun in one hand, and saddlebags in the other. "Come on," he said, "I'm headed to the livery stable. I'll introduce you to the owner, Eagan Smith. He'll get you fixed up."

Smith, a young man with a barrel-shaped body and eyes so brown they were almost black, listened quietly as Bliss explained what was needed.

"Don't be giving us no broken down nag," Bliss told the man. "This here's a Texas Ranger, and we need your best. Give him something with a little gumption and get-up-and-go."

Smith looked Caleb over for a moment. "I have what you need," he said.

After the deputy's directives, Caleb was afraid Smith would trot out a devil horse, but a few minutes later he was throwing a saddle over the back of a beautiful buckskin mare.

Bliss and Eli saddled their own horses while visiting with the livery owner, inquiring in turns about his family and his business.

From the corner of his eye Caleb kept a close watch on the deputy. He would've been willing to bet that the old man couldn't stay in the saddle, and would only slow them down, or worse, get himself hurt. Yet Bliss sat a horse with ease. In fact, he looked almost fierce with a Volcanic repeating pistol on his hip and the shotgun in a saddle scabbard.

Eli had slipped a Winchester repeating rifle into his own scabbard. He caught Caleb staring at it. "What's wrong?" he asked.

"I'm feeling a mite under-armed," Caleb admitted.

Eli grinned as he handed him a canteen of water. "Don't worry, baby brother. I've got your back."

Caleb was surprised that he found a measure of comfort in the jesting remark.

Since Bliss had lived in the area the longest, and knew the people, he volunteered to go homestead-to-homestead in the outlying wooded areas to the west, checking on everyone, while Eli and Caleb searched around the river.

Eli gave the old man a stern look before he took off. "Bliss, don't sit around talking to each and every person you come across. We need to make short work of this. Just make sure they're okay, and that there's no sign of the missing outlaw."

"I won't visit any more than's necessary," the old man drawled.

"What you consider necessary and what I consider necessary are usually different," Eli said. "Get in, get what information you can, and get out."

Bliss nodded. "I won't linger...unless they're talking about something I need to know." He tugged on the reins, turning his horse toward the woods. "Or unless they're cookin' something good, and they offer me some. Or," he hollered over his shoulder as the horse took off at a trot, "it's a good-looking widow woman."

Eli grinned and shook his head. "Make it quick, you old coot."

Caleb and Eli searched for miles up and down the Moccasin Rock side of the riverbank, with no luck at all. They then moved inland up into the cedar breaks, checking out a few dilapidated structures, including an abandoned log cabin. They came up empty-handed all around.

When they paused to water the horses, Eli took his hat off and swiped an arm across his brow. "It rained an uncommon amount here in the past few months. Sure has caused things to green up good."

Having fought his way through high weeds, brambles and briars for the past hour, Caleb merely grunted in acknowledgement. They'd come across tramped-down spots, but no footprints, at least not human ones. There was plenty of evidence of wildlife around the river.

"You know this area better than I do," Caleb said. "Where do you think we should head next?"

"There's a little town called Boone Springs to the east of us. It's the first one you come to after you cross the Brazos here. There's no bridge, so when the river's swollen up like it is now, the only way for most people to cross is to take the ferry."

"There's a ferry?"

"Yeah, not as impressive as it sounds," Eli said, "but considering that people have been swept away trying to cross on horseback, it's better than nothing. It'll hold two wagons and six horses. A man named Jones Morton runs it."

The ferry man, as he was known locally, was a big, bearded fellow who lived in a little shack near the river. The ferry was tied to a tree on the Moccasin Rock side. There was a bell attached to a post outside, and a sign that read: "Holler if you need help." Eli rang the bell and hollered.

"The only people I've crossed over was them men with those fancy tools and equipment," Morton told them when he appeared.

Before Caleb could question that, Eli explained. "A team of surveyors came in to town last week. They're doing preliminary work for a bridge here. They spend part of their time in Moccasin Rock, at the boarding house, and part in Boone Springs."

Caleb hadn't seen any men except the old preacher at breakfast. The surveyors must be in Boone Springs now. Eli thanked the man, and the Calhouns set out to search some more.

"It looks like this might not happen as quickly as I'd hoped," Eli admitted a bit later. "If you need to go on and report to headquarters, or search elsewhere, I'll keep looking and get word to you if I have any luck. I got a gut feeling Bob's still in this area, but I can't promise that."

Squinting as he looked out across the river, Caleb watched a red-tail hawk as it swooped low over the water and then back up over the cedar trees. He knew what Captain Parnell would say. *This is your mess, you clean it up.*

Caleb turned to Eli. "If it's all the same to you, I'd like to stick around and see this through. I'll need to contact my captain again and let him know what's happening. He's on his way back from Amarillo to Austin, so I'm not sure when or where the messages will catch up with him. But I'd better keep trying."

Eli nodded, then took the canteen from his saddle and drank heartily.

Sweat trickled down Caleb's neck. Removing the cork from his own canteen, he took a big swallow, then removed his hat and poured a little of the water over his head.

"You fixed for a place to stay?" Eli asked. "Most nights I bed down at the jail. I'm planning on building a house on some land I recently bought. For now there's only a one-room cabin out there. It's not much, but you're welcome to stay. The only hotel in town burned down awhile back."

Caleb nodded as he ran his fingers through his wet hair. "Yeah, so I heard. That's why I'm at the Horton place. Couldn't find any other accommodations. Didn't realize at the time that I had family in the area."

Eli studied him for a moment without speaking. "I don't really know how to ask this," he finally said, "but do you need anything? In the way of money or supplies?"

"Nah, I'm fine," Caleb said. "Thanks, though." *How much should he tell this new brother?* He was enjoying the chance to get to know Eli, yet the subject of money was tricky territory. He himself had been given every opportunity and privilege that wealth could afford, yet he suspected that hadn't been the case for Elijah and Nathaniel.

Caleb's money had come from his mother's side of the family, not his father, still it seemed strange to know that his own flesh and blood might have had needs that weren't met.

"So, you'll stay on at the boarding house?" Eli asked.

"Yes, I talked to Mrs. Horton this morning. She seemed glad of the chance for extra income."

"From what I've heard, they've had it rough since Bob's been gone," Eli said. "Can't imagine how upsetting all this must be for them. I never did get a chance to ask you last night, but what made you stop and let Bob see his family to start with?"

Caleb didn't want his brother to think of him as a pushover, yet he answered honestly. "Because Bob begged me. He kept saying he was innocent, saying that he could prove it, but he needed to talk to his family. I wasn't buying it. He finally asked me if he could at least tell them goodbye. Then right before we left, I got the telegram, supposedly from the sheriff here."

Eli nodded, but didn't say anything.

"Considering the circumstances, I feel real foolish now," Caleb admitted. "Since we were coming through anyway on the way to Austin, I thought, 'Why not?' I guess I should've been thinking 'Why?' I can't believe I fell for this."

"Is Mrs. Horton mad at you for trying to hunt him down? Could get awkward there."

"No, that's the strangest thing. I think they're really decent people. They've treated me very well. Although the daughter's acted a little strange. Sorta flustered when I'm talking to her. I think she may be…interested in me."

Eli looked at him, one brow raised. "Can't be the first time that's happened."

"Well…no. I'll have to be careful, though. If she were to take a serious liking to me…" He let his words trail off. *What in the world made him start this conversation?*

Eli grinned. "A real heart-breaker, are you?"

Caleb grunted, turned away and urged his horse onto a nearby trail. Apparently he wasn't ready to discuss money *or* females with his brother.

"Let's split up and search for a while," Eli called after him. "I'll see you in town."

"Sounds like a good idea," Caleb said over his shoulder.

An hour of hard searching later, with nothing to show for it except a few bug bites and one tired horse, Caleb was headed back to town when he spied a woman walking along the trail—a gingham-clad figure wearing a faded yellow sunbonnet, and carrying a big stick. Abigail Horton.

Caleb reined in his horse as she drew closer. "Hi, Abby. What are you doing way out here?"

She opened and closed her mouth several times before finally blurting, "I came out here to pick berries."

"Alone, and on foot? Is that safe?"

"I walk everywhere," she said with a shrug. "We don't own a horse or a buggy. Since we live in town, and seldom go anywhere, we've never needed one. It's not that far out here."

Caleb studied her, noting the tell-tale flush creeping up her cheeks. *What was that all about?* "Doesn't berry-picking require a bucket or a basket of some sort?" he asked. "How were you planning on carrying them?"

She glanced down as if surprised by her empty hands, then

reached up and untied the string beneath her chin. She yanked the bonnet off and held it in front of her. "In this."

Caleb was certainly no berry-picking expert, but it sure didn't seem the most sensible idea to him. Wouldn't that stain? And why did she look so guilty? He was about to question her further, when a movement in the bushes drew his attention.

The Remington was in his hand before he realized he'd reached for it. Henry Barnett stepped forward. The young man paled when he saw the gun, yet he pushed toward Abby anyway and took his place beside her as if he belonged there. *Picking berries, huh? So that's what they call it in Moccasin Rock.*

Caleb was surprised by a little pang of disappointment as he slipped the gun back into the holster. They might not be getting married yet, but obviously she wasn't averse to Henry's company. Why should he care? He was only passing through. And besides, he didn't want her getting attached to him, anyway.

Straightening in the saddle, Caleb mentally gave himself another reprimand that his captain would've delivered verbally had he been present. As long as he was in Moccasin Rock, Caleb was going to act like the lawman he was, and be on his best behavior.

He managed to assume what he hoped was the stoic, steely expression that had taken him a while to perfect, and a bored tone. "Well, I guess I'd better get on back to town. Good luck with your berry picking." He tipped his hat to them. "Looking forward to a nice cobbler or pie."

Caleb chuckled at the guilty expression that crossed her face.

So much for being on his best behavior.

Chapter Six

ABBY TOOK A deep breath as the ranger rode on toward town. One down, one to go. She turned toward Henry.

"What are you doing out here?" she snapped. "I thought you were going to leave me alone."

He seemed taken aback by her abrupt change of mood. "You're not the only one who likes to take walks, Abby."

Dismayed, she placed a hand on his arm. "I'm sorry, Henry. Hope you enjoyed your walk. I suppose you need to be getting on back to town now." She tried to control the hopeful sound to her voice.

He smiled. "Nope, I can help you pick berries."

"Thanks, Henry, but I really don't need the assistance."

His brows drew together. "How are you going to get enough berries for pie in just your bonnet?"

"It doesn't take many for a pie or two. Even if it did, how do you plan on carrying any berries at all?"

Uncertainty flitted across his face.

"Henry, go home."

Abby regretted her blunt dismissal when he flinched. "I'm only trying to help, Abby."

"I know, and I appreciate it," she said. "Truly I do. What I really need though is some time to myself. It's not about picking berries. That was an excuse to get Ranger Calhoun to leave. I really would love some time alone. I have a lot to think about." While it wasn't the whole truth, it wasn't a lie.

Henry visibly perked up. She'd said the right thing. Unfortunately, he jumped to the wrong conclusion. "I'm glad you're willing to give us some thought," he said. "I told you I wouldn't pressure you anymore, but I'm still hoping you'll come around to my way of thinking."

She opened her mouth to set him straight, and then thought better of it. Maybe he'd leave her alone sooner. "Thank you, Henry. I do have a lot on my mind."

"I understand. Are you sure you don't want me to stay though? It's so remote out here."

"We're not that far from town," she reminded him. "Plus, I have my walking stick. Besides, I figured you'd have chores waiting for you."

His shoulders slumped. She'd finally hit upon the right argument. Most of Henry's time was spent helping his aging parents. He was the last of five children born to Horace and Clara Barnett, and the only one to survive to adulthood.

Henry's parents relied on him for nearly everything around their busy farm. With the help of a few hired hands, the Barnetts grew a variety of crops, including corn and watermelon. However, they made most of their money raising and selling donkeys and mules—and Henry did most of the work.

"Yeah, there are always chores." He gave her a sad little smile before striking off toward town. "See you later."

She waited until he had cleared the bend in the trail before she continued on to the area where she remembered the cave being. The river rushed along below, glinting like a ribbon unfurled in the sunshine, the waves dashing at the bank.

Abby halted as she neared the bluff. She'd spotted the blackberry bushes and plum thickets easily enough, but they'd grown wild and tangled now, and she couldn't tell where the cave entrance was. Or had been. She pulled, snagging her hair and clothing on brambles and thorns. Stepping back to go at it from another angle, she heard a rustling noise behind her.

An arm pulled her backwards before she could react, and a deep voice whispered in her ear, "Did anyone follow you?"

"Daddy!" She turned and threw her arms around her father. "You did send me a message."

"Yes, and I'm glad you understood." He stepped back and looked at her. "You always were the smartest little girl I knew, and the prettiest."

"Oh, Daddy. I'm hardly a little girl."

"I know." He shook his head. "And Robby's shot up several inches. I can't believe how much I've missed. I feel like I've been gone for years instead of months."

Her father had changed, too. His hair had grown longer and shaggy, and he hadn't shaved in a good while. His hair was still dark, but the whiskers were gray. There were lines around his eyes that she didn't remember seeing before, and he'd lost weight. His appearance was almost gaunt.

"That's what I don't understand," she whispered. "Why did you miss anything? Where have you been?"

Her question had him looking past her shoulder. "Are you sure you weren't followed?"

"I'm alone. Although Henry and that ranger didn't make it easy."

At the mention of Caleb Calhoun her father paled. He tugged her a few feet away, pushed aside some bushes and then led her to the opening of the cave. Crouching down, he entered first and then motioned for her to follow. It was a tighter fit than when she was young. Once they were both inside, he pulled her back a few feet from the opening. "Are those two working together?"

She blinked, waiting for her eyes to adjust. "No, Ranger Calhoun stumbled across me as I was headed here. I think Henry might have followed me."

Her father, apparently accustomed to the darkness, located a match and then lit a stub of a candle. He placed it in a makeshift candle holder he'd rigged from a tin can. The resulting light, small and weak as it was, was welcome, and the smell of the burning wick helped offset some of the dank, musty odor surrounding them.

When he raised the candle, creating a wavering shadow all around, he motioned for her to come in a bit further. She did, and then cringed when something crunched beneath her feet. Her father moved the light closer to her, illuminating the bones of some animal beneath her boots.

Abby shuddered, just as a low moan echoed through the cave. Hand to her throat, she whispered, "I guess you were right all those years ago, something is living in here."

Her father chuckled softly. "There have been some critters here, obviously," he said, pointing to the bones, "but that sound came from one of my gang." He said the word "gang" with such sarcasm that Abby knew instantly there was more to the story than she'd heard. Not that she'd heard much.

"Who is he?"

"Name's Nash Latham. He was the one who took me from the boarding house last night. I wouldn't have thought he had the sense or the guts to pull it off, and I don't know where he got his hands on a badge. Probably don't want to know. He's the younger brother of the gang's leader, and the only one who managed to get away when the law came riding in. He's actually a nice enough kid, but he sure has kept some rough company all his life."

"Daddy, please tell me what's going on."

Bob Horton held a finger to his lips, and then stepped toward the rear of the cave. She started to follow him. He motioned for her to stay. Carrying the candle, he approached the man curled up on the ground and looked him over.

Apparently satisfied with what he saw, he returned. "Wanted to make sure Nash won't hear this. He drank himself sick last night and has been in a stupor for hours. He's starting to come around though, so I need to make this quick." He took a deep breath. "Look, no matter what you heard, I'm not an outlaw."

Relief flooded through her. "I knew that. Why does everybody think you are?"

He countered her question with one of his own. "What all has your mama told you?"

Abby shrugged. "Not much. When you left, she said you were looking for work."

"Well, that's the truth of it." He rubbed his hand across his jaw. "I saw an advertisement in the newspaper saying that railroad officials were set up in a hotel in Dallas. They were hiring men to lay track from Jenkins Gap to Cartersville."

"You were planning on building railroad track?"

"Yeah, not the brightest idea I've ever had," he admitted. "But the boarding house wasn't bringing in enough money. It did all right when the railroad was being built through here, yet it never has been steady income. Although I've taken odd jobs here and there, a man needs to provide for his family. I was letting y'all down. Desperation is the only way I know how to describe what I was feeling."

Blinking back tears, Abby said, "I'm so sorry you felt that way. I had no idea."

Her father's expression softened. "I didn't want you to know. I decided that if I could get on with the railroad—where the pay was better than anything around here—I could send the money home. As much as it pains me to admit this, I was also thinking about the fact that you need to be free to marry." He glanced away. "I was afraid that you weren't accepting Henry's proposals because you felt an obligation to help at the house."

Abby wouldn't lie to him about her desire to leave home, but she didn't want him to think he'd stood between her and true love. "I'm not ready to get married yet," she told him.

"Maybe not, but getting my hands on some cash, for all our sakes, sounded like the right thing to do at the time."

"Was Mama a willing party to this plan?"

He grimaced. "Not at all. She pleaded with me not to go. She said she didn't mind living poor. She did mind living without her husband. The way she grew up, well, family is important to her."

Abby knew the truth of that statement. Growing up in an orphanage had left Irene Horton clingy with the ones she loved.

"She warned me that it wouldn't work," he said, "which only made me want to do it more. Not very smart, yet that's the way it was. Of course, that wasn't the only reason I was determined to go. I really didn't want her to have to work so hard all the time."

It's been worse since you left. Abby didn't voice that thought. He obviously had enough to deal with without her laying guilt on him.

Although she didn't say it, he did. "I only made things worse."

"Your plan didn't work out?"

"To put it mildly. They had all the able-bodied men they needed—more able than me, for sure—probably before I even left Moccasin Rock. When I boarded the train for home, I was lower than I've felt in a long, long time. I could hardly stand the thought of facing your mother."

"Oh, Daddy. I'm sorry."

Her father acknowledged her concern with a pat on her arm. "Then the strangest thing happened. The man sitting next to me on the train turned out to be a writer. He'd written a dozen of those little dime novels and was making more money than he ever had before. He traveled all over the west, writing about outlaws, lawmen, folklore and legends. He wrote the stories as fast as he could, and sent them back to his publisher. Money was deposited into his bank account in Kansas City. I was fascinated by that. I started telling him about the stories I used to make up for you."

Abby knew where this was headed, and it made her furious. "His name was H.D. Roberts and he stole your stories," she said. "That is simply outrageous. Isn't there anything you can do?"

Her father smiled. "Let me finish. That man was intrigued by my stories, but he didn't steal them. Before we parted company, he gave me the name of his editor at a publishing company in New York, and encouraged me to send a story to him. I got off the train in the very next town, checked into the cheapest hotel I could find, and wrote up the story about Abby and the wolves. I added details to make it more of a folklore tale. I mailed it off, sent a telegram telling the editor to be expecting it—and included the name of the fellow who referred me—then I prayed and waited."

She stared at him in astonishment. "So you simply stayed there to see what would happen?"

He nodded. "I took a job cooking and cleaning at a café near the railroad. Your mother wasn't expecting me back yet anyway, and I couldn't face her without something to pin our hopes on. If the editor hated the stories, or I didn't hear from him within a few months, I would've come home, tail between my legs. In the meantime, I planned to send y'all every dime I made, from any kind of work. It didn't take as long as I'd expected to hear from the editor. I got a telegram a couple of weeks later. He loved the story and wanted more."

Her mouth dropped open. "So you're H.D. Roberts?"

Her father smiled. "Yes, instead of using Robert Dale Horton, I switched it to Horton Dale Roberts."

"Daddy, that's wonderful."

He ducked his head, almost bashful. "Oh, I was thrilled. I headed home, more encouraged than I had been in months, trying desperately to figure out what to write about next. And yet again, a fellow passenger on the train changed everything. Only this time it wasn't a stranger."

A sound outside drew Abby's attention. She held up a finger to her lips. She needn't have bothered. Her father stopped talking and appeared to be holding his breath as he watched the cave entrance.

After what seemed an interminable time with no additional noise, he whispered, "We'll finish this later. You need to get on home." He paused, placing both hands on her upper arms. "I'm gonna come barreling outta here at full speed if you call for help, Abby. I'd rather be recaptured than have something happen to you. So don't make any noise unless you need me."

She nodded, not wanting to do anything that would put him in any additional danger, yet she really wanted to stay right where she was until he answered her questions. All of them. *Why did you let us think you were dead, Daddy?*

"When you get back to town, I need you to do me a favor," he added.

She pushed everything else to the back of her mind. "Anything. Tell me what to do."

"Take the train to Fair Haven as soon as you can and send a telegram to Jim Adair, U.S. Marshal, Abilene, Kansas."

Numerous questions raced through her mind. She asked only one. "Can't I send it from Moccasin Rock?"

"No, too risky. The message I want you to send is something that only Marshal Adair will understand, but it's strange enough that if anyone finds out you sent it, they'll wonder what's going on. They might show up at the house to ask you about it, and I don't want your mother tangled up in this. I didn't have a chance to tell her much last night, and in hindsight that's for the best. She looked so tired and unhappy, and I'm the one who's done that to her. I don't want her involved until this is resolved."

He glanced back toward the other man again. "Nash is not all that bright, or I'd get him to help. He's not a bad kid, yet my instincts are telling me not to rely on him. I'd rather leave you out of this, too." He raised his hands in a helpless gesture. "I don't know what else to do."

"I can handle it," she assured him. "I won't let you down."

"Thank you, Abby. Although that ranger seems honest enough, there's a price on my head. And most worrisome, someone shot at us as I was being transported to the train. It barely missed me. The ranger thought it was someone shooting at him, since Nash managed to get away, but I'd gotten a glimpse of Nash disappearing in the other direction. Someone wants me dead."

A chill crept over her. She would do whatever was needed to keep him safe. "What should I tell Marshal Adair?"

"Send these five words: Old Blue's running loose tonight."

Abby blinked, not sure she'd heard him correctly. "What?"

He repeated the words and then pushed her toward the entrance. She turned and gave him a fierce hug, and though he started to return the embrace, he suddenly grunted with pain and eased his arms down to his sides.

"Daddy? What's wrong?"

"I'm recovering from a little incident, it's nothing. Now go on."

She dug her heels in. "I'm not leaving until you tell me."

He put a hand to her shoulder. "I was shot. I'm fine now. Really. It only pains me every now and then. Please go. Get out of here. Send that telegram as soon as you can."

She gasped, wanting to hear more about his injuries, but he was pushing her forward again.

"I'll be back as soon as I can," she whispered over her shoulder. "Do you have food?"

"Some. I'm not sure where Nash got it, and it's not exactly home-cooking, but we'll be okay for at least a couple of days."

Abby turned around again at the last moment, kissed him on his scruffy cheek and crept to the opening. She crouched down and waited several moments. All she heard outside was a bird chirping. With one last look behind her, she said a silent prayer for her father and wriggled through the opening.

Her thoughts were as tangled as the plum thicket. There were so many questions she hadn't had time to ask her father. *They'll have to wait.*

Abby's gaze darted here and there on the horizon, searching for any activity or motion. Nothing. Maybe it was a deer they heard. Swallowing the lump of anxiety and fear in her throat, she started home. Sure, that's what it was. *Only a deer.*

Chapter Seven

ABBY MENTALLY REHEARSED the upcoming conversation with her mother as she climbed the steps of the back porch. Yet no matter how it began, the imaginary discussion came to a screeching halt when she got to the, "I need to go to Fair Haven right now, no matter how busy we are, and I can't tell you why," part.

Squaring her shoulders, Abby took a deep breath. She could do this. She was already harboring a fugitive, had lied to a Texas Ranger, and crept into a cave—occupied by an outlaw no less.

When she walked through the back door, her mother looked up from the breadboard. "Where did you get off to, Abby? I was starting to worry."

The tone was pleasant, the question a reasonable one, yet Abby found herself discomfited at the invisible bonds that seemed to pull tighter each week.

"I went for a walk." She draped her bonnet over a hook near the back door, and took a deep breath before turning towards her mother. "Mama, I ne—" Abby paused. If she said she *needed* to go, her mother would be even more worried, and wouldn't rest until she knew the whole story. "I want to catch the next train to Fair Haven."

Her mother had started kneading bread dough, but stilled and studied her daughter. "Whatever for?"

"I'd like to pick up a few things at the mercantile there."

"Silas doesn't have what you need?"

Abby hated to do it, but she was going to have to guilt her mother into letting her go. "Mama, I need a little time away from here."

Her mother's mouth dropped open. "Oh, Abby. I'm so sorry. Of course, go, get away for a while. Why don't you take Robby with you? He came in from the Wilson's a few minutes ago. I sent him upstairs to change clothes."

"Maybe next time," Abby said. "I need to hurry if I'm going to make it to the station on time."

Her mother wasn't easily dissuaded. "Please, take him with you. I worry about you alone."

"I can take care of myself," Abby protested.

"I know, sweetheart. But if anything happened to you, I don't think I could bear it."

Her mother's usual anxiety was more trying today. "Nothing is going to happen," Abby said. "Even if it did, Robby wouldn't be much protection."

"He could run for help," Irene said, then waved a hand. "You're right. Of course nothing's going to happen. But I was also thinking that Robby might enjoy a chance to get away, too."

Abby groaned. *Brilliant move, Mama.* Now she'd have to take her brother. "I'll go up and get him."

"Wonderful. Thank you, Abby. Please be careful when you get to Fair Haven. Things can go wrong in a heartbeat."

Was she thinking about what had happened to her husband? Abby was trying to think of a way to reassure her that everything would be okay, when it dawned on her that her mother didn't seem particularly distraught, or overcome with worry…at least not about Bob Horton.

"Mama, did you know that Daddy was still alive?"

Her mother's startled gaze flew to hers, and then dropped. "No, I didn't."

Abby wasn't about to let the subject go. Obviously her mother knew more than she was letting on.

"Mama, please."

Sighing, her mother wiped her hands on a rag and sank down on one of the kitchen chairs. "I was stunned to see him at the revival," she admitted, "but I wasn't as surprised as you were, I suppose, because deep in my heart I never felt like he was dead."

Irene's lips quivered and she stared down at her hands, twisting the plain gold band on her ring finger. "I just knew, bone-deep, that I would see him again, this side of Heaven I mean." Tears burned Abby's eyes, but she didn't interrupt.

Her mother drew in a deep breath. "Don't get me wrong, I was angry at him when he showed up, because he was obviously in trouble, and I hadn't wanted him to go in the first place, and…well, I could go on, but that's between me and your father."

Abby tried hard to keep the accusatory tone from her voice. "Why didn't you say something sooner?"

"What was there to say? I didn't really know anything. When that coffin was returned here, I felt like I was the one who died. I went through the funeral in a daze. I felt as if time had stopped and I was waiting for something. Yet I didn't know what. Thankfully, I had you children, and this house, and the boarders to tend to. I didn't have time to dwell on anything."

What her mother said was logical, yet it still didn't explain why she wasn't more concerned now. "You seemed to be keeping something from me last night."

Irene Horton stood, smoothing her apron as she spoke. "Your father and I had a moment to talk, and he assured me that he was innocent. I was devastated when Ranger Calhoun told us about the gang. Yet after giving it some thought, I simply don't believe it. I'm still furious with Bob for leaving in the first place, but I know this has to be a mistake. Your father hugged me as he left, and he whispered to me that the young man who'd come for him was on his side. I feel guilty for not telling Ranger Calhoun about that, although I won't betray my husband. Bob's a good man. He said he didn't know when he'd be back, but he would be back—for me not to worry."

Abby hugged her mother before going up to get Robby. "He's right, Mama, you shouldn't worry." *I'll be doing enough for the both of us.*

***

Caleb swung back around to the livery stable, and asked Eagan Smith if anyone had purchased or hired out a horse. Smith answered in the affirmative, and Caleb was excited until he caught the man smiling. He realized Smith was talking about Caleb himself and the buckskin.

His next stop was the mercantile. "No, ain't seen nary a soul," said the owner Silas Martin, a portly, balding man with a droopy mustache. "Well, I seen a few, but Bob Horton wasn't one of them." He scratched his chin, thoughtful. "Come to think of it, there was a fellow in the alley earlier. Don't believe he ever came in, though."

"What did he look like?"

"Didn't get close enough to tell, his hat was pulled low."

"Do you remember what he was wearing?"

Silas shook his head. "No."

"Well, thanks anyway," Caleb said. "If you see him again, will you let me know?"

"Sure thing," Silas said.

Caleb then stopped by the jail, where Bliss reported that he'd also came up empty-handed. "No one's seen hide nor hair of Bob Horton," the old man said, "and I didn't even hear any interesting stories."

Eli returned a short time later, reporting the same results. "I've gotten word back from all the lawmen in the surrounding towns, and none of them have seen Bob either. They've agreed to keep their eyes open."

"Appreciate you checking," Caleb said as he dropped into a chair. "What about unusual activities," he asked both men. "Anybody around here report any stolen livestock, clothing, food, that sorta thing?"

Eli shook his head, while Bliss looked thoughtful.

"What are you thinking?" Eli asked the old man.

"You recall that Silas had a few things turn up missing recently? Seems like it was some cigars, and some sort of miracle elixir." He pushed his hat back. "Although if it was really a miracle, seems like it would cost more than fifty cents a bottle," he muttered.

Eli grinned and then opened his mouth. Before he could say anything, Bliss was talking again.

"Then Big John Finley came in here all riled up about somebody stealing some jugs of whiskey. Only piddlin' things, but it coulda been Bob Horton, I guess."

Eli nodded. "Yeah, except all that happened several days before Caleb and his prisoner got here."

"That's true," Bliss said. "Although, there was a fellow in here a little bit ago that reported a missing mule."

Caleb leaned forward. "You think maybe Bob took the mule?"

Bliss tipped his hat back even further and scratched his head. "Well, I considered that, until I remembered that's the mule that likes to run around town with that pig that belongs to Adger Wilson. The two of them enjoy an outing every now and then," the old man concluded. "Doubtful there was any theft involved."

"That's true," Eli said, "not unusual for those two."

Caleb was about to say, "I don't understand," and then decided he might as well give up on that expression until he left Moccasin Rock.

After leaving the jail, Caleb headed to the telegraph office to do what he'd been dreading all morning—sending another telegram to his captain. Hopefully it would catch up with him soon. As much as he hated to do it, Caleb had to let him know that Bob Horton was still at large.

Afterwards, Caleb returned to the train station. He'd checked with the clerk at the depot several times, and no one matching Bob's description had purchased a ticket. There was still the possibility that the outlaw would try to sneak aboard at the last minute, so Caleb settled down to wait and watch.

He was sitting on a bench, back against the outer wall of the depot, chewing on a matchstick and trying to decide what to do next if Bob didn't show up, when the train pulled into the station. He really only needed to watch for someone trying to sneak on the train and out of town, yet his natural curiosity kept his eyes focused on the people departing from the passenger car.

The first one to make it down the platform steps was a dapper older man, half dragging, half carrying what appeared to be a salesman's sample case. The man stopped just beyond the steps and took off his derby hat. He swiped a handkerchief across his forehead and then proceeded on toward town. The next passenger was a gray-haired woman carrying a small, red-headed child, and those two were followed by a young couple who had eyes only for each other.

Caleb heard the next passenger before he saw her. Boy, was she putting up a fuss. He shook his head as he listened to her complaining about how uncomfortable the seat had been, and about the heat, the noise, even the smoke and the cinders. That must've made for a very long trip for the others. Caleb leaned forward, even more curious, as the woman neared the steps to the platform.

He spied first a pair of delicate green boots with high heels, pointy toes and a dozen or more buttons, followed by a green silk dress clinging to a nicely-curved figure. The hat she wore was such an arresting and bizarre spectacle—a profusion of feathers, bows, flowers, even a tiny stuffed bird—that his eyes were drawn there next, skipping completely over the woman's face.

She was down the steps, across the platform and standing in front of him before he'd gotten a good look at her. Pretty. Very pretty. Dark brown hair, big brown eyes. Eyes that were looking him over in much the same way he studied her.

Warning bells went off in his head.

Suddenly the woman smiled and placed one dainty hand on her hip.

"Well, well, if it isn't Caleb Calhoun. Just who I was looking for."

The matchstick dropped from his lips as he shot to his feet. "Jenna?"

"Sure is. I was headed to Austin, and was annoyed at the delay here. Now I'm grateful. I've been looking for you for a while, sugar doll."

Caleb was too stunned to verbalize the half-dozen thoughts racing through his mind, so he settled for one little word. "Why?"

She adjusted her hat, causing the bird to wobble. Caleb knew exactly how the little fellow felt.

"I got tired of waiting on you," Jenna said. "We can be married as easily in Texas as we could in Colorado."

"M…married?"

She reached out to hug him, then stilled. "You're not about to tell me you forgot, are you?"

"Forgot what?"

Her eyes narrowed. "That you proposed to me."

Mind racing, Caleb tried to recall any such conversation. Taking his hat off, he shook his head and then ran his fingers through his hair. "I did?"

She stomped one of those ridiculous boots on the platform. "Are you telling me you don't remember one of the most important moments of my life?" Her words started out quietly enough but had changed to a high-pitched screech by the end.

He glanced over his shoulder at several gawking bystanders

before taking her hand. "Calm down, Jenna. You're making a scene. Now refresh my memory."

She drew in a deep breath. "After your father's funeral, you said you'd be back. That if I needed you before then, you'd be there even quicker. That I could count on you. That you'd always take care of me." Each word was bitten off, teeth bared.

Caleb slapped his hat on his head, his own irritation taking hold. "Now that wasn't a proposal and you know it. I meant that I'd be there to *help* you, if you needed me. You get yourself on back to Truett. We are *not* getting married. I don't have time for this... or for you."

He braced for the next round of screeches, and was dismayed when she burst into tears instead. Caleb glanced around, awkwardly patting her back.

The sound of footsteps drew his attention. The boy he'd seen delivering groceries to the boarding house approached. He slowed when Caleb frowned.

"What is it?" Caleb snapped.

The boy flinched and backed up. Caleb felt about an inch tall. He hadn't meant to sound so gruff. He gentled his voice. "Did you need to talk to me?"

"You've got a telegram, sir." The boy thrust a piece of paper at him and scurried away.

The message was from his captain. It was short and to the point. "Find Bob Horton. Now. Or I'll hire Jenna Nolan. Obviously she knows how to track a man."

Caleb crumpled the telegram in his fist. It took effort to unclench his jaws enough to speak. "So you talked to my Captain? How? Why?"

Jenna nodded, reaching into her small, beaded handbag and removing a lace-trimmed, monogrammed handkerchief. After dabbing her eyes, swiping at her nose, and sniffing delicately, she answered him. "I stopped in Amarillo and went to the Ranger headquarters there. You said after you got out of the army you were planning to join the Rangers. When you didn't answer any of my letters, I decided to come out and surprise you."

He stared at her, blinking rapidly, unable to say a word.

She placed a hand on his arm. "I figured even if those Rangers didn't know you, they could tell me where to head next. So I told them all about you, and how handsome and smart you are, and how you were probably the boss of all the rangers by now."

Caleb closed his eyes and swallowed hard. *Would he ever be able to live this down?*

Jenna was still chattering away. "I explained that I needed to find you. There was a real nice man there, I can't remember his name, but it started with a P."

"Parnell," Caleb muttered. "Captain Joshua Parnell."

She smiled at him. "Yes, that's it. I was thrilled when he said he knew you."

Caleb's mortification gave way to aggravation again. "I can't believe he told you where to find me. You could've been some sort of lunatic for all he knew."

"Oh, Captain Parnell didn't want to tell me at first, but when I explained about our getting married, and began to cry, he smiled real big and put me on the train. Said you deserved to be reunited with me. Wasn't that sweet of him?"

Caleb swallowed about a dozen curse words before replying. "Yes, I'm sure it was pure kindness on his part. Come on, you can rest a while before we make arrangements to send you back."

"Oh, Caleb. I can't go back." She took a deep breath and then let out a wail. "I sold everything."

Something akin to panic began to replace his earlier confusion. "Then buy it all back."

"I can't," Jenna said. "I was robbed. I'm destitute. I have no money and nowhere to go."

He grasped her arm. "Were you hurt?" He didn't give her time to answer. "Where did it happen? I'll help you track the money down. We'll file a report and…as soon as I take care of business here, I'll investigate the robbery myself."

"That's the problem, I don't know for sure where it was." She pressed the handkerchief to her eyes again. "I've gotten on and off so many coaches, wagons and trains since I left Truett. The money was secure in my valise one day, and when I checked several days later it was gone."

He couldn't believe his ears. "Surely you left most of the money in the bank. Right? You wouldn't have tried carrying all that cash all this way."

"Everything I had is gone," she whispered on a sob. "I honestly don't know what I'm going to do."

Caleb shook his head and choked back a groan. Jenna could be manipulative. He'd witnessed it plenty of times growing up, but these tears were genuine. She was devastated…and literally hanging from him. He guided her into the depot and over to a corner away from the curious stares on the platform.

Pulling Jenna close, he made soothing sounds, mostly because he didn't know what words to say. Although he had no intention of marrying her, he sure didn't want to see her hurting. Could this day get any worse?

He glanced up to find Abigail Horton staring at him from across the depot, an odd expression on her face. She looked…hurt. And for some strange reason that hit him like a punch to the gut. The day *had* gotten worse.

He pulled free from Jenna and stepped toward Abby, not sure what he should say, or why he felt he needed to say anything. Before he could reach her though, she lifted her chin and stormed away, dragging a young boy by the hand toward the ticket desk. Now where were they going?

Caleb wanted to follow them, but Jenna was still crying, loudly, behind him. "Come on," he told her. "Let's see if there's room at the boarding house for you. We'll decide later what to do."

Jenna's tears had tapered off to an occasional hiccupping sob by the time they reached the Horton's, then started again when Mrs. Horton regretfully informed them that no room was available.

"I'll have to stay at a hotel," Jenna said after taking her hanky out again. "You can loan me some money, can't you, Caleb?"

Caleb exchanged glances with Mrs. Horton, dreading the next few minutes. "Of course I'll take care of the money. But the only hotel in town burned down recently. That's why I'm staying here."

He braced for a fresh onslaught of weeping, and was horrified when she merely shrugged and gave him a calculating grin. "Then I'll have to stay with you, won't I?"

Caleb was relieved when Mrs. Horton didn't gasp or faint at the comment, though she did give Jenna a hard look. "Are you two married?"

"No," Caleb blurted.

"That's true," Jenna said, with another sidelong look his way. "But we've known each other since we were children."

"Well, you're not children now," Mrs. Horton said. "I'm afraid I can't allow you to share a room. If you truly have no place else to turn, you'll have to stay with Abby."

Jenna's expression turned wary. "Who's Abby?"

"My daughter."

"I have to share accommodations with a child?"

Mrs. Horton shook her head. "No, Abby is a young woman, a good deal older than you. She's twenty-two."

Jenna's mouth dropped open. "I'm twenty-three."

Irene Horton didn't say it, but her raised eyebrows seemed to imply that the young lady sure wasn't acting her age.

Mrs. Horton turned to him. "Ranger Calhoun, will you help me get a cot from the attic?"

"Cot?" Jenna started to say something else. Looks from both of them shut her up.

"I'd be glad to get it, ma'am," Caleb said. "And thank you for helping Jenna out."

They were on the second-floor landing when Miss Culpepper called up from the bottom of the stairs. "Mrs. Horton, it smells like something might be about to burn down here. Do you want me to tend to whatever you've got cooking?"

Mrs. Horton paused, clearly torn between her duties in the kitchen and helping him with Jenna's plight. "I'll take care of this," Caleb told her. "You can go on back down."

"Thank you," she said, guiding him to the attic entrance. "The cot should be over against the north wall. Hopefully Abby will be home soon, and she'll bring the linens." Hurrying toward the stairs, she called out, "I'll be right down, Miss Culpepper."

Caleb pretended he didn't know that her daughter was absent. "So Abby's away?"

"She's taken the train to Fair Haven," Mrs. Horton said over her shoulder. "I'm glad for her to get away, and I'll be more glad for her to return. She left rather unexpectedly, and I'm short-handed in the kitchen."

So Abby left in a hurry, huh? What was so important in Fair Haven? *Or was it a who?*

Chapter Eight

"HE OWES YOU no explanations," Abby muttered to herself as she settled into her seat on the train. "You don't even know him, and it's no concern of yours who that woman is. Why in the world do you care?"

Robby turned to her. "Who are you talking about?"

"Nobody important."

He leaned his head back against the seat. "I knew you wouldn't tell me. Nobody ever tells me anything anymore."

Abby glanced down, surprised by the look of frustration on her little brother's face, and ashamed of herself for not realizing how much their father's reappearance had confused him. "I'm sorry, Robby."

She knew better than to hug him. At eleven, he was already shying away from demonstrations of affection from his mother and sister. He was growing up before her eyes. Robby had the same dark hair and deep blue eyes as their father, and it was easy to see what he'd look like as an adult. Abby had also inherited eyes that color, but the reddish brown hair of their mother.

"It's just that there's so much going on, and I don't understand most of it myself," she admitted.

"Can you at least tell me what happened to Daddy?" he whispered. "Is he a bad outlaw like they say?"

"I *can* tell you that much—he's not." What else could she say that would bring him comfort but not give away their father's secrets? "He was with the wrong people, and got caught up in something he couldn't find a way out of. It will all be sorted out, soon."

"Where is he now?"

She hesitated. "Well, you know he came home for a little while last night, and then left again, right?"

He nodded. "And the lawman's looking for him."

"Yes. I imagine we'll hear something as soon as he finds him. There's been some confusion. It'll all be straightened out soon."

"I hope he doesn't shoot Daddy before he can explain what happened."

That simple, fervent wish went straight to Abby's heart, echoing her own worst fears. She reached for Robby's hand and squeezed it. For once, he didn't object. "It'll be okay," she whispered.

Fair Haven was packed. Since it was Saturday, the day when country people were most likely to come to town, there were sturdy, weather-beaten wagons vying for space with buggies and fancy carriages. Horses and the occasional mule were tied to every available hitching post, and people were standing in little clumps, chatting and visiting as if it were a garden party.

Pushing their way through the crowd milling about the boardwalks, Abby led Robby into the general store. Just inside, she drew in a deep breath and let her gaze roam at will.

The place was a veritable feast for her senses and Abby soaked it all in. There were jars of candy—lemon drops, licorice, peppermint sticks, wintergreen lozenges and rock candy on display—as well as the various confections, including pink and white bonbons and chocolate fudge stacked on squares of waxed paper.

She merely glanced at the more practical goods—including churns and paddles, Mason jars and coffee grinders, but lingered over the colorful bolts of fabric, the lace trim, and ribbon, beads and buttons. And several ready-made hats. *Oh my.* A sign below the display proclaimed that these were the creations of Mr. Monroe's Millinery, and that custom orders could be placed at his establishment down the block.

She didn't know who Mr. Monroe was, but the man was obviously an artist. The hats were incredible creations, every bit as beautiful and tempting as the candy. Abby had exchanged her sunbonnet for her Sunday hat before leaving home, but it paled in comparison to these. She self-consciously fingered the brim of her own more practical straw headpiece, and gave the hats on display one more lingering glance. Even these hats were nothing compared to the masterpiece that Ranger Calhoun's friend had been wearing. Where did a person find a hat like that? Created especially for that woman, no doubt.

Abby turned away from the millinery section and thoughts of the beautiful woman, and waited to see what would capture Robby's attention. He was fascinated with many of the books, and so was she, yet she couldn't let her little brother linger there. Daddy hadn't mentioned the wolf story in years, so she didn't think Robby would recognize it, but better safe than sorry. So she steered him clear of the dime novels. Besides, Mama wouldn't have approved anyway.

The toys were another matter—there was no pulling him away from those. There were tops, drums, dolls, balls, trains, boats and wooden horses. Unfortunately, most of them were beyond what her meager funds would allow. Until they knew the outcome of her father's plight, she couldn't squander the money she had. When Robby stopped beside a small wooden game—a little triangular puzzle board with pegs you moved around in specific designs—she knew they'd found the right thing.

She also picked up some medication for Miss Culpepper and a few last-minute things her mother had mentioned, and they made their way to the front. The storekeeper rang up their purchases on a cash register with fancy silver scroll work and a bell that echoed throughout the building when he entered each price. Although this store was better stocked and more efficiently laid out than Martin's

Mercantile, when the clerk took her money without a greeting she missed Silas Martin and his less impressive establishment.

They were on their way out when she noticed the bulletin board by the door. It wasn't the various handbills and pamphlets—advertising everything from patent medicines to tobacco products—that held her attention. It was the wanted poster for the Latham gang. Five hundred dollar reward for their leader. Dead or Alive.

Abby's stomach twisted. Her father was right; there were people who'd be willing to do anything for that kind of money.

"I need to take that down," the clerk said, when he noticed what she was reading. "I heard that the law caught up with them." He paused to shoot a stream of tobacco into a spittoon near his feet. "I say good riddance to bad rubbish. Men like that are a scourge, a bane, a veritable plague on society. Vermin, pure and simple."

Abby, face burning, hurried Robby outside before the man could share any more of his thoughts. Once on the boardwalk, she took a few deep breaths, then found a bench within sight of the telegraph office. She instructed Robby to sit there and wait for her. "I won't be long. Why don't you play with your puzzle until I return?"

"Where you going?" he asked, but he'd already begun moving the little pegs around.

She smoothed his hair down with her palm, cupping his head for a moment when he didn't jerk away. "One more errand to run. Will you stay put?"

Robby nodded, distracted, and was still as absorbed when she returned from completing her task. He hadn't even noticed she was gone. Mission accomplished. She'd sent the unusual message her father had given her, and signed her name. She would check back before they left town to see if there'd been a reply.

In the meantime, they could look around a bit before the return trip home. "Come on," Abby said, "let's take a walk. I'll put your puzzle in my bag." He slipped the board and pegs back into its canvas pouch and pulled the drawstring before handing it to her.

Together they studied every building, person and fancy convey-ance they stumbled across. A woman with two infants nestled inside a large carriage paused and smiled indulgently as Abby admired the babies' intricately-smocked matching gowns.

Robby spared a passing glance at the twins, but appeared more interested in the carriage itself. Abby knew her brother well enough to know that he was probably thinking of other ways he could use those oversized, spoked-wheels—probably affixed to some home-made contraption as he raced headlong down the nearest hillside.

Around the next corner, people were gathered to watch a boxing match, though the crowd was too thick for them to get more than a glimpse. Robby was particularly disappointed by that, until they came across a man with a pet monkey on the next corner. Abby enjoyed the sight of her brother laughing at their antics more than she did the antics themselves.

At a restaurant with a huge front window, she paused, taking in the diners in their finery, and the large chandelier—each candle lit even though it was daylight. What would it be like to eat a meal that you hadn't prepared? Then her attention was captured by the waiters, bustling here and there. They moved even faster than she and her mother.

"Come on," Robby said, pulling on her arm. "That's boring, let's go."

If Fair Haven was this busy, what would New York, Chicago or Boston be like?

She and Robby crossed over to the town square and sat on the grass near a pond to eat the sandwiches Abby had brought along. Before they returned to the train station, she stopped by the tele-graph office once more. Leaving Robby on the bench again, she popped inside long enough to discover that there'd been no reply.

Abby was disappointed, but all she knew to do was pray—and try to keep her secret from Ranger Calhoun.

***

As the train rattled and steamed back toward Moccasin Rock, everything seemed to speed by faster than it had on the trip out. Abby's
feet grew heavy as she and Robby disembarked and headed home to
the mountain of work she knew was waiting for her. Robby spotted several of the Wilson kids as they neared the house and took off
in their direction at a run. "Hey fellas, look what I got," he said,
clutching the puzzle in his hand.

"Don't be long," Abby reminded him. "You've got chores to do
before bed."

"I know," he called back.

She climbed the steps, crossed the wide porch, and pasted a
smile on her face before entering the kitchen. Her mother was stirring something on the stove. Abby placed the items she'd picked up
in Fair Haven on the table.

"I wish you could've gone with us, Mama. There were so many
people, and such an interesting bunch." She removed her hat and
reached for her apron without a wasted motion. When there was no
reply, Abby turned around.

Her mother stood stock still, staring at her with a strange
expression. *What's going on?* Mama couldn't know what she'd done,
not this soon. Abby tried to keep a guilty look from her face, and
then realized that her mother was the one who looked remorseful.

She tensed. "What's wrong, Mama?"

Her mother abruptly came to life with a burst of energy, stirring
and chattering away. "There's nothing wrong, in fact it's wonderful
news. We got a new guest while you were gone."

Abby's shoulders slumped in relief. "Oh, where did you put
them? Did Reverend Wainright decide to leave after all?"

"No, he's still here."

"If that's the case, we don't have room for anyone else. There's
nowhere for them to sleep."

Her mother finally stopped fidgeting with everything and looked Abby in the eye. "I'm sorry, dear."

Abby rubbed at her temples, trying to keep a headache and panic at bay. "Sorry for what?"

"We put her in your room."

Her heart sank. *Please, tell me you didn't move Miss Culpepper in with me.* "Her?"

"Yes, a friend of Ranger Calhoun's arrived in town and needed a place to stay."

The woman from the train station. Abby bit back an angry response, not sure if it was because the woman was to stay with her, or because she was a friend of Caleb's. Either way, Abby was not happy. Her room was the smallest and the plainest in the house. She understood that the best of everything needed to go to the paying guests. She was okay with that. At least that plain little space had been hers and hers alone. A place where she could think and dream. *Maybe this is all a bad dream.*

She followed her mother through the hall and up the stairs calmly enough, but her first glimpse inside her room only served to worsen her mood. There was indeed a cot tucked away in the corner, and "she" was sprawled across Abby's own bed.

Her mother introduced them with a quick, "Abby, this is Jenna Nolan," and then scurried from the room without making eye-contact with her daughter. Abby nodded, her attention already captured by the other woman. The fact that Jenna was impossibly beautiful—even travel-weary and somewhat rumpled in appearance—only added to Abby's annoyance.

Who are you?

Before Abby could decide on a polite way to voice that very question, the woman greeted her with a complaint. "I couldn't seem to get comfortable on that," she said, pointing to the cot.

"I'm afraid it's the best we can do." Abby stepped around a large, leather suitcase that the woman had opened in the middle of the floor. Two huge trunks, topped with several hat boxes, were shoved against the wall, leaving only a small pathway to her own bed. Abby battled frustration, knowing it was due in part to fatigue and concern over her father. It wasn't fair to take it out on their newest boarder.

Jenna Nolan eyed the cot again, and then ran her hand across the quilt on Abby's bed. "This one is so comfortable."

"I'm sorry if these accommodations are not what you're accustomed to, but I'm not giving up my own bed."

There was no immediate hysterics, but Jenna sniffed a couple of times and Abby braced for a tearful scene like she'd witnessed at the train station. Only this time, instead of crying hysterically, the woman pressed her fingers to her eyes and moaned. "I'm so tired. I've been traveling for weeks."

"Weeks? Where did you come from?"

"Colorado."

Abby's interest quickened. "What are you doing here?"

"I was trying to find Caleb."

She'd already guessed that much. "Why?"

"Because we're going to be married."

Abby was too stunned to speak for a moment. *He kissed me while he was betrothed to someone else?* Pity kiss or no, that was simply outrageous. She finally murmured, "Congratulations, I'm sure you'll be very happy," yet she suspected her words sounded as hollow as she felt. "When is the big day?"

The girl ran her hand over the quilt again. "I'm not sure, yet. Caleb and I haven't worked out all the details."

A chilling thought occurred to Abby. What if he'd duped this girl? What if he had a whole string of girls across the country that he'd kissed within minutes of meeting them? She concentrated on keeping her voice level, hopefully betraying none of the turmoil roiling inside her. "How long have you known Ranger Calhoun?"

"Since the day I was born," Jenna said, a dreamy smile replacing the pout. "He's a little older than I am, but our parents were the dearest of friends. Our property bordered his. We grew up together."

Abby was relieved, somewhat. This girl was probably the first he'd kissed, though she definitely wasn't the most recent. What a scoundrel he was. She thought back to the long list of names that the clerk in Fair Haven had called the outlaw gang. Yes, a couple of them also described Caleb Calhoun.

"How long have you been betrothed?"

Jenna looked away, her eyes not meeting Abby's. "I didn't know I'd be subjected to an inquisition," she sniffed. "Do you treat all your guests this way?"

Abby stiffened. "I'm sorry if I offended." She whirled around to leave and nearly ran into Caleb in the doorway.

He looked straight into her eyes. "I'm sorry. But—"

She didn't know what he was apologizing for—his friend's behavior, or his. She wasn't in the mood for either. And she wasn't interested in hearing anything else he had to say.

"Please, don't give it another thought, Mr. Calhoun." She pushed at his shoulder, intending to flounce by him, but it was like hitting a brick wall. Her heart stuttered for a moment when he reached out to steady her. Anger, that's all it was.

"Excuse me," she said in her iciest voice. "I have work to do."

He moved aside without a reply. She risked a glance at him, expecting to see shame, or embarrassment, yet he was staring at her, mouth tight, brows drawn together. Caleb Calhoun was angry. With her. *Of all the nerve!*

***

To Abby's relief, Ranger Calhoun was not present for supper. By the time the meal and cleanup were over, she was too tired to worry about their encounter. As always, she readied the kitchen for the morning. The more she could get done in advance, the more smoothly things would run the next day. After cleaning the stove, she laid the wood for the next fire, then swept the floor and did a final wipe down of all the surfaces.

Afterwards she pumped water—not even bothering to heat it—and carried it to what Mama had started calling the bathing room. It had been the laundry room before the hotel burned down. Her mother was trying to make what few amenities they offered sound grander, she supposed.

Granted, the room did contain a large galvanized tub, but it also contained several smaller tubs, bars of laundry soap, and a rub board. In hot weather they hauled the tubs out and washed clothes on the back porch, so it really didn't matter what they called the room anyway.

Since Abby was the last of several people to use the tub that day, she scrubbed it good before adding the water. She then reached into the far recesses of the cupboard and removed an embossed leather case. She ran a finger over the top, and then popped it open to admire the celluloid comb, brush, and toothbrush nestled inside. There was also a tin box that held a bar of lavender-scented soap.

She'd received the travel kit as a gift from a friend, but was loathe to use it now. She would someday, though. Abby wasn't sure when, or even where she'd go, but she would leave Moccasin Rock, and take the perfect little travel kit with her. After admiring everything for a moment, she closed the lid and pushed it back inside the cupboard.

In the meantime, she'd use her plain wooden hairbrush, comb and toothbrush, as well as the bar soap they purchased from the mail-order catalog in bulk. At least they didn't use lye soap anymore.

After washing and drying, Abby put on her gown and wrapper, tying the belt in a knot. She then opened the door, only a crack, to make sure there were no men in sight. The hall was empty, so she made a run for the stairs. She couldn't risk a scandal.

One of the church ladies, Mrs. Myrtle Dunlop, had been outraged the first time Irene Horton rented a room to a single man after Bob Horton had disappeared. Luckily, the outcry had died down quickly enough.

Since then, they'd rented rooms mostly to couples or older people. Until now. In the space of a few days, they had allowed five men into the house. If word were to get out that Abby had been seen in her nightclothes outside her room—even though she was covered head-to-toe—there would be more trouble.

Thankfully, the surveyors were spending the night in Boone Springs and wouldn't return until sometime tomorrow. Reverend Wainright and Ranger Calhoun shouldn't be a problem. Still, she flew up the stairs…then stumbled at the sound of a door softly clicking shut somewhere down the hall.

Hand to her throat, she slipped into her room. Someone had been watching her. Who? *The ranger? The preacher?*

Her insides trembling, Abby started toward her bed in the darkness. She remembered Jenna, yet forgot the suitcase in the middle of the floor until she smacked her shin against the lid. Biting her lip, she groaned softly to herself.

Jenna stirred. "Do you have to make so much noise?"

Abby didn't respond. She couldn't. *Please, Lord, give me patience.*

Untying and removing her wrapper, she slid into bed. Yet despite her exhaustion, rest eluded her. One worried thought after another raced through her mind.

What if whoever was watching her had followed her to the cave? What if Jim Adair never got the message? Was there anybody buried in that grave with her father's name on the headstone? Her father was depending on her, possibly for his life. *And Caleb Calhoun was engaged to be married.* Even more worrisome, why did she care? She'd been fascinated by him, but no more so than anyone else who'd stayed here. Well, maybe a little more.

Abby squeezed her eyes shut, determined to sleep. Counting sheep didn't help at all. She'd count boarders instead. Who all had confirmed they'd eat with them tomorrow? Everyone except the surveyors.

Not all the boarders took their meals at the house. Occasionally they'd dine at Moccasin Rock's only eatery, Bony Joe's. Despite the almost skeletal appearance of the proprietor there, a good, hearty meal could be purchased at all hours of the day.

Abby let out a sigh of frustration. She'd give counting sheep another try. Still it didn't work. Because now they were all wearing Stetsons. *Goodness, what was wrong with her?*

A moment later she was startled by a whisper from Jenna. "Abby?"

"Yes?"

"I've decided to let you help me with my wedding plans."

Surely she'd not heard that correctly. "What did you say?"

A yawn sounded from Jenna's direction. "I said you can help me with my wedding. I doubt there's a lot of excitement in this town. Thought you might enjoy some fun. No need to thank me."

Thank you? Ooooh. Counting to ten, Abby tried to summon an appropriate Christian reply. Words that showed her disinterest in such an offer and yet didn't involve telling Jenna to stick her head in a bucket of water.

Unfortunately, before Abby could say anything at all, she heard Jenna snoring...like a congested buffalo. *Ha! Hope you enjoy listening to that the rest of your life, Caleb Calhoun.*

Chapter Nine

HER MOTHER WAS already peeling and slicing fruit when Abby made her way to the kitchen the next day.

"Morning, Mama."

"Good morning. Did you sleep okay?"

Abby popped a slice of peach in her mouth and gave a vague murmur to avoid a direct answer.

"The survey team won't be in until later," her mother said. "So breakfast shouldn't take long."

The two women spoke little as they prepared coffee, oatmeal, and sliced fruit. Abby then drained the water from a huge pot of dried pinto beans she'd left soaking overnight. She'd let them cook through the morning and then add chunks of ham. The midday meal on Sundays tended to be simple.

Her mother met each of those arriving for breakfast—Miss Culpepper, Reverend Wainright and Robby—with the same cheerful greeting as Abby added fresh water to the pot.

Abby almost dropped the pot, beans and all, when she heard her mother greet Ranger Calhoun, and the deep-voiced response. "Good morning, Mrs. Horton." He then offered a hello to the others. Since Abby had her back to him, she couldn't tell if the greeting had included her. *Not that she cared one way or the other.*

She busied herself with her chores until her mother spoke-up. "Abby, you better eat something."

Her stomach rebelled at the thought of food, but she grabbed a piece of bread so her mother wouldn't worry. "I am, Mama. I want to get this finished. I also need to heat a kettle of water to wash the dishes."

Irene Horton nodded as she rose from the table. "If you'll excuse me, everyone, I've got some things to attend to upstairs. Come on, Robby, it's time to get ready for church."

Robby obediently followed her from the room. Then his voice rang out loud-and-clear from the hall. "Oh, Mama, I went to church a hundred times last week, do I have to go?"

Abby cast an uneasy glance at Reverend Wainright, but the man continued with his meal as if he hadn't heard a word.

Although her brother's statement embarrassed her, part of Abby's discomfort was due to the fact that she'd had similar thoughts—fleeting though they were. Yet, she actually couldn't imagine missing church. No matter how tired she was, or how reluctant she was to go, once she was there, the sermon was always balm to her soul. She especially needed that today.

"Can I get anyone more coffee?" she asked now to fill the silence. After topping off Reverend Wainright's cup, Abby began a steady stream of inane chatter directed at him and Miss Culpepper—anything to avoid personal interaction between her and Caleb Calhoun.

Finally, though, the older people left, leaving only the two of them. Caleb didn't seem to be any more anxious to converse with her than she was with him. And that suited her fine. Really.

Abby cleared the dishes from the table, scraped them clean, and placed them in the dish pan. She then poured hot water over them. *Why was he lingering? He'd had time to finish three meals.* Abby wet a rag and wiped down the counter. She could go and get dressed herself, but it seemed rude to just walk off and leave the man here alone. Finally, when the silence stretched out unbearably, Abby felt she had no choice but to fill it.

"Ranger Calhoun, will you be joining us for church today?" *You sure could use a dose of the Lord's word.* Although Abby hadn't expressed her thought aloud, she was startled by his reply.

"Nope. The churches I've been to were long on ceremony and stifling tradition, and short on forgiveness and not judging folks."

Embarrassment swept through Abby, even though he had no way of knowing what she'd been thinking.

"I would hope that's not what you'd find at our church," she said. "There are some traditional, old-fashioned ways we cling to, but I find them comforting, not stifling. And there's not a lot of ceremony. We're pretty simple folks."

Nodding, Caleb speared a piece of peach on his plate and popped it into his mouth. He chewed, swallowed and then gestured toward her with the fork. "What about the judging part?"

"Judging is up to God," Abby said, perhaps a bit too primly. She crossed to the stove, stirring the pot of beans, briskly, despite the fact that they didn't need to be stirred. She stopped when some of the liquid sloshed over the side.

"I see," Caleb said. "So, you didn't assume that I was a philanderer after talking to Jenna last night?"

"No, of course not." But of course she had. "Although you did kiss me about five seconds after meeting me," she said in her own defense.

"I explained that, and I apologized. Which brings us back to the forgiveness part."

She thought about that for a moment. "I do forgive you. Although I think you're confusing the issues," she added. "The forgiveness you need from God is something entirely different."

He pushed his plate back. "True. But isn't the forgiveness of humans, one to another, in the Bible, too?"

Abby drew in a deep breath, determined to keep her voice calm despite the urge to scream in frustration. "*But* you're engaged to be married and you kissed me. I have a right to be upset."

His expression was one of long-suffering. "See, there's the problem. I'm not engaged. You didn't even give me a chance to explain."

Abby's heart gave a strange little lurch. "You're not?"

"Nope. So even if you didn't judge me, you sure misjudged me."

"Jenna said that—"

He held up a hand. "Jenna says a lot of things. Take it all with a grain of salt."

Abby bit her lip. *Should she tell him?* "Jenna Nolan truly believes you're getting married," she finally blurted. "She even asked me to help with the wedding."

Caleb, who'd just taken a drink of his coffee, made a strangled sound and sat the cup down with a clatter. "She what?" he wheezed, when he could finally speak again.

"Jenna asked me to help plan the wedding ceremony. Sounds to me as if she's pretty sure there will be one."

Caleb inhaled deeply, cleared his throat and gave an emphatic shake of his head. "No. I made it quite clear. There will be no wedding." Shrugging, he added. "I have no idea why she's pretending otherwise. To be honest, there's no telling what she'll say next."

Sudden understanding filled Abby. *Oh my.* "Is Jenna... disturbed?"

Laughing, Caleb leaned back in his chair. "No, not in the way you mean. She is, however, spoiled rotten and self-absorbed, among other things."

"Oh." Abby picked up his plate and carried it to the dishpan.

"So, as long as we're straight on that," Caleb said, "I'd like to apologize again for that kiss. I occasionally do things without thinking them through first. I meant well."

She turned and stared at him, genuinely puzzled by the man. "Do you indulge in that sort of behavior on a regular basis? Seems to me you would've been punched in the nose, or at least slapped a few times."

Rubbing his jaw, Caleb laughed again. "Oh, I have been."

"And yet you still haven't changed your ways."

"Actually, I have. I've been the epitome of exemplary behavior for a while now. Until I got here."

"Sorry Moccasin Rock has been such a trial for you."

A smile tugged at the corners of his mouth. "Thanks."

Striving for a nonchalant appearance she certainly wasn't feeling, Abby leaned against the counter. "So tell me, how many times have you kissed girls you didn't know?"

Caleb's smile disappeared. "That's none of your business," he said. "Although I will tell you that I've never kissed any while I was engaged."

"How many times have you been engaged?"

The smile was back. In fact, he was grinning from ear to ear now. "My my, Miss Abigail," he said softly. "You sure do seem interested in my personal life. Any particular reason?"

Abby whirled around, draped the rag across the rim of the basin and then straightened it with shaking fingers. "I…I am not interested. I was only making conversation. Your affairs are none of my concern, I assure you."

That statement only made him chuckle.

A blush warmed her face as she turned to face him again, determined to change the subject. "So you're not coming with us to church? You really are welcome, you know."

Pushing back his chair, Caleb stood. "Thanks, but I'm headed out to search for your father."

Abby sucked in a breath, all thoughts of Caleb and other women fleeing her mind. "If you do find him, please don't hurt him," she whispered.

Caleb's expression softened. "I will do my best to make sure that nothing bad happens to him. But I have to take him into custody. You understand, don't you?"

"Unfortunately, I do." *Marshal Adair, you'd better hurry.*

***

Abby washed the dishes after Caleb left, still hoping that Jenna would make an appearance. She wasn't interested in the girl's company, but she desperately wanted some time in her room, alone, to get ready for church. Abby finally made her way upstairs, tapping on her door in case Jenna was up and preparing for the day. She pushed it open when there was no answer. "Jenna?"

The other girl was still asleep. From the way the sheets were twisted around her, it appeared as if Jenna's night had been as restless as her own. *Good.*

Shamed by her own thought, Abby softened her voice. "Jenna? Are you going to church? You're welcome to join us."

Other than a snort, and an indecipherable mumble, there was no response.

"I need to wash up and change into my good clothes," Abby said. "I'd like some privacy for that. If you don't want to go to church, that's fine. However, I need you to give me a few minutes alone."

After a bit more prompting, Jenna finally sat up, blinked and yawned. "Fine, I'll leave. However I need to get dressed first. If you don't mind waiting outside."

Abby clenched her teeth and moved to the hall without further comment. She stood there, tapping her toes while she waited. And waited. "Jenna, can I come in now?"

When there was no answer, she opened the door to find the girl curled up on the cot again.

"Jenna, you said you were getting up to dress. I need my room."

The other girl rolled over to glare at her. "I've decided I'm not ready to get up. You'll have to wait." That statement set off an argument that lasted for several moments.

The fact that the woman's nightgown was fancier than any of Abby's dresses only added to her annoyance.

Hearing a door open and close further down the hall, Abby peeked out to see her mother leaving her own bedroom and heading toward the stairs. "Fine, I'll get ready in Mama's room," Abby said, as she snatched her clothing and a towel. "You can have the place to yourself."

She bit her tongue, not daring to say anything more…until Jenna's next statement sent her over the edge.

"That's wonderful," the other girl said while stretching. "I don't believe I'll accompany you to church. I'm still exhausted from my travels. I'll be ready for breakfast in about an hour, though. Perhaps some eggs, toast and bacon. And I'd like to dine up here."

Abby watched in disbelief as the woman closed her eyes, sank down, curled up, and pulled the sheet over her head.

"You will get oatmeal and sliced fruit," Abby snapped, "like everyone else. And you'll eat it in the kitchen or you won't eat at all. Furthermore, I don't care if you ever go to church. Although on second thought, I've never met anyone who needed it more."

The sound of footsteps in the hall had her whirling around in the doorway. Reverend Wainright merely nodded as he passed by, eyes straight ahead, not indicating in any way that he'd heard her tantrum. Abby was mortified nonetheless.

She groaned aloud when Caleb passed by a moment later, also without comment. But his lips were twitching, and the look he gave her was full of amusement. Obviously he'd heard her.

***

At the last minute, Jenna announced that she'd changed her mind and wanted to accompany the others to church. After what Abby had said earlier, she didn't feel like she could leave the girl behind. So she waited in the parlor along with the others as they listened to Jenna moving around upstairs at a snail's pace.

When a door opened, they all rose. Until a voice called out, "Can someone give me a hand with my dress?" The others sat down again as Abby headed up.

Abby gasped when she entered her room. Clothing—a variety of colors, designs and fabrics—was strewn over every available surface, and a good portion of the floor.

Mistaking Abby's reaction for one of admiration, Jenna smiled as she ran her hand across the skirt of the sapphire blue dress she was wearing. "It is beautiful, isn't it?"

Abby merely nodded. In her own light blue gingham, she felt like a pale imitation of what a woman should look like. Drawing in a frustrated breath, she sat to work fastening the shiny jet buttons that ran down the back of Jenna's dress. "How did you manage this while you were traveling?"

"I started out with a maid," Jenna said. "Unfortunately, the woman came down with a mysterious illness before we were halfway to Texas. After that, if there was another woman nearby I asked for help. If not, I wore something simple. Luckily, it seemed like there was always someone willing to assist."

While Abby worked, Jenna studied her reflection in the bureau mirror. "I also had trouble doing my hair this morning."

Ignoring the hint, Abby finished with the buttons. "It looks fine to me," she said. Jenna had gathered it in a low chignon.

"It's so plain," the other girl protested. "I normally wouldn't be caught dead with my hair like…" Jenna's eyes met Abby's in the mirror and her words trailed off. Their hairstyles were the same. Neither spoke as they joined the others downstairs.

The walk to the church—a small, whitewashed structure at the edge of town—took only a few minutes.

Pastor Wilkie Brown, a tall, lanky red-haired man, met them inside the front door with a shy smile. "Good morning, Horton family and friends."

A quiet, unassuming man, Pastor Brown was new to Moccasin Rock, and to the Lord's service. Yet he knew the Bible backwards and forwards, or so said the deacon's committee who'd interviewed him. Already the congregation loved him.

As everyone returned the greeting, Abby noticed that her mother's "Morning, Pastor" lacked some of the enthusiasm that it normally contained.

She reached out and gave her mother's arm a squeeze. It was difficult enough to have your husband return from the dead, but then to discover that some people believed him to be an outlaw was a lot to handle.

After introducing the pastor to Jenna, Abby followed her mother to their usual seat. About halfway up the aisle she realized that Irene Horton was avoiding the gazes of those around her—every eye turned their way, people leaning in to whisper to their friends. Abby's heart ached for her mother. *Lord, please help Mama today.*

Was Caleb Calhoun right? Were they being judged? She didn't want to think it of the close-knit community she'd grown up in, and yet at the very least, they were being talked about. Abby thought back to times when she'd discussed others—not in a mean-spirited way—and realized how unpleasant it could be for those who were the topic of such conversations.

Considering the circumstances, Abby wouldn't have been surprised if Reverend Wainright sat on the other side of the church. She was pleased to see him follow the Horton family into their usual pew, right along with Miss Culpepper and Jenna. What an odd little group.

Abby smiled at Henry and his elderly parents, seated in the pew directly ahead, and then leaned in to greet them. She worried, belatedly, that they might snub her, but both Mr. and Mrs. Barnett offered a warm welcome to her and the visitors. The Barnetts were much older than her own parents and Abby had always thought of them as grandparents. She should have known they wouldn't treat her or her family any differently.

Leaning back, Abby began to relax. Although the revival had been memorable in more ways than one, it was good to be attending services in the church house again.

The piano had been moved from the adjacent tabernacle and was back in its place to the left of the pulpit. Miss Hattie, looking starched and serene, was also in her customary place on the piano bench.

Once the service started, Abby made an effort to push everything else from her mind and let the hymns wash over her, soothing her troubled soul. Pastor Brown's sermon on the power of prayer was also a much-needed respite from her worries. She realized that though she'd offered up some anxious, hastily uttered prayers over the situation with her father, she had not truly poured out her troubles to her Heavenly Father. She'd been trying to handle everything on her own. She needed to take it all to the Lord. Abby spent the invitation time praying for His guidance.

After the service, they'd barely cleared the church steps when Myrtle Dunlop, the owner of the bakery in town and self-appointed morality patrol, strode up and planted herself right in front of Irene Horton.

Myrtle was a thin little woman with a pinched face and a pinched attitude. Abby had often wondered how someone so sour could produce such sweet confections.

As usual, Myrtle's bonnet strings were tied so tightly they pressed in to what little flesh she had. Her mouth was a hard, thin line, and when it opened, her words were anything but sweet.

"I would think you might have the decency to stay home," Myrtle hissed, "seeing as how your husband is such a despicable human being. We have young folks in this church, and children can easily be led astray. And for all anyone in this town knows, you may have aided your husband in his heinous activities, all the while pretending to be a poor widow. And to think I brought you sweet rolls after the funeral!"

Unprepared for a verbal assault of such magnitude, Abby was so stunned she couldn't summon a reply. Her mother, who stood beside her with her mouth hanging open, didn't seem to be doing much better.

Reverend Wainright, Jenna, Robby and Miss Culpepper wore

varying degrees of shock on their faces. Surprisingly, it was the elderly spinster who leapt to the Horton family's defense.

"How dare you speak that way," Miss Culpepper said, "and within feet of the Lord's house. You should be ashamed of yourself. You know absolutely nothing about Bob Horton, other than a bit of gossip. There could be any number of reasons he was found in the company of those outlaws. Maybe you should wait until you actually know something before you talk about it."

Mrs. Dunlop was stricken silent. She opened her mouth several times, and then snapped it shut and turned on her heel, her boots sending little bursts of dirt flying as she stomped across the yard to her own family. A few stragglers who'd witnessed the scene darted sympathetic glances in the Hortons' direction. Henry and his parents crossed over and shook hands with them. Abby was grateful for their friendship and support.

A silence enveloped the group after the Barnetts departed. Reverend Wainright cleared his throat a couple of times, as if he wasn't sure quite what to say, before grinning and gesturing toward the church house. "I think maybe that woman needed to go back in for a second helping."

Everyone smiled, and Abby appreciated his effort to lighten the mood. As they headed for the house, she studied the normally timid, whiny Miss Culpepper, intrigued by her sudden burst of assertiveness. The woman's color was still high, and she was almost quivering in her indignation. *What had come over her?*

Just then, Miss Culpepper glanced at Abby and groaned. "Oh, dear. I fear I might've overdone, I feel a sick spell coming on."

Abby sighed. Whatever it was, the change had been short-lived.

Chapter Ten

DESPITE WHAT HE'D told Abby, Caleb had merely walked around the block and waited for everyone to leave for church before returning to the house.

He found the place quiet and still, as he'd hoped, and began his search in the attic. He didn't think Bob Horton would be foolish enough to sneak back in to hide in his own home, but Caleb had long ago learned that people, especially desperate people, did some strange things. Even if he didn't find Bob, he might find evidence that the man had been in touch with his family.

Caleb had given the attic space a quick once-over when he'd retrieved the cot for Jenna, and had found nothing unusual. Now he examined everything a little more carefully. There were several rolled-up rugs, an old chest of drawers, as well as a cradle and a child's rocking chair. Also a number of crates, trunks and even a couple of barrels, but none of them were large enough to conceal a full-grown man.

A portion of the space had been cleared for the Horton's young son to sleep. Caleb smiled at a few of the items on an overturned crate by the boy's bed. Several snail shells, a wad of string, and an empty glass jar with holes poked through the rusty lid. And even a plug of tobacco. Mrs. Horton would tan his hide if she knew about that, Caleb suspected. There was also a blanket on the floor, wallowed out. An animal of some sort had slept up here. But there was no sign that Bob Horton had been here recently.

Caleb searched the second floor next, beginning with the two rooms rented by the team of surveyors doing the preliminary work on the bridge. He didn't know where they'd spent the night, but Mrs. Horton had mentioned that they weren't expected in until later in the day. Both rooms were surprisingly tidy. One had a pallet on the floor next to the wall. On the bureau tops there was some loose ammunition but no guns, a few coins, a ledger and journal with some notes about their work, pen and ink, and an ornate gold letter opener. Caleb whistled softly as he examined the opener. *Nice!*

The only personal effects in the preacher's room were a suitcase, a battered old leather satchel, and some clothing. He didn't bother with any of it. Although Caleb didn't have more than a passing acquaintance with God, he didn't figure messing with one of His messengers was a brilliant move. Besides, there was no way the old man was involved in Bob's disappearance.

He moved on to the room of the older woman they'd introduced as Miss Culpepper, and was surprised to discover that the door was locked up tight. Caleb considered picking the lock. But had the woman left with the rest of the group? He thought she had, but the way his luck was going, he would open the door and find the woman sleeping inside. Then she'd either shoot him, or scream and whine until he wanted to shoot himself. The door was probably locked because she didn't want anyone pawing through her unmentionables. Caleb didn't plan to paw through them, and he definitely wouldn't mention it if he did. He moved on.

Caleb opened Abby's door and stepped inside, and then stepped back out to make sure he'd entered the right room. It had been neat and clean the day before when he'd set up the cot. Now, it looked as if someone had shot a peacock and let the feathers fly.

He surveyed the array of colorful dresses, petticoats, gloves and stockings tossed around the room. Jenna had to be responsible for this. Caleb was going to have a little talk with her. He didn't want his friend to cause any unnecessary work for the Hortons. Stepping around the debris, he glanced inside the wardrobe. Abby's clothing was hanging neatly inside, yet he felt strangely reluctant to search through them.

Caleb closed the wardrobe door, and then crouched down to peer under the bed. He found only a box, filled with memorabilia typical of a young girl. None of it helpful. On the dressing table he found a stack of postcards, the top one from New York, with "Wish you were here," scribbled across it. It was signed by C.G. Lovell. *Who was he?* Maybe Abby wasn't as innocent as she appeared. *Interesting.*

Mrs. Horton's room was larger than the others. There were two windows instead of one, on either side of a fireplace, and the bed was full-sized, instead of a single like the other rooms. It was furnished as simply, though. He checked under the bed, where all he found was a pair of men's boots.

In the wardrobe he found shirts and several pairs of trousers. If Irene Horton had believed her husband dead, why hadn't she disposed of these things? *Just one more thing that didn't add up.* Or maybe she was saving them for her son.

A noise outside drew his attention. Had someone returned early? Easing the wardrobe door shut, he crossed to a window that overlooked the lot next to the house. He lifted an edge of the drapes with one finger and peered down. The only thing he saw was a scruffy-looking mutt lurking near the garden's edge.

Caleb smiled. The dog's coat—white with black patches—matched the hairs he'd seen on the blanket in Robbie's room. The pup was watching the back door with an intensity and wariness resembling some of the criminals that Caleb had dealt with. That dog probably spent the night here, but obviously he didn't live here. Caleb headed downstairs to continue his search.

The parlor ran across the front of the house, and the kitchen ran the width of the back. In between, there were two rooms on each side of a wide center hallway. Caleb continued his search on the right side of the hall.

He'd made use of what they called the bathing room the evening before, so after a brief peek inside, he explored the others. The next room on the right was being used for storage. There were ladders, gardening tools, buckets, a chair that needed the cane seat repaired, and even some sections of fencing. Caleb was baffled by the odd assortment until he remembered that he'd seen no outbuildings except for a chicken house and privy. They had to store these sorts of things somewhere.

The first room on the left held a quilting frame, a spinning wheel, and a large sewing box with long wooden legs and a needle-point canvas on top. All of it appeared to be well-used. The Hortons kept busy.

The last room was a study, with a large bookcase on either side of a fireplace. Caleb did a quick perusal of the books lining the shelves and was surprised by the selections. There were leather-bound volumes of poetry, the complete works of Shakespeare, law books and even a medical book. Were all of these Bob's? If so, what would make an obviously intelligent man take up a life of crime?

After deciding there was nothing further to learn there, Caleb searched the pantry, a good-sized area, and the root cellar, a tiny space accessible through a trapdoor in the pantry floor. He explored everything thoroughly, making sure there was no one hiding in the shadows. There wasn't, and there was no sign that anyone had recently.

Back in the kitchen, he uncovered a plate on the counter and helped himself to an oatmeal cookie before heading out to search the town. Since most of the businesses were closed, it didn't take him long to make his rounds. He looked into any and every unlocked structure he passed—including sheds, stalls and barns, and once again, he came up empty-handed.

He settled down in one of the chairs on the Hortons' front porch and thought about what he'd discovered during his search. Despite the one locked door, and the clothing belonging to Bob Horton, he didn't think there was significance to any of it.

Caleb pushed to his feet as the returning church-goers approached.

Abby's steps faltered when she spotted him. "I'll have dinner on the table in about forty minutes," she announced to everyone in general, yet she continued to stare at Caleb, brow furrowed.

Caleb looked her in the eyes and shook his head. *No, I didn't find your father.*

Abby didn't respond, yet he knew she'd understood when her expression and her shoulders relaxed. She turned to her brother, "Change out of your good clothes," she reminded the boy as they passed through the gate and up the front walk. "I'll do the same, and then I'll meet you in the kitchen and tell you what I need from the garden."

Robby groused a little, and pulled away when she patted his back, but he obeyed.

Once everyone was inside, Caleb went to his own room to wash up, and then joined the others in the kitchen. Miss Culpepper offered to help serve the food, and Mrs. Horton shooed her away, reminding the older woman that she was a guest.

When Robby returned from upstairs, barefoot and clad in overalls, Abby sent him outside for onions. "Don't forget to give them a good shake, and then rinse them under the pump before bringing them back inside," she said.

Once the meal was on the table and everyone was seated, Mrs. Horton turned to Reverend Wainright. "Would you do us the honor of saying grace?"

"Of course."

Caleb suppressed a yawn, but then listened with growing amazement as the old man began talking to God. That was the only way he could describe it. Caleb had always thought of God as far away, distant. Yet this man was speaking as if God were here with him... with them. The words were simple, yet full of quiet reverence. For some reason it gave Caleb goose bumps. He rubbed his arms and listened to the chorus of "Amens" from the other diners when the preacher wound it up.

Everyone ate their fill and expressed their compliments to the ladies. Afterwards, Reverend Wainright announced that he was plum tuckered-out and was headed upstairs to get a little shut-eye. One-by-one, the others drifted off as well, most of them expressing similar intentions.

Although Caleb wasn't a bit sleepy, he went to his room anyway to mull over the situation with his missing prisoner. He was sitting on the bed, trying to decide where to search for Bob Horton next, when a board creaked in the hallway.

It normally wouldn't have attracted his attention, but since he'd heard no footsteps, he was instantly alert. Someone was sneaking around. He eased the door open and crept down the hall. Abigail Horton had started down the stairs on tiptoe.

"Hey, there," he said.

Abby gasped and nearly toppled down the stairs. She turned, one hand on the banister and one pressed to her throat. "Ranger Calhoun, I'm sorry to have disturbed you."

Caleb grinned. "And I you."

Even if he'd had no desire to know what she was up to, he would have enjoyed watching the color rise in her face. Of course, if he'd been smarter, he could've followed her. Now she wasn't about to leave. Even though teasing and flirting with her, even verbally sparring with her, was quickly becoming his favorite pastime, he couldn't let it get in the way of his mission.

"Where you headed?" he asked, knowing full well she wouldn't tell him the truth. His real question was whether she'd been on her way to see Henry, or her father.

She gripped the banister harder. "Down for a glass of water. It's rather warm up here today."

"That it is," he agreed.

Caleb left his door open as she headed on downstairs, and then put a hand over his mouth to keep from laughing out loud when she returned a few minutes later, making a big production of walking down the hall and shutting her door.

Abby definitely wasn't going anywhere as long as she knew he was watching. And he would be watching.

He'd just have to be smarter next time.

***

Caleb joined the Horton house residents as they congregated on the wide front porch that evening, where the breeze made the heat bearable.

Abby swayed in the porch swing, snapping green beans into a round enamelware pan. Miss Culpepper and Irene Horton sat in chairs across from the swing, hands busy with some sort of needle work. Robby perched on the porch steps, totally captivated by a small wooden puzzle in his hands. Henry Barnett, a recent arrival, sat beside him, and was nearly as fascinated as the boy.

"I lost one of the pegs," Robby said, disappointment lacing his words.

"I can make you a new one," Caleb offered. He wasn't sure why, but it bothered him the way Robby kept his distance and sent him fearful, distrustful looks. Mrs. Horton and Abby seemed to understand why he was still here, yet as far as Robby was concerned, Caleb had a feeling he was "that man" who wanted to put his father in jail. "If you've got a piece of wood, I've got my knife right here," he added.

Henry glared at Caleb. "I'll make Robby a peg if he needs one." The young man then whipped a beat-up old pen knife from his pocket and set to work on a chunk of wood that Robby provided.

Caleb held up both hands, palms out. "That's fine, only trying to help."

He'd been watching Henry and Abby closely to see if there were any signs of a romantic relationship between the two, yet so far it appeared to be exactly what Abby had said. Henry was smitten, yet she regarded him only as a friend. Perhaps they had been picking berries, although Caleb hadn't seen any evidence of them. Maybe Henry had taken them home.

"I'm the best whittler in Moccasin Rock," Henry declared with another scowl in Caleb's direction.

Caleb understood the young man's attitude was more about the kiss he'd given Abby than it was about anyone's woodworking skills. Yet it annoyed Caleb anyway. He felt a spark of pure devilment as he sauntered over to the porch swing where there was room for another person on the seat by Abby. He glanced over to make sure Henry was watching before he sat down, and was stunned when the preacher stepped through the screen door and swooped in behind him.

The old man didn't address Caleb, although he spoke to Abby. "Hope you don't mind if I sit beside you."

"Of course not," Abby said, scooting over a bit. "Make yourself comfortable." She then darted an embarrassed glance at Caleb. Apparently, they both knew what was going on. That old coot was trying to keep them apart.

Caleb shook his head. Oh well, that was probably better for everyone in the long run. As far as he could tell, the man hadn't said anything to Abby's mother about what he'd seen. Caleb didn't want to rock the boat. He chose a spot on the steps near Robby and Henry, turning sideways to lean against the porch posts so he could see everyone.

"Where's Jenna?" he asked.

"She has a headache," Abby said, her tone dry, "and wasn't sure she could stand the excitement of sitting on the porch."

Caleb choked back a laugh. That sounded about right. There was a slowness to life in Moccasin Rock, and especially on the Horton's front porch, that Caleb found soothing. He doubted if Jenna felt the same way.

The assembled group chatted about the weather for awhile, and then discussed the morning's church service. That led to a discussion of favorite hymns, and Caleb noted with interest that everyone agreed that *Amazing Grace* was their favorite. He knew he'd heard the song before, but since he avoided church, it had been years ago, and he couldn't recall even a fragment.

The discussion then turned to someone named Myrtle Dunlop and the fuss she'd made after church. Caleb didn't really understand what had happened, although he knew that something had hurt the feelings of the Horton family. He found himself offended for their sake. And saddened. Yet it was Bob Horton's fault he reminded himself. The man had deceived everyone and lived an outlaw's life. His family deserved better.

Caleb was considering taking another jaunt around town and then checking the area down by the river again, when Robby began talking about his trip to Fair Haven. Everyone was laughing within a few minutes, and Caleb especially enjoyed seeing it all through the eyes of a young boy.

"And the monkey danced," Robby was saying, "and he had on the same clothes as the man."

"The same clothes?" his mother asked.

"They were dressed alike," Abby clarified, "with matching vests and hats—black, trimmed with green ribbon."

"He had a big mustache," Robby said. "The man, not the monkey. And there were two other men fighting and everyone was hollering real loud."

Mrs. Horton's hands stilled. "Goodness. That's sounds terrifying. I'm not sure you two should go off alone again."

"It was a supervised boxing match," Abby said. "They were separate events. We were never in any danger." Her tone was calm, her fingers never faltered as she continued snapping beans, yet Caleb sensed tension in her words.

"The man in the store called the outlaws vermin," Robby added. This time, Abby did react. Color filled her cheeks and she opened her mouth, but whatever she was going to say was lost in Robby's next remark.

"And there was a dog, the biggest one I've ever seen, and it walked right over to me and laid his head in my lap."

Abby's hands stilled, a puzzled expression crossing her face.

"It had brown and white hair, and big eyes," Robby continued. "I thought it was a bear at first. Then the lady said it was a Saint Ber…something. I can't remember. I want a dog like that. Can we have one, Mama?"

Mrs. Horton smiled. "Well, if he's as big as you say he was, wherever would we keep him? And what would we feed him?"

"I could feed him table scraps," Robby said. "And he could sleep beside my bed. If you don't want me to have a big dog, maybe I could find a little one somewhere."

Caleb smiled. He had a feeling he knew which little dog Robby had in mind.

"I don't remember seeing a large dog in Fair Haven," Abby said. "When was that?"

"It was the second time you went into the tel—"

In one swift movement Abby rose from the swing, tripped over the preacher's foot, and dropped her pan. Caleb caught Abby, and several people tried to catch the pan, but the green beans flew everywhere.

Her hands were shaking as she bent to scoop them up.

"All that hard work," Caleb said, grabbing for as many beans as he could reach. "I'll help you snap some more."

"Oh, that's okay, but thank you," she said. "I'll do some more tomorrow. The chickens can have these. If you'll excuse me, I remembered something I need to do. Robby, can you give me a hand for a moment?"

She hurried inside, dragging her little brother behind her. Caleb wasn't sure what the kid was supposed to help her with, but his remarks about the dog had sure upset her.

Or was it something else about their trip to Fair Haven that had her in such turmoil?

Chapter Eleven

DAWN WAS BEGINNING to break when Abby hit the trail that led to the river the next morning. Though in a hurry, she paused to admire the vivid shades of red, pink and orange streaking across the eastern sky. Such displays of God's beauty never failed to amaze.

After a few minutes, she adjusted the packed canvas bag slung over her shoulder and resumed her journey. She was taking her father food, candles, soap, towels and some extra clothing. It should be enough to keep both of the fugitives fed and clean until help arrived.

The dew was heavy, and the bottom of Abby's dress was wet by the time she arrived at her destination. She'd have a hard time explaining that when she got home, unless she could sneak in and change without her mother seeing her.

She glanced behind her one more time, and then reached for the bushes that concealed the cave entrance. A hand grasped her arm and pulled her back.

She turned, expecting to see her father, and found herself staring into the eyes of a young man about her age. He looked more worried than dangerous. He wasn't much taller than Abby, but he was on the stocky side. The battered derby hat he wore was nearly the same shade of gray as his eyes.

The man peered at her through the little round lenses of a pair of spectacles, blinking repeatedly. She wasn't sure if he was having trouble seeing or trouble believing his eyes. Despite his obvious confusion, his grip on her arm was firm.

"Who are you?" Abby hissed.

"I was about to ask you the same thing," he replied.

Her father's voice sounded from the cave entrance. "Nash, let her go. That's my daughter, Abigail. She's brought us some provisions."

Abby's mouth fell open. *This was one of the outlaw gang?*

The young man dropped her arm and gave her a hesitant smile. Except for mumbling a soft thank you when she handed him several cookies and a biscuit with bacon, he said nothing else. Nash then glanced once more at Bob, and at his nod, disappeared through the cave entrance.

Abby pulled more food from the bag for her father, her heart heavy at the dark circles under his eyes…and the hope in them. *I've let you down, Daddy.* She opened her mouth to tell him about failing to reach the marshal, but he held his hand up to silence her until they had made their way into the cave. Once her eyes adjusted to the dimness, Abby realized the other man had disappeared. *How big is this cave?*

Her father was biting into a biscuit as he guided her further inside, and groaned softly as he sat down, back against the wall.

"Oh, this tastes good. I've missed your mother's cooking, and yours. Thank you, Abby." He took another bite, swallowed, and then said, "Did you have any trouble getting to Fair Haven?"

Abby shook her head. "No, I got there okay… but I didn't get a reply from the marshal. I'm so sorry."

He waved away the apology. "May take a while. There's no telling where he is. Hopefully he'll get the message soon and send someone to help. How are your mother and Robby holding up?"

"They're doing okay. I have to hurry and get back to the house before the ranger realizes I'm gone. You didn't get a chance to tell me everything last time. Don't keep me in suspense. Who was the second man on the train?"

Her father swallowed the last bite of the first biscuit, and then placed a hand on his stomach with a satisfied sigh before beginning his story. "The man was Jim Adair. He was my best friend growing up. We'd lost touch through the years. Jim wasn't the same skinny kid I remembered. I was stunned to discover that he's a U.S. Marshal now." He shook his head, as if still finding that hard to believe.

"Jim had been investigating a string of robberies by the Latham gang," he told her. "He said that every time they got close to capturing them, someone tipped them off. There had to be someone, Jim said, maybe even someone in law enforcement, who was giving them advance notice on where and when large shipments of cash and gold would be coming through, and more importantly, when the law was closing in."

A chill ran through Abby. "A crooked lawman?"

Her father nodded. "Or maybe one of the gang members had a sweetheart that was related to a lawman, or some other family connection. They considered all kinds of scenarios."

"So how did you get involved?"

"Jim said he wished he had someone on the inside, someone unknown to both the gang and the lawmen, who could infiltrate—or at the very least, spy on them, and figure out what was going on. I volunteered."

Abby gasped. "Daddy, why would you do something like that?"

"Because I realized I could help Jim, and myself." He looked at her, sorrow in his eyes. "I was desperate, Abby. I had to do something to make money." He glanced away a moment before going on. "Jim wasn't interested in my help, though. In fact, he flat out refused. As that train rolled on through the night, I kept trying to change his mind. I wanted to do it, not only for him, but because I could get stories out of the experience. I could write more books. I could take care of my family. I would be writing about a gang, from the inside. Jim wasn't having any part of it, though. He told me to go on home. And I was planning to. But then an opportunity arose and I took it. Figured I could let Jim know what was going on later."

She stood there, staring down at him in disbelief as he bit into a cookie. "Why didn't you at least tell us what was going on?" Her voice broke, and she swallowed several times before she could speak again. "Do you know how devastated we were when we thought you'd died?"

Her father groaned, reached out and tugged her down beside him. "That was not part of the plan, at all. I'm so sorry. I planned to send a message saying that I was okay and I'd be home as soon as I could."

"So what went wrong?"

"Nothing, at first. The train stopped in Jackson Junction, and I'd gotten off to stretch my legs. The gang hit the bank there. I was outside when it happened. When everybody else ran out, I ran in."

She stared at him, aghast. "Daddy, you could've been killed."

He swallowed hard. "I nearly was. If it wasn't for the fact that they were literally stunned to see someone walk right up to them, unarmed, I'd be dead right now. Before they could react, I started talking."

"I know you have a way with words," Abby said, "but what could you possibly say in a situation like that?"

"I made up this huge story, right off the top of my head, about the bank doing me wrong and cheating me, and that I wanted revenge. I told them I hoped they took every single dollar when they left."

"And they believed that?"

"Well, I thought they did. They shoved me out of the way, tied up the teller and took the money. They'd already killed another teller, when they first rushed in. He was on the floor behind the counter. I didn't find that out until later. As the gang ran out, one of them pointed his pistol at me, and *invited* me to ride out with them. I didn't have a horse, so he untied one from a hitching post and threw me the reins. He was pointing the gun at me, so I did what he said."

"And just like that you were a member of the gang?"

Her father shook his head. "Nope. That goes to show how naïve I was, and how much I'd underestimated the intelligence of Webb Latham. After we'd been riding for about thirty minutes or so, they blindfolded me and somebody else led the horse along for another little while."

"They didn't want you to know the exact location of their hide-out?" she guessed.

"Exactly. They hadn't said much while we were riding, but once we pulled up to this old shack, they all started talking and arguing, at once. Some were saying to kill me right away, others wanted to know who sent me."

She held her breath, not really wanting to hear what came next, yet knowing she needed to. "Is that when you were shot?"

He shook his head. "No, Webb was still toying with me at that point. He knew all along that I was up to something, he just didn't know what." Her father paused. "Webb had the coldest eyes I've ever seen. He wasn't making idle conversation when he told me I had two choices. Tell him the real reason I was there…or die."

"So you told them about Marshal Adair?"

"No. I told them the truth, but only part of it. I confessed that I'd had an ulterior motive in approaching them. Webb had already cocked his gun when I blurted out that I was a writer working on a dime novel."

Abby gasped. "Seems to me that would've gotten you killed even quicker."

"You'd think so, but Webb Latham was fascinated by that. He and Nash were both avid readers of those books—especially the ones written about them. It bothered him a lot that some of the facts were wrong. Webb wanted me to tell their side of the story. The man was looking forward to being immortalized."

"So you actually became part of the gang?" Abby whispered. "You rode with them?" She couldn't keep the dismay from her voice.

"Never got the chance. The next morning, Webb decided I needed a better horse. Stupid me, I thought we were going shopping."

"He stole another one?"

"Yes, and shot the old man riding it clean out of his saddle." His voice shook, and he paused for a moment, seemingly lost in memories that were too horrible to share.

"I tried to help the man," her father finally said, "and Webb threatened to shoot me, too. I knew that fellow was only minutes from death, and I wasn't going to ride off and leave him to die alone. I dismounted and knelt down to grab hold of his hand, praying with every breath. That's when I saw the gun in the man's other hand. He didn't realize I was trying to help him. He shot me, and then Webb, before dying a few minutes later."

Abby was so horrified she couldn't speak.

"The other outlaws grabbed Webb and headed back to the hideout. They left me there."

She squeezed his hand. "So how did you survive?"

He glanced toward the back of the cave. "Nash. The others tolerated him because he was Webb's little brother, but they didn't pay any attention to him. He managed to get me back to the shack all by himself."

"Were you aware of what was going on?" The thought of him wounded and at the mercy of outlaws was too terrible to comprehend.

"Off and on. I was hurt pretty bad, and Webb was in worse shape. He died a few days later, and it hit Nash hard. He was lost without his brother."

Abby's own gaze drifted toward the back of the cave. *What a strange life that young man had lived.*

"When the other outlaws dug a shallow grave behind the hide-out, Nash threw a wall-eyed fit," her father said. "He's normally quiet and even-tempered, but Nash demanded they give Webb a Christian burial. Said it was important to their mother. When they stopped laughing at him, I thought they were going to shoot him. All of a sudden, Forde Devlin, Webb's right-hand man, grinned at the others and said he would handle everything. He told Nash not to worry, prayers would be spoken over Webb's body."

"How did they manage that? Did they bring a preacher to the hideout?"

Her father shook his head. "No. I only pieced some of this together recently, thanks to Nash, but apparently Forde convinced everyone to say that I had died, and to ship my body home."

Abby's mouth dropped open. "Why in the world would they do that?"

"Because that way, even if it was under another name, Webb could have a decent burial—with hymns sung, and a preacher to pray over him. It was a huge joke to Forde, but believe it or not, it satisfied Nash. Then, when I recovered, the gang planned to have me ride along with them, pretending to be Webb Latham when they made some big raid they were planning. They figured that people would fear them as long as they thought Webb, a cold-blooded killer, was the one in charge. Certainly more effective than being led by a mild-mannered writer."

"So they hadn't cared whether you lived or died, but they were willing to make use of you anyway?"

His expression tightened. "Yes, they were ruthless and rotten to the core."

"So Webb Latham is buried in the grave that has your name on it?"

Her father nodded. "While I was recovering, the rest of them came and went, doing some small penny-ante type crimes. But they were planning something much bigger. I was in bad shape for weeks, and then my wound became infected."

"Oh, Daddy, I'm sorry."

He waved his hand as if dismissing the weeks of pain. "They got so disgusted that they quit messing with me. They wanted me to get better—they just didn't want to have to work at it."

"What did you do?"

"I couldn't do anything. If it wasn't for Nash I would've died. He brought me food and water, and even bandages and some medicine—although I'm not sure what it was. When the pain got really bad, he'd pour something down my throat and I'd go back to sleep again. Once I started waking up for longer periods of time, he brought me reading material that he'd stolen. Mostly dime novels. The day he walked in with my own book, I was stunned. I hadn't realized it had been published. Although it had been a while since I sent it off, I couldn't believe the turnaround time on those things."

Despite his current bleak predicament, he smiled at the memory of seeing his first work in print.

"I'd only been up and moving for a little while," he continued, "when they announced that it was time for the big heist they'd been planning. They had all sorts of maps, schedules, and coded messages. All I know is that it came from someone outside the gang. I pretended to relapse because I knew they'd want me to ride with them if I could sit a horse. Forde stood over me and said I was going to ride, even if they had to tie me into the saddle."

"Sounds like he was as evil as Webb Latham," Abby said.

Her father nodded, a grim look on his face. "I decided I was going to cut and run as soon as we all saddled up, even though I knew there was a good chance they'd shoot me in the back. Before it came to that, we heard horses riding in—so many it sounded like thunder. There were men shouting and then gunfire exploded all around me."

Everything he told her matched what Caleb Calhoun had said.

She nodded, encouraging him to continue, although she knew what happened next.

"The place was swarming with lawmen," he said. "To avoid being shot I surrendered immediately. Three of the gang were killed. And one managed to get away." He gestured toward the back of the cave. "Pure luck, I suppose."

"Did you try to tell them about Jim?"

He nodded. "Every time I opened my mouth, someone told me to shut it. I even told them that I ran a boarding house in Moccasin Rock, but one old lawman threatened to shoot me if I didn't keep quiet. I kept hoping, praying, that Jim would come riding up any minute. He didn't. Then, right before Forde Devlin died, he looked at me, grinned, and said, "Guess we reached the end of the line, boss.""

Abby groaned. "No wonder everyone thinks you're the leader."

"Exactly. I don't mind admitting I'm scared, Abby. I never did learn who the mastermind is, yet he may know who I am."

Her heart sank. "What can I do, Daddy?"

"You've done all you can for now. Jim's the only one who can get me outta this, the only one who can vouch for me. I should have listened to him and never gotten involved to start with. He'll probably want to shoot me himself, but he won't let me hang for something I didn't do."

Hand to her throat, Abby closed her eyes in an effort to erase the image that brought to mind.

"I asked the telegraph operator in Fair Haven to send any replies on to the Moccasin Rock office," she said. "I'll let you know as soon as I hear anything. And I'll keep bringing you food as often as I can."

If I can sneak away without Caleb Calhoun following me.

Chapter Twelve

CALEB DIDN'T HAVE time to dwell on where Abigail Horton had disappeared to that morning. He'd noted her absence, and the fact that he'd have to get up earlier if he was going to follow her next time—then forgot all that when Eli sent a message to the boarding house. Caleb had visitors waiting at the jail—Texas Ranger Captain Joshua Parnell, Garrison Becker, a stockholder of the B&H Central Railroad; and Mason Hawthorne, president of the First State Bank & Trust of Fair Haven.

The moment Caleb walked through the door, the railroad executive lit into him. Becker was a pompous, puffed up man who was obviously used to being the most important person in any room. His thin black hair was parted in the middle and he wore a fashionable suit with a pointed, standup white collar that pressed into the fleshy area of his jaw. He held a big cigar, and gestured at Caleb with it as he ranted and raved.

"I've lost lots of money to those degenerates," he shouted, "probably more money than you'll see in a lifetime. I want to see them all pay for their crimes, every single one of them. I can't even imagine how you allowed this to happen."

Caleb listened, hat in hand, biting back the impulse to respond. Captain Parnell had warned him the last time he'd popped an idiot in the mouth that it had better not happen again. But *that* man had insulted his horse, his gun, and then his mother—if a man couldn't respond to that, what was the point of being a man? So far this blowhard was only insulting him. He could take it.

It was Captain Parnell who finally stopped the tirade, with a simple lift of a finger. As Becker sputtered to a stop, the captain said, "He's my man, if he needs hollering at, I'll do it."

Becker, who'd been all bombastic bluster a moment ago, nodded and stepped aside. He might treat a young ranger with derision, but he wasn't foolish enough to treat a seasoned veteran that way. Captain had earned the respect, though, and Caleb knew it. Hopefully he would too, someday.

The captain, a square-jawed, stocky man with short gray hair and a scar that ran from the bottom of his left ear across his cheek and all the way up into his hair line, settled his steely gaze on Caleb.

Captain had never told anyone how he'd gotten the scar, and when asked he always answered the same, "Ask the other fellow." Since rumor had it that his opponent had died in the battle, that wasn't possible.

"What do you have to say for yourself?" Captain Parnell asked Caleb now. "What sort of excuse do you have?"

His words sent a little shiver of apprehension down Caleb's spine. Becker had only irritated him with his remarks, while the captain's softly-spoken words were another matter.

Caleb glanced at Eli. Although his brother hadn't said much, his stoic, unruffled expression lent a certain comfort to Caleb. When they made eye-contact, Eli gave an almost imperceptible nod, as if to say, "Well, get on with it."

Caleb drew himself up and looked the captain in the eye. "I have no excuses, no explanations."

Captain Parnell seemed taken aback by his bluntness. "At least you're not going to try my patience by pretending this was someone else's fault."

"No, sir."

The banker, a short man with spectacles and a closely-trimmed gray beard, stepped forward. "I'm not interested in what happened," he said. "I want to know what happens next. Where all have you looked for Webb Latham, or Bob Horton, or whatever he's calling himself?"

Mason Hawthorne wasn't as obnoxious as Becker, but Caleb still wasn't sure he liked him. After a quick glance at Captain Parnell, Caleb provided the search details.

"We've combed the countryside and nearby towns, and done a thorough search through each and every business here," Caleb said. "And I've gone through the Horton family's boarding house from top to bottom."

Hawthorne frowned as he fingered his gold watch fob. "What about searching other homes in the area?"

"No, sir," Caleb said. "Was kinda hoping it wouldn't come to that. We've talked to everyone, but we haven't pushed."

"Nosing around in people's houses is a good way to get shot," Eli added.

"Well, we can't stand around here and do nothing," Garrison Becker barked.

"We're not standing around," Captain Parnell said. "We'll track him down. We've already got teams of riders fanned out in every direction." He took a map from his pocket, unfolded it, and spread it out on Eli's desk. Captain then marked an area he wanted Caleb to search, as well as where he would look.

Eli looked on as they made their plans, and during a lull, spoke up. "I think it'd be better if Caleb stayed here."

Captain Parnell's gaze sharpened. "Why's that?"

"Based on a possible sighting, I believe that Bob Horton is still in the area. And if that's the case, he's likely to reach out to his wife or daughter. They could lead us to him. It wouldn't hurt to search further afield, but I really believe the man's hiding out somewhere around here."

"Let's go talk to his family now," Becker said. "I'll get the truth out of them."

Caleb's temper flared again at the thought of this man brow-beating Abby and her mother.

Eli held up his hand. "You'll be making a mistake if you put them on guard. Caleb is the logical one to keep an eye on the family. He's staying in the boarding house with them. They're good people. They seem as surprised by what Bob was up to as anyone else in town, and they don't appear to resent Caleb for doing his job. Let him get further acquainted with them. If they know where Bob is, they might lead Caleb straight to him. One way or the other."

The captain nodded. "Makes sense. So they don't resent him, huh?"

Eli folded his arms across his chest and looked Caleb directly in the eyes, a smile tugging at his lips. "Nope. In fact, I believe the daughter might be a little sweet on him."

Caleb glared at him. *See if I ever tell you anything again.* Eli's smile widened and Caleb realized he was being paid back for the punches.

The captain turned to Caleb. "Do you agree with your *brother*?"

Caleb groaned. *So they'd already had that discussion. Or maybe Captain had figured it out for himself. Not much got past the man.*

"I don't know if she is or not," Caleb admitted. "But she was acting a little strange. I'll try to figure out what's going on."

Captain Parnell frowned. "Does she know you're betrothed?"

Eli looked at Caleb, brows raised. "You didn't mention that."

"I'm not," he hastily assured his brother and his captain.

"That young woman who stopped in the offices at Amarillo said you asked her to marry you," the older man said.

"She was mistaken," Caleb said through clenched teeth, adding belatedly, "Sir." *Blast Jenna's hide.*

His captain stared at him, eyes narrowed for a moment, but all he said was, "I see."

I doubt it. Changing the subject, Caleb asked, "Have there been any sightings of the gang member who got away?"

Captain Parnell shook his head. "No, and the trouble we're having there, is that nobody really knows what he looks like. No one knew what any of them looked like. We have men searching for him in every direction. We'll find him. You concentrate on finding the one you let get away. Hopefully, Mrs. Horton and her daughter will provide some answers."

Garrison Becker stepped closer to Caleb, leaned in, and nudged him with his elbow. "Be as charming as you need to be, and do whatever it takes," he said with a leering wink. "You understand what I'm saying? Is the daughter pretty? That'll make the work a lot easier."

Caleb seethed as he fought the urge to slam his fist into the man's face.

The captain frowned at Becker before returning his attention to Caleb. "I wouldn't put it like that. However, I do want you to stick close to her, Calhoun. You better not let her out of your sight."

"Yes, sir."

Mason Hawthorne removed his spectacles, polished them on a pristine linen handkerchief and placed them back on his nose before addressing Caleb in a mild tone. "Ranger Calhoun, I've lost a great deal of money because of the Latham gang. I want Bob Horton behind bars or six-feet under—doesn't matter which. I don't care how you accomplish it. Just get it done."

Caleb didn't say anything. He wasn't sure he could verbalize his thoughts without a whole string of obscenities.

He had a preacher keeping him away from Abigail Horton, and a boss pushing him closer. Plus a banker and railroad executive who didn't care how low he had to sink as long as he accomplished what they wanted. He knew better than to speculate on whether a day could get any worse.

***

Caleb Calhoun was gone when Abby returned home. She slipped in through the front door, changed her dress, and headed for the kitchen. She was immediately thrust into the beehive of activity that filled her normal day.

Fortunately, her mother was likewise occupied and didn't have time to question her absence.

Unfortunately, their newest boarder had nothing to occupy her time and therefore kept up a litany of complaints. As Jenna Nolan droned on and on, Mrs. Horton suddenly thought of a dozen chores she needed to complete upstairs. Abby wished she'd thought of them first.

"What do you do for fun in this town?" Jenna asked Abby.

The girl's voice was just short of a full-blown whine, and Abby was ready to smack her with a skillet.

"Sometimes we go to the river," Abby said. *Or I could put you to work peeling potatoes.*

Jenna's expression brightened. "The river sounds promising. What do you do there?"

Abby shrugged. "Sometimes we fish, and sometimes we sit and talk."

"Oh. Do you ever get in the water?"

"Not when we're in mixed company."

Jenna's brow furrowed. "Mixed company? What does that mean?"

"You know, when the men are with us."

"But it's so hot."

"Well, occasionally, we remove our shoes and stockings, and cool our feet."

Jenna made an exaggerated gasping sound. "Oh my, how scandalous."

Heat filled Abby's face.

Before she could say anything, a deep voice startled both women. "Please forgive Jenna."

Caleb stood in the back doorway, frowning. "She was raised as the only child of a man who wanted a son more than anything in the world," he said. "Tomboy doesn't even begin to describe her. She's used to throwing herself recklessly into large bodies of water, and whatever else she has a mind to."

Jenna faced him, arms crossed, her pretty face marred by a pout. "You act as if I'm completely unladylike, Caleb Calhoun. I love fancy dresses, shoes and hats. I've attended etiquette classes and a session of charm school in Denver, and I've successfully hosted everything from tea parties to weekend house parties." She stomped her foot. "I am a genteel young woman, and you know it."

"When it suits you," Caleb agreed. "Though more often than not, you do whatever wild thought passes through that head of yours. It's not every girl who would've started out for Texas, alone. It's a miracle that all you lost was your money. You could've been killed."

Jenna suddenly smiled at him. "I knew if I could find you, you'd take good care of me, sugar doll."

Abby was stunned by the girl's forwardness.

Caleb didn't seem to care for it either. "Cut that out," he growled.

Jenna put her hands on her hips and batted her eyelashes. "Whatever's the matter, sugar? I'm only being ladylike."

To Abby's amazement, they began arguing. And she couldn't leave. There was work to do. She tried to concentrate on preparing dinner—humming to herself as she worked—but the sound of their exchange couldn't be ignored. Abby stilled when it dawned on her that there was no real animosity in Caleb and Jenna's squabbling. He was chastising her about cleaning up after herself and not making extra work for Abby and her mother. And she was griping about him ignoring her.

As they continued to bicker, Abby realized that the argument was actually along the lines of what she and Henry got in to every now and then. How odd.

Speak of the devil. Henry smiled at her as he entered the kitchen from the hallway, but stopped short when he saw the others. Although he greeted Jenna politely, as he had at church, when he looked at Caleb, Henry's eyes narrowed and his jaw tightened.

As the other couple resumed their argument, only quieter, Henry drew closer to her.

"Hey, Abby. I came to see if we could talk for a moment. Alone."

"Not now, Henry. I'm busy."

He glanced over his shoulder at the others then lowered his voice. "Are you sure you don't have time? I've got something to tell you."

"I said I didn't want to marry you," she whispered fiercely. "I thought you were going to leave me alone."

Henry took a step back. "I said I have something to tell you. Not something to ask you." He stared at her intently, and not with his usual affectionate expression.

"Okay, I can spare a few minutes out on the front porch," she said. "I can't be gone for long, though."

"That's fine," he said.

She followed him down the hall, careful not to make any noise when they passed the old preacher snoring softly in the rocking chair in the parlor.

Abby eased the screen door open and then closed, and motioned to the porch swing. Once they were seated, Henry seemed hesitant to talk. Finally, he blurted, "I saw you, Abby."

She turned to face him. "What do you mean?"

He cleared his throat. "Out at the river this morning."

Though her heart pounded, Abby tried not to overreact. "I've taken to enjoying a walk each day."

Henry shook his head. "I saw you at the cave. I saw your father."

Abby was off the swing in an instant. Shaking her head, she placed a finger to her lips. Henry clammed up immediately.

Grasping the screen door, Abby eased it open and checked the parlor. The preacher's eyes were still closed. She settled down in the swing again.

"Henry, please promise me you won't say anything," she whispered.

"Why?"

"Just don't tell anyone," she pleaded. Grabbing his arm, she added, "I can't go into detail yet, but it would mean a lot to me."

He scowled at her. "Why should I care about your feelings? You obviously don't care about mine."

"That is not true. Even if it were, this isn't about my feelings. This could very well be a matter of life and death."

"I thought that Ranger was taking him to trial. He hasn't been sentenced to death."

"A trial is the plan. But my father doesn't believe he'll make it there alive. There's been a reward offered, and someone might still try to collect."

Henry pushed against the porch with his boot, setting the swing in motion. "He may be telling you that so you'll help him escape. I've always liked your father, but sometimes people aren't who we think they are. It's only logical to assume he'll have to pay for his crimes." He turned worried brown eyes her way. "I'm sure it would be awful for you, but you should turn him in before you get caught up in something that takes you down with him."

Abby stuck her foot out and stopped the swing. "That's just it, my father doesn't need to pay," she whispered fiercely. "He didn't do anything." It was clear that Henry didn't believe her. "Will you trust me on this?"

He studied her for a moment. "I disagree with you, strongly, but I won't say anything. For now. You be careful going down there by the river, though. I'll go with you next time."

"Thank you, Henry, but that's not necessary. Going to the river…" She snapped her mouth shut as Ranger Calhoun stepped out onto the porch.

"Did I interrupt something?" Caleb asked.

"Not at all," Abby said, forcing a smile to her face. *How much had he heard? At the very least the part about the river.* Heart pounding, she struggled for a logical explanation. "We were talking about a picnic. I'll go gather what we need."

Caleb and Henry spoke at the same time. "Now?"

"I want to go," Jenna said, peeping out from behind Caleb.

Ignoring her, Abby looked at Henry. "I thought that's what you had in mind. A picnic. Down by the river. Did I misunderstand?"

"N…no," he said, finally catching on. "Sounds like fun."

"I want to go," Jenna said again, louder this time.

Henry glanced at Jenna and then back at Abby before motioning to the buckboard parked in front of the house. "I'm finished making deliveries. Wagon's empty. I guess we can bring along whoever wants to go."

"Wonderful," Abby said, jumping to her feet and hurrying inside. In the kitchen she explained to her mother about the impromptu outing as she began gathering the food.

Caleb had followed her back into the kitchen. "I'd like to go, too."

"Of co…course," she stammered. "The more the merrier." Apparently he thought nothing odd of her explanation. *Thank you, God.*

Even though the picnic had begun as an act of desperation, Abby was truly looking forward to it.

She looked at her mother. "What about you, Mama?"

"I think a picnic is a fine idea, Abby. You all go on. I'll stay here and get caught up on some work."

Guilt shot through Abby. "Do you want me to stay and help, Mama?"

"No, absolutely not. I want you to go and have some fun."

Miss Culpepper popped in from the hall. "I'll stay here and help your mother. I'm not much on outdoor dining. Between the bugs and the breezes—fresh air often makes me nauseous—I'm usually miserable at picnics."

I don't doubt that for a moment. Abby shook her head. Although

Miss Culpepper was annoying, she had to admit the woman was incredibly cheerful about her apparent lack of fortitude.

"You go on now," the older woman said, "I don't mind pitching in."

"Thank you, Miss Culpepper. I really do appreciate it. Don't overdo, okay?" *I don't want to hear about it when I return.*

"You're welcome, and don't worry about me. I'll plod along here at my own pace."

While Abby gathered food, her mother found a large wicker basket. Since Abby had already done most of the cooking for dinner, she divided the prepared food—leaving some for those staying at the house and taking the rest.

After packing the basket she grabbed several blankets from a cedar chest in the parlor and thrust them into Jenna's arms. The woman blinked at her, and then gave a shrug and carried them to the buckboard.

The young people were at the front door when the preacher straightened in his chair. Yawning, he pushed to his feet. "Fresh air and sunshine sounds mighty tempting. Mind if I tag along?"

Abby hid her shock, she hoped. *Why did he want to go with them? Was he still planning on causing her grief because of that scene he'd witnessed?*

Gripping the basket handle until it cut into her fingers, Abby said, "We would love to have you, Reverend Wainright. There's room for everyone."

He smiled. "Thank you. And please, call me Preacher."

Chapter Thirteen

ABBY, JENNA, CALEB and Robby settled into the back of the wagon, while Preacher perched on the seat beside Henry as they headed toward the river. Thankfully, without her even mentioning it, Henry went in the opposite direction of the cave.

They had almost reached their destination when Sheriff Elijah Calhoun and Deputy Bliss Walker rode up. "You're welcome to join us," Abby said to the men as the wagon rumbled along. "We've got plenty of food."

Before Eli could respond, Bliss said, "I don't recall ever runnin' away when the words food, welcome and plenty was all strung together in the same sentence. Much obliged."

Abby chuckled to herself when Eli shot him a disgruntled look, but he didn't argue with the man. Abby had always liked the old deputy. Their paths didn't cross often, but when they did, he always brought a smile to her face. He was full of interesting stories—some of which were believable.

The riders fell in alongside the wagon, and Eli asked Caleb how the search was going. Although Abby tried to hear the answer, Jenna was chattering away to Robby about how to make a whistle from a blade of grass. She decided she liked Jenna better when she was sullen and pouty.

Henry slowed the wagon, and Caleb and Robby hopped off while it was still rolling. Once it stopped fully, Jenna rose, and then waited, hands on hips, giving Caleb a pointed look until he stepped over to help her down. Smiling, Jenna tightened her arms around his neck and held on for a moment even after she had both feet on the ground. Caleb, seemingly used to such demonstrations, managed to appear bored and annoyed at the same time.

Abby, annoyed at both of them for reasons she didn't want to examine too closely, jumped from the wagon on her own. She wasn't waiting around for a man to help her down. She was proud of her independence and agility. Right up until the moment her shoe caught in her petticoats and she pitched forward, landing in a heap at Caleb's feet.

He appeared to be battling a smile as he pulled her up. He lost the battle completely when she lost her balance again and landed in his arms.

"I was going to offer you a hand getting down," he whispered with a grin, "but helping you up has been even more fun."

Caleb's green eyes sparkled in the sunlight and Abby was positive she'd never seen a more arresting sight in her life. Heat flooded her face when she realized she was staring. Her hands trembled as she brushed grass from her skirt, something that suddenly demanded all her attention.

She stepped back as Henry reached her side. "You okay, Abby?"

"I'm fine," she muttered. "Could you hand me the basket and blankets?"

After selecting the perfect grassy spot, Abby spread the largest blanket and began laying out the food—fried chicken, potato salad, deviled eggs, baked beans, cornbread and fresh peaches.

She was pleased when Jenna began to assist, but then realized the girl only wanted to see what food was available. After everything was laid out, Reverend Wainright said a brief blessing, thanking God for the food, the beautiful day, and the company.

Preacher and Bliss each grabbed a piece of chicken and a slice of cornbread, and ambled over to sit beneath a bent and gnarled live-oak tree. They leaned against the trunk while they ate, their stories punctuated by occasional laughter. They weren't acquainted and Abby was surprised at how well they got along. Perhaps the only thing they had in common was age, but it seemed to be enough.

Caleb sat down cross-legged on a corner of the blanket with a plate of food balanced on one knee. Henry anchored another corner of the blanket, facing Abby, then twisted around a bit so that his back was turned to Caleb. Despite his childish pique, Henry ate heartily. Even if he wasn't enjoying the company, he was enjoying the food.

Henry reached for another piece of chicken at the same time Caleb did. Abby held her breath, expecting Henry to start growling at any moment. All he did was shoot Caleb a withering glance, while the ranger looked about as bored as he had with Jenna.

Jenna surprised Abby by talking briefly to Henry, without a single whine, although it was about food. Eli had taken the horses down to the river for a drink. When he returned, Abby once again offered him something to eat. "We have plenty," she assured him.

"I've got to admit, those peaches sure look tempting," Eli said.

She tossed one to him. "They're delicious."

"Thanks."

Eli bit into the fruit, then balanced himself on his boot heels near Caleb. Abby leaned toward them, trying to overhear their conversation, even though she was in danger of tipping over and landing in the food. Unfortunately, Jenna was once again talking, this time to both Henry and Robby. Abby sighed when the men rose and walked away.

Abruptly, the conversation beside her stopped. Abby glanced up to see Jenna studying Eli and Caleb.

"So he finally found one of them," the girl said softly.

"What?"

Before Jenna could respond, Henry tugged on Abby's arm. "Come on, Abby, let's go for a walk."

"Not now, Henry. It's too hot."

Muttering under his breath, Henry rose to his feet and wandered down toward the river. Abby saw him a few minutes later, walking out on a large, low-hanging tree limb, parallel to the rushing water.

Worried, she was about to call out to him when Jenna addressed her. "Are you going wading?"

"No, I don't think so," Abby said. "The water's too high."

Besides, Caleb and Eli were walking back toward the pallet, still deep in conversation, and Abby hoped to learn of their strategy in the search for her father. If she heard them mention a cave, maybe she could get word to him and give him a chance to escape.

Jenna waved a bee away, and then made disparaging remarks about the heat, the boredom, the bugs, and Texas in general, and stomped back up toward the trail.

Robby immediately took off after her, pestering her about learning to whistle. Abby was ready to intervene if Jenna was rude to her brother, but she didn't rebuff the boy. In fact, they seemed to be chatting amiably as they walked along.

Caleb returned to the picnic blanket, and Eli walked over to talk to Bliss and Preacher.

"Where'd everybody go?" Caleb asked.

"Henry's down by the river, and Jenna's teaching Robby how to whistle with a blade of grass."

They heard a shrill, high-pitched trill just then, and Caleb smiled. "Better watch Jenna. She's a worse influence than most boys ever thought about being. She'll have him jumping out of trees, and throwing coins on the railroad tracks before you know it."

Abby wanted to ask Caleb more questions about Jenna, about

the two of them, but he stretched out flat and pulled his hat down over his eyes.

She turned her attention to Henry. "I do wish he'd be careful," she muttered. She was talking to herself and was surprised when Caleb responded.

"It's not like he's in the top of the tree. A fall from that distance wouldn't harm him at all."

"He can't swim," Abby explained.

Caleb raised up on one elbow and glanced toward the river. "He's fine. If I have my guess, he's showing off."

Henry stared in their direction. When Abby motioned to him, he stepped further out onto the limb. Suddenly he slipped, and teetered a moment before righting himself. Abby's gasp of horror had everyone looking toward Henry. Except Caleb. He laid back down, hat over his face again.

She motioned for Henry, who once more flailed his arms.

Abby sighed in disgust. *He was showing off.* She was turning away when a crack reverberated through the air, followed by a loud splash. The tree branch, and Henry, landed in the water.

Crying out, she rushed toward the river.

***

Caleb groaned and tossed his hat to the blanket. Abby could get herself killed trying to rescue that idiot. He pulled off his boots and dropped his gun belt. *Of all the dumb stunts.* If Henry didn't die, he might just kill him.

Even if Abby knew how to swim, and had the strength to tow him in, her skirt and petticoats would weigh her down. "Abby wait," Caleb shouted.

He scanned the water as he dashed to the river's edge, calling out for Abby to stop, and mentally cursing Henry for each rock and twig that bruised his feet. His heartbeat jumped a notch when he saw no signs of Henry…until he spotted that blond hair bobbing up and down.

Pushing past Abby, Caleb dove in and swam toward the floundering man.

When he reached him, Henry latched on, pulling them both under. Caleb came up spitting water and gasping for air, and yanked Henry up with him. The young man hadn't said a word, although his death grip on Caleb spoke volumes. Once again they went down. When they surfaced a second time, Caleb shouted, "Stop pulling at me. Be still or you're gonna kill us both."

Caleb felt a moment's sympathy as Henry's wild, wide-eyed gaze connected with his. "Be still and let me get a good grip on you," Caleb said softly. Henry loosened his hold on Caleb's shirt, and then immediately panicked again. "Don't make me knock you out," Caleb threatened.

It took two more tries before Caleb was able to get a good enough grip to start towing Henry to shore. Although lanky, the young man was surprisingly solid. As soon as they were in shallow water, Henry jerked away and stumbled forward on his own.

Caleb slipped a few times on the slick river bottom, the water-soaked denim of his pants weighing almost as much as the man he'd rescued, but eventually they were both on dry land.

Staggering a few feet forward, Henry collapsed face down as soon as he reached a grassy patch. Abby flew toward him, kneeling as she reached his side.

Caleb—hands on his knees, chest heaving—worked to catch his breath. Grumbling, he turned away, annoyed by the sight of the two of them, and happened to catch a glance at Eli.

His big brother was calmly putting on his boots, and then his gun belt. It took a moment for it to sink in.

Eli had been watching, ready to come to his aid. The knowledge that he had someone, two someone's, hit him hard. *He really had family again.* Dripping water, Caleb rubbed his hands across his eyes and walked toward his brother.

"You okay?" Eli asked.

"I'm fine. He was panicking, almost took us both under. Can't blame him for being scared." He shot a disgusted glance at Henry and Abby. "Although he does seem to be making the most of his near-death experience."

Eli laughed. "That, he does."

Despite the fact that he was soaked through, Caleb did a slow burn as he watched Abby fussing over Henry. Instead of being grateful for his help, Henry seemed angry, glaring at Caleb over the girl's head.

Finally, Abby turned to Caleb. "Thank you for saving Henry's life."

Henry objected immediately. "That man did not save me," he sputtered, water trickling from his hair and onto his face. "I could've gotten out of there…eventually."

Caleb didn't even try to hide his disgust. "You were in over your head," he said as he shook water from his own hair, "and going down for the third time. And you very nearly took me down with you."

Abby glanced from one man to the other, dismay evident in her eyes, and then seemed to realize that Caleb was every bit as wet and miserable as Henry.

Rushing to the picnic spot, she tossed the remaining food and dishes into the basket, grabbed the blanket from the ground and hurried back to wrap it around Caleb. She pulled it tight, her warm fingers brushing his throat in the process.

Caleb protested at first, but when she began fussing over him, he stilled. She took one of the kitchen towels she'd brought along and motioned for him to sit on a nearby fallen log. Once he was seated, she moved behind him and began drying his hair.

Caleb was shocked at how good it felt. Eyes closed, he leaned into her hands, letting his shoulders relax. He opened his eyes to see Reverend Wainright and Bliss chuckling together. At him.

A quick glance at Eli revealed that he, too, was smiling, although he did have the good manners to turn his head when he caught Caleb looking.

Jenna chose that moment to return, with her usual dramatic flair. Racing past everyone else, she threw herself forward, nearly unseating him. "Oh, Caleb, sugar. What happened? Are you all right?"

Caleb stood, removed Jenna's arms from around his neck, and turned to Abby. He gave a brisk nod in an effort to recapture some of his dignity. "Thanks, Abby, but a few minutes in the sunshine is all I need."

He walked to the wagon, pulled the blanket from his shoulders and laid it over the sideboard to dry. Jenna trotted along beside him, chattering like a magpie about nearly "losing him."

"I'm fine," he told her. "Really, it was nothing to worry about. Henry was the one in danger."

As Jenna continued to chatter on, Caleb eyed Abby with concern. While he was experienced enough to enjoy a moment for the moment's sake and nothing more—and he had indeed enjoyed her care—she was every bit as smitten with him as he'd feared.

She'd all but abandoned Henry to rush to his aid. Caleb was going to have to tread lightly here. No matter how tempted he was to pursue her—and he was sorely tempted—she would eventually come to resent him, or even hate him.

Because he would only be playing, and Abby was the sort of girl who'd be playing for keeps. Caleb gathered his resolve around him much like the blanket he'd discarded. He'd do the right thing, no matter how difficult it was.

Besides, even if he were to allow himself to return Abby's feelings, there could never be a future for them. Especially once he hauled her father off to prison.

Chapter Fourteen

CALEB FINALLY GOT to meet the surveyors—introduced only as Fredrick, Cecil and Joseph—when they joined the boarders for supper that night. Although educated, the men were a bit on the ragged side. They lit into the meal like they weren't sure when they'd get another. He'd discovered that they were sleeping in tents when they stayed in Boone Springs. Probably didn't get any home-cooking over there.

They were friendly fellows, at least two of them anyway. One of them didn't look up from his plate long enough for anyone to find out. Caleb planned to take them aside later and ask if they had come across anyone fitting Bob Horton's description.

In the meantime, he watched Abby as she watched them, marveling at the way her eyes lit up as the men answered questions about the places they'd been.

When Fredrick, a scrawny, balding fellow with an Adam's apple that bobbed up and down constantly, mentioned that he was from the east, Abby leaned toward him.

"Have you ever seen New York?"

He nodded and swallowed a mouthful of ham before he answered her. "Why sure I have."

As the man described the sights and sounds of that bustling

city, Abby asked him question after question, wanting to know all sorts of details. Caleb shook his head in amazement. The girl was simply mesmerized.

Then it dawned on him that Abby was looking at that surveyor the same way she had at him the first night. What Caleb had taken for interest in him had merely been interest. *Abby was fascinated by...life.* Any life beyond Moccasin Rock. The heat of embarrassment washed through him.

Caleb heard little of the conversation for a while, and contributed nothing, caught up in his own humiliating thoughts. Luckily, no one seemed to notice. Everyone was captivated by the surveyors' stories of all the places they'd traveled.

All three of the men had worked enough prairie jobs that there were also stories of Indian skirmishes to share. Preacher got in on those. The old man had traveled Texas when it was still a wilderness, encountering hostile natives, wild animals and even an outlaw or two. Preacher had several friends who'd been felled by Indian arrows. Caleb was as fascinated as everyone else, which made him forget his own problems. For a while.

When the meal was over, Fredrick excused himself to the front porch for a smoke. Caleb followed him, tossing out a few questions while the man opened a pouch of Bull Durham tobacco and rolled a cigarette. Fredrick answered Caleb's questions as willingly as he had Abby's. Unfortunately, he hadn't seen anyone matching Bob Horton's description.

"Have you heard anybody talking about the gang, or any rumors at all?" Caleb asked.

Fredrick nodded, patting his pockets as he searched for a match. "Folks seem relieved that most of them are dead. And they're hoping you find the last two."

While they were talking, the screen door opened, and Cecil stepped out. The man skidded to a stop when he saw Caleb. "Didn't know you had company," he said to Fredrick, then turned and hurried back inside.

"What's with him?" Caleb asked. "It usually takes more than five seconds for someone to decide they don't like me, although not much more in some cases."

Fredrick laughed as he took a long drag on the cigarette. "Cecil doesn't like lawmen. Nothing personal. We're in and out of a lot of different towns, and sometimes there are lawmen ready to blame us for whatever goes wrong. We like to keep our heads low, get our work done, and move on."

Caleb nodded his understanding, but the other man's reaction had sure seemed personal to him.

Fredrick took a few more puffs from the cigarette, then dropped it and snuffed it out with the toe of his boot. "I'll let you know if we see or hear anything about the Latham gang," he said.

"Appreciate it."

Caleb settled into the porch swing after Fredrick left, his thoughts jumping back and forth between Bob Horton and Abigail Horton. How could he have been so stupid as to think she'd been infatuated with him? He couldn't even stand the thought of looking at her right now.

The sun had begun its slow slide into the horizon when the screen door creaked.

"Caleb? Everything okay?" Abby asked.

He answered without looking at her. "Yep, everything's fine." Embarrassment hit him again. Did she know what he'd thought when they met? That's what he got for teasing and flirting with her.

"Did that man know anything about my father?"

His gaze flew to hers. "No." It didn't surprise him that she'd known what he was up to, but he was startled that she was so open about it. She stood there, twisting a corner of her apron. Was her anxiety for her father's well-being? Or did she know more than she was telling? He needed to find out. Pushing his personal feelings aside, he patted the seat next to him. "Join me?"

She hesitated briefly. "All right, I guess I can spare a few minutes."

They chatted about the weather, something that all Texans did regularly, Caleb noted, before he broached the subject. "What did your father do before…" he paused, and Abby finished his question.

"You mean before he became a desperate outlaw and turned to a life of crime?" She apologized for her cutting tone. "It's only that my father is not what you believe him to be. I wish I could convince you of that," she added.

He responded casually. "Why don't you try one more time? Tell me about him. Convince me that I'm wrong."

Now she was the one hesitating.

Come on, darlin', tell me what you know.

She tilted her head to one side, clearly weighing how much to say. "I just know my father. And he's not that kind of man."

Caleb suppressed a sigh of frustration. "So what kind of man is he?"

"He's kind and quiet. The very epitome of the word gentleman."

"I thought the same thing about my own father," Caleb said. "And I would've beaten the tar out of anybody who said otherwise." He paused, not sure why he wanted to tell her this. Yet somehow it felt right.

"You discovered you were wrong?"

"Yes, I recently found out he had another family before he married my mother. He walked away from them."

"Are you talking about the sheriff and Dr. Nathaniel?" she asked. At his nod, her eyes widened.

"You knew nothing about them?"

"Never even had an inkling that I had siblings. It was only a coincidence that I landed in the same town as them."

Abby looked thoughtful for a moment, like maybe she wanted to disagree with him.

"You don't believe in coincidences?"

She shrugged. "I don't know, that's a little over my head. However, I do believe that sometimes what people call coincidences are really part of God's grander plan for us. Maybe your coming here wasn't happenstance, is all I'm saying."

Caleb wasn't about to argue with her. While he didn't know about any "grander plan", everything that had happened was too strange for him to explain away.

She looked at him, compassion in her eyes. "Coincidence or not, that must've been quite a shock."

"To say the least. I have two blood relatives in this town, and I don't know a thing about either one of them."

"I wish I could help you," Abby said, "but I'm not well-acquainted with them either. They haven't been in Moccasin Rock long. Eli stopped a robbery at the bank here about a year ago. He'd just arrived on the train. I'm not sure if he meant to get involved, or even why he'd stopped here. Witnesses later said he walked right into the shootout and gunned-down the two robbers. Some said his demeanor went beyond calm, that he was expressionless, eyes devoid of any emotion. Others said it seemed as if he didn't care whether he lived or died. Our previous sheriff was killed in that robbery, and Eli was offered the job. No matter what had caused him to act the way he did, the town officials decided that he wasn't afraid to fight."

Didn't care whether he lived or died? Why? "I can't imagine what would bring him to that point," Caleb admitted.

"Me either," Abby said. "But, I will say he's changed since then."

That eased his mind somewhat. "What do you know about Nathaniel?"

"Not much. He arrived about six months ago. And it was definitely no coincidence. He's mentioned to others that he was searching for Eli. Our previous physician had retired a couple of years ago and moved down to Houston to be with his daughter.

His office was just sitting there. I'm not sure what the arrangements were, but Dr. Nathaniel got in touch with him and made some sort of deal. He moved into Doc's old place and set up shop right away."

Caleb appreciated the information, yet he had so many more questions. "To be honest, I'm really struggling to make sense of any of this," he said.

"So you can't ask your father?"

Caleb shook his head. "He passed away. My mother's gone, too."

"I'm sorry," Abby said. "What about asking Jenna? At the picnic she said something about you 'finally finding one of them' and she was looking right at Eli. Do you think she has any answers?"

Caleb wasn't sure he'd heard her correctly. "She said what?"

Even after Abby repeated herself, it took a moment for Caleb to comprehend what she was saying. Jenna knew something about his family that he didn't know? *How? Why?* It didn't make sense. All thought of discussing Bob Horton's whereabouts flew from his mind.

"I'm not sure what she could possibly know," he told Abby. "But I'd like to ask her about it. Will you excuse me?"

"Of course. I hope whatever you discover will put your mind at ease."

***

After a brief search inside the house, Caleb found Jenna with Robby near the edge of the Horton's garden. They were both bent over something in the gathering dusk. He'd seen the boy there earlier, barefoot, one strap of his overalls hanging from his shoulder, hoe in hand, working between the rows. Caleb knew perfectly well that Jenna wasn't much on hard work. So what were they doing?

Robby spotted him and to Caleb's surprise, waved him over. "Hey, look at what I found."

Caleb smiled when he saw what was causing the excitement. A

grass snake. The boy scooped it up, holding the small reptile loosely in one hand, allowing it to crawl in and out through his fingers and up his wrist before securing it with the other hand. "I'm going to keep him," Robby said.

Jenna was rattling off instructions a mile a minute, telling Robby how to care for the snake.

Caleb shook his head. Some women might've been scared— some men for that matter—but Jenna was in her element. She'd been this way as a kid, too—an unusual girl and now a unique woman.

As she laughed and talked with Robby, her brown eyes flashing with humor, Caleb almost wished he loved her. Although she had a list of shortcomings that wasn't exactly short, she'd always been a good friend, and his feelings for her felt safe and familiar. She was also one of the prettiest girls he'd ever seen. Caleb sighed. He sincerely hoped she found the right man some day. He didn't know when that would happen, but he did know it wouldn't be him. She deserved someone who would love her with all his heart.

"You might want to ask your mother about keeping that," Caleb told Robby when Jenna paused for a breath.

Caleb then took a moment to admire Robby's new pet before turning his attention to his old friend. "You got a minute?"

Jenna glanced up at him, brows raised.

"I'd like to talk to you, in private," he said. "I want to ask you something."

She immediately straightened and gave him a dazzling smile as she brushed dirt from her hands. "Of course, Caleb. I always have time for you."

He motioned her toward the back porch and waited until she was seated on the steps before easing down beside her.

Robby pushed the snake into his pocket before he scurried inside looking for his mother.

As the screen door slammed shut, Caleb tried to figure out

exactly how to begin. Jenna placed a hand on his arm. "What is it, honey?"

Taking a deep breath, he said, "Abby told me you made some remark about me 'finding' Eli at the picnic. Is that true?"

Her smile faded. "Oh."

"Did you say that?"

Jenna shrugged, clearly bored now that she knew what he wanted to ask her. "Yes, I was surprised you'd finally found one of your brothers. I'm happy for you. Your father would be too."

Incredulous, he stared at her. "How did you know I even had brothers?"

She returned the look, eyes wide. "You mean you didn't know?"

"I had no idea." He stood and started pacing back and forth in front of the porch. "Tell me everything you know. And when you discovered it."

"Well, the second part is easier. You remember when your father first started getting sick?"

He nodded. "I was away at school and eventually ended up coming home for awhile."

"Right. Well, before you did, your father would often ask me and my father to come visit him."

"Why?"

"He was lonesome, I think. Needed someone to talk with."

Caleb experienced a pang of guilt, although there was nothing he could've done at the time. "Even if that was true, how in the world did something like that come up? Why would he tell you and not me?"

She shrugged and glanced away. "Truthfully, he didn't tell me. I overheard it."

"Oh." Although somewhat mollified, Caleb was still confused. "What exactly did you hear?"

"That was a long time ago. I don't remember it in detail."

He bit back the impulse to push. It wouldn't do any good to

rattle Jenna. She could be easily distracted; and even when focused, her thoughts were often difficult to follow. "Please, tell me what you do remember."

She dropped from the top step to a lower one, and leaned back on her elbows. "As best as I recall, your father was talking about his two other sons and...he was crying."

"Crying?"

"Yes. Papa and he were talking about something, and tears were sliding down his face."

"You don't remember any of what they were saying?"

Jenna shook her head. "Just something about his sons. It was unsettling, and a bit frightening, to see a grown man cry. That's all I was aware of at the time."

Caleb stared at her in astonishment. "I don't understand this. Why didn't he tell me? Why didn't you?"

"Seriously, Caleb, I thought you already knew. I figured it probably bothered you to talk about it. So I never brought it up."

"Why did you think it would bother me?"

Standing, she straightened her skirts and adjusted the satin belt around her waist. "Because your father was hurting badly, and I didn't want to bring up anything that might cause you the same kind of pain. I figured you'd tell me when you were ready. I had no idea that you didn't know."

After she'd gone, Caleb stood there, unable to move. Why had his father not told him about his other family? Why had he left them to start with?

Mrs. Horton burst through the doorway, a firm grip on Robby, who had a less than firm grip on the wriggling snake. "Oh, Mama, slow down, you're scaring Mr. Wiggles."

"I'm going to do a lot more than scare him if you dare bring that thing back in this house, young man."

Caleb smiled. Robby's indignant expression, and Mrs. Horton's frustrated one, brought back memories of his mother's reactions to some of Caleb's own antics. Even though his mother had been hard on him, and wanted him to be something he wasn't interested in becoming, he'd never doubted that she loved him.

And his father had been the best companion a little boy could hope for. Amos Calhoun had been the perfect father.

Or had it all been a lie?

Chapter Fifteen

ABBY PULLED A wet towel from the basket at her feet, twisted it in a wringing motion, and then snapped it out with a flick of her wrists before securing it to the clothesline with a pin.

She reached behind her for another towel, only to touch something furry instead. A scream died in her throat when she turned and encountered the big brown eyes of a raggedy dog—front paws perched on the basket, the tip end of a pink tongue sticking out.

"What are you doing here?" she whispered fiercely. "I told you last time that you can't stay. Mama will have a fit. She said it's hard enough to look after all the humans who live here."

The pup, a black and white spotted mutt, wagged his tail, completely undaunted by her scolding. Abby bent down to get a closer look at him. He cocked his head to one side, tail fanning faster as he awaited her appraisal.

"It won't do you a bit of good to charm me," she said. He gave a little yap, which had Abby glancing over her shoulder. There was no one in sight. "Okay, fine. Wait here. I'll be right back."

Hurrying into the house, she returned with a piece of ham. "After you eat this, you'd better skedaddle," she said. "Mama just came down the stairs."

The dog gobbled the ham and ran, as if he understood every word she said. Wiping her hands on her apron, Abby laughed and returned to her chores. She wasn't sure where the little fellow belonged, but he'd dropped by several times lately. Now that she thought about it, he'd looked a little thinner and more ragged with each visit. Maybe he didn't belong anywhere. She'd better start leaving food and water out for him. Although Mama might not want him living in the house, she sure wouldn't want the poor boy to starve.

Abby sighed. The dog's problems were easier to fix than her own. It had been a week since her father escaped custody and taken shelter in the cave, and she hadn't been able to visit him in nearly that long. Caleb Calhoun was watching her every move. And for some reason that was disturbing in more ways than one.

It wasn't only that she was being watched—it was that *he* was watching her. Abby had spent the biggest part of her life in the boarding house kitchen, either learning to cook or cooking, and yet lately it seemed almost foreign to her. And it was his fault.

Why was she so unnerved by Caleb? *Guilt, no doubt.* Thankfully, Henry had agreed to keep taking food to the cave while they waited on word from Marshal Adair. If Caleb discovered her father's hiding place, it wouldn't be because he'd followed her.

Abby ran a hand up the back of her neck, gathering a few loose tendrils that had escaped the bun she'd fashioned that morning, and re-secured them with a hairpin before taking another towel from the basket.

The last time Caleb had tried to learn what she knew about her father, he'd gotten side-tracked by his own father's secrets. She might not be so lucky next time. Ranger Calhoun could be very charming when he wanted to be. She'd have to watch every word she said in his presence. If he tried to question her again, maybe she could keep him distracted by talking about some mind-numbing topic. But what? *How about potatoes? That's about as mind-numbing as it gets.*

Turning back for another towel Abby let out a yelp and pressed a hand to her chest. Caleb was leaning against the back porch railing, watching her. "You nearly scared the life out of me," she said.

He grinned, straightened and crossed over to her. "Sorry. I thought you might have time to talk. Before I was sidetracked the other night, you were about to tell me about your father."

So much for turning his attention elsewhere. Abby turned back to the clothesline and continued on with her chores. "Well, as I've mentioned before, for most of my life, he's run the boarding house here with Mama. But he was a bookkeeper before a massive fire destroyed our home, our whole town, in fact, back in 1871."

He handed her a towel from the basket. "So y'all came here from Chicago?"

"No, we came from Peshtigo, Wisconsin. There was a fire there the same night, the exact same time, in fact, as the one in Chicago. The death toll was actually higher in Peshtigo. More than fifteen-hundred people were killed."

She turned in time to catch a look of amazement on his face.

"I didn't know that," he said.

"For some reason, the other fire captured the attention of the nation, the world, while the Peshtigo fire was quickly forgotten," Abby said. "Maybe because the Chicago fire was supposedly started by Mrs. O'Leary's cow kicking over a lantern in a barn. True or not, that extraordinary story spread as rapidly as the fire."

Caleb nodded. "That's what I've always heard."

"The Peshtigo fire, on the other hand, started as a forest fire. Before it was over more than a dozen communities were destroyed. Including ours."

He studied her. "That was a long time ago. Do you actually remember it?"

She shook her head. "No, only vague images—but I remember

the desperation and despair. And I remember Daddy trying to keep me from drowning."

"Drowning? I thought it was a fire, not a flood."

"It was a raging fire storm," she explained, "consuming everything in its path. Folks were running, submerging themselves in whatever water they could find—wells, ponds, creeks, and the Peshtigo River."

Abby cleared her throat. "That's where we went," she added. "We stayed in the water for hours. We were fortunate to have survived both the fire and the river. Some died from the cold water, and others drowned. The fire jumped across the river at one point and burned for miles on the other side."

"I can't even imagine a fire of that magnitude," Caleb admitted.

"I was fortunate to be too young to understand the worst of it," Abby said, "although I'm sure my parents can recall the horrifying detail even to this day."

She paused, a hand resting lightly on the clothesline, the other on her chest. "I do have one memory," she said softly. "There was a flurry of embers flying around us. Daddy curled himself over me, keeping my head above water, as the sparks rained down on him. His back was burned, but he kept me sheltered."

Caleb's expression softened. "No wonder you don't want to believe the worst of him. The man's your own personal hero."

It warmed her heart that Caleb understood how great a father Bob Horton was. Now if she could only get him to believe that he was no outlaw.

"So y'all moved here afterwards?" he asked.

Abby nodded as she pinned the last towel in place. "Daddy's family all died in the fire. Mama was an orphan so when they left Wisconsin, all they had was each other. And me. This little town is all I've really ever known."

"Moccasin Rock seems like an odd choice for starting over, especially for a bookkeeper. How did you end up here?"

She knew what he was getting at. "Are you thinking that maybe I didn't know what Daddy was up to?"

He ducked his head for a moment, and then looked her in the eye. "Yes. Desperation could make a man do strange things. Especially if he's trying to care for his family."

So much for convincing him of her father's innocence. "From what I've been told, there's a simple explanation for our coming here," she said, trying not to become defensive. "Some of the people who came in to help clean up after the fire talked a lot about Texas, and all the opportunities here. There was nothing left for us in Wisconsin. Daddy took what little money he had, and a few precious mementoes they salvaged from the ashes, and we headed to Texas."

Abby placed the empty laundry basket on the back porch, and picked up a metal pan. She crossed to the garden, knowing he would follow. "At first, he and Mama took work here at the boarding house to pay for our room and board," she continued. "Eventually, the elderly owners sold the place to them. If it wasn't for all the activity from the railroad being built a few years later, we probably wouldn't have made it."

Green beans made a soft pinging sound as Abby plucked them from the vine, and tossed them into the pan. "Eventually though, everyone moved on to the next town and we were nearly empty here. Periodically it's better, but it's so unpredictable. Of course, until another hotel is built, we won't have to worry as much."

Abby stopped to tie up a drooping bean vine, and Caleb reached out to help her. His hand brushed against hers and a fluttering sensation swept through her stomach. Her breath gave a little hitch before she could stop it.

Thankfully, he didn't seem to notice. "When did *you* start working here?" he asked.

"I can't remember a time that I didn't work here. There's always been something to do."

"You'd rather be doing something else?"

"It's not that, really. I don't mind the hard work. I just feel… trapped at times."

"Trapped?"

Abby lowered her head. "That sounds so dramatic now that I hear it aloud, but I've watched my mother struggle to keep this place going, and raise her children, and be a good wife, and friend and neighbor, and she's done it all well. Yet she's tired all the time, and…trapped. I don't want to end up that way."

Head tilted to one side, he studied her. "What do you want?"

Unsure if she should share her dreams, Abby hesitated a moment. "I want to travel."

"Where?"

She shrugged. "Everywhere. Anywhere."

"Don't you want to marry and have children of your own some day?" Caleb stilled and then made a gesture as if to physically pull the words back.

Abby suppressed a smile at his obvious discomfort and answered him matter-of-factly. She knew there was nothing personal about the question. "Oh, I do," she said. "First though, I want a chance to see something, anything, past Moccasin Rock and Fair Haven. I had planned on leaving before now. My parents have paid me a little here and there when they could, and I've made some extra money by sewing. I'd save nearly every cent. Then times got really tough, and I gave the money to Mama."

"Did you have enough saved to get you where you wanted to go?"

"To be honest, it wouldn't have gotten me far," Abby admitted. I'd planned to take work eventually. You see, I wasn't going alone. I planned on meeting a friend. We were going to New York together."

Strangely, that seemed to bother him. "What friend?"

"Her name is Catherine Gloria Lovell. She invited me to accompany her and her brother, Richard, on their travels."

"C.G. Lovell," Caleb murmured.

It took a moment for Abby to realize what he said, and what it meant. *He'd searched her room and seen the post cards!* She started to confront him about it, but then reconsidered. He was only doing his job. And she knew he hadn't found anything incriminating about her father.

"The Lovell family stayed here some years ago," she continued. "Catherine and I were close to the same age, and when they left, we kept in touch. She and her brother are photographers now, and traveling a great deal. Such an exciting life. Catherine's always sending me postcards. She invited me to join them. So I saved every bit of money I ever earned and planned to do that. I knew I would need to find employment at some point, but I wanted to go so badly. It seems like such a childish dream now, although it was important at the time."

"So what happened?" he asked. "Why didn't you leave?"

"Like I said, times got really tight, and I gave Mama what I had saved. Then my father passed away, or at least we thought he did, and it wasn't only my money she needed. She needed me. There's no way she can run this place alone."

"Does your mother know that you'd planned to meet up with your friend?"

"No. She had so much to worry about already. I was trying to decide how best to tell her, when...when we got the news about Daddy."

"That must've been rough." His sympathy seemed genuine, yet Caleb's next question had her on guard again. "Any idea why he led y'all to believe he was dead?"

Abby clamped her mouth shut and shook her head. She'd told him everything about her father that she was willing to. To her surprise, the next words out of his mouth had nothing to do with Bob Horton.

"I'm honestly not sure you'd like big cities such as New York or Boston, at least not long-term," Caleb said.

"You've seen those places?" She couldn't control the excitement in her voice. Didn't even try.

"Yes, and more."

"More?"

"I've been to Europe."

"Oh my," Abby sighed. She peppered him with questions, delighted when he answered each one, even going into detail when she asked about the clothing, the food, and the houses. *How long had he saved for a trip like that?* She couldn't even imagine.

"Where do you live when you're not seeing the world?" she asked when he'd answered all her other questions.

"I have a rented room in Austin near Ranger headquarters."

"So you don't travel much anymore?"

Caleb shook his head. "No. I'm usually up to my neck in work. I wouldn't have it any other way though. I enjoy what I do."

They talked a little more about his travels as they left the garden and returned to the porch. "What was the most unusual meal you've ever eaten?" she asked.

"Hoe cake," he answered promptly.

Abby raised her brows. "I figured you'd describe some elaborate feast in France. What's so strange about a hoe cake? They're just made from corn meal."

"That's true. But this one was actually made on the blade of a hoe."

"Are you serious?"

He smiled. "Yep. Not much of a story. All I'll say is that I found myself in a situation where all that was available was cornmeal and water. And no skillet."

Abby laughed. "I can see why that was the most unusual thing you've ever eaten. So what's the most elegant meal you've ever had?"

This time he did describe a meal he'd eaten in Paris. She was silent for several moments, just savoring the description.

"One last question," she said. "What's the most memorable thing you've ever seen—something you won't ever forget?"

He opened his mouth, then closed it again, an odd expression on his face. "That's tough. I'll have to get back to you on that one."

Caleb left shortly afterwards, Abby watching as he made his way down the alley. *What adventures he'd had!* Closing her eyes, she tried to imagine herself standing on the streets of New York or Boston or Philadelphia.

With a gasp, Abby opened her eyes. In every single scenario, she'd pictured Caleb Calhoun standing beside her.

"You'd better get such foolish notions out of your mind," she whispered to herself as she headed inside. "There's work to do."

Chapter Sixteen

CALEB ENTERED THE jail to find both his brothers inside. Eli was polishing the Colt, and Nathaniel had his boots propped up on the edge of the desk. "Glad I caught you two together," Caleb said.

Having decided to tell them what he'd learned about their father—though it wasn't much—Caleb was now trying to figure out how to say it.

No matter how it all unfolded, he hoped this discussion would go better than his most recent one with Abigail Horton. When he'd caught up with her at the clothesline, alone, his intention had been to learn as much as he could about her father.

Instead, Caleb had learned something about himself—he couldn't flirt and tease Abby for the fun of it anymore.

When she'd asked him what he'd never forget, the first thing that popped into his mind was "A girl from Moccasin Rock." Before those words passed his lips, Caleb had realized that she might take a comment like that seriously.

Even though he knew now that Abby wasn't as smitten with him as he'd thought, Caleb was appalled at how casually he tossed statements like that around in the past. He'd made some sort of vague reply to her question and high-tailed it out of there—before he was tempted to say, or do, something worse. He was starting to feel a little off balance around that girl, and he didn't like it one bit.

"Do y'all have time to talk," Caleb asked his brothers now. He snagged a chair from in front of the stove and positioned it next to Nathaniel.

Eli opened the desk drawer and dropped the rag inside before twirling the gun twice and slipping it into his holster.

Caleb smiled at the flashy move that was at odds with his brother's reserved demeanor.

"What's on your mind?" Eli asked.

"I was wondering if maybe we could talk about our father."

His brothers exchanged a quick glance. Nathaniel dropped his feet to the floor and straightened.

Eli frowned. "What about him?"

Inhaling deeply, Caleb told them about his conversation with Jenna.

"I was shocked, and frankly disbelieving, that she might know something about my father that I didn't," Caleb said. "It turns out she did. She knew I had brothers and I never even had a clue. I wish I'd discovered more, but I know now that whatever caused Amos Calhoun to leave y'all behind, it didn't bring him happiness."

Neither of the other men said a word. Caleb fell silent, too. They'd learned something about their shared parentage, yet not enough to answer any questions. The silence stretched on for a while, each brother seemingly lost in his own thoughts and memories.

Caleb had noticed before the striking resemblance Eli had to Amos Calhoun, but he took the opportunity to study Nathaniel now. This brother's hair and eyes were a lighter shade of brown than either Eli or their father. He was also a bit leaner. But he had the same features—that same brow, straight nose and firm jaw line. Calhoun, pure and simple.

"Thanks for letting us know," Eli finally said. "I'd give anything for a few more answers, but it doesn't look like that's meant to be. At least he talked about us to somebody."

A thought occurred to Caleb. "I do have a great-aunt I could speak to."

His brothers leaned forward, clearly interested in a possible familial link. "On my mother's side," he said, and then added, "Sorry," when they both seemed to collapse a little.

"Her name is Victoria Edgers," Caleb said. "She's from Boston. When I was a boy we visited her there every few years, and she would come to Colorado as often as possible. She's been here in Texas, down in Austin, for several weeks now, trying to talk me into visiting her."

"You don't want to see her?" Nathaniel asked in surprise.

"I would rather take a beating than to have to spend any time with her," Caleb said, "but if there's even the slightest possibility she might know something about our father, I guess I'd better check it out."

Eli gave him a puzzled look. "You're not fond of her?"

"You could say that. She never forgave her sister—my grandmother—for marrying a down-on-his-luck gambler while on a trip to Denver. Although my grandfather gave up that life, and, as far as I know, was a good family man after that, he was never good enough for the Edgers family. They were true bluebloods. Even the fact that Grandfather's gambling nature paid off, big time, when he invested in a Colorado silver mine, didn't make a difference. Grandfather didn't need their money, yet from what I understand, he always craved their acceptance. That never happened."

Caleb pushed to his feet and began pacing back and forth in front of the cells. "Then, when my mother was born, Aunt Victoria swooped back in, pinning all her hopes of an advantageous, socially superior union on her little niece, Julia. My mother spent her younger years trying to live up to Victoria's expectations and standards."

"I'm gathering she didn't succeed?" Nathaniel said.

"Nope, because despite my great-aunt's best efforts, my mother married even further beneath her than my grandmother had—to a dirt-poor Texan named Amos Calhoun. Victoria was furious. And instead of telling her aunt to mind her own business, my mother tried to garner her approval by making *me* into the perfect little gentleman. She even sent me to live with Aunt Victoria for a while. I can't tell you how much I detested everything I was subjected to—fancy dinners, dance lessons, etiquette lessons. I wasn't the only little boy who went through that sort of thing, but all of it seemed to matter so much to my mother and aunt, more than I mattered to them. I began acting up and causing trouble. Victoria eventually sent me home."

His brothers didn't say anything, so he continued.

"My father was my rock, my friend, and without a doubt saved my sanity. That seemed to make Aunt Victoria angrier. She had absolutely no use for Amos Calhoun."

"Sounds like your aunt and I have something in common," Eli said.

Caleb snorted. "I guarantee you that's the only thing. She's an annoying, sanctimonious, wealthy woman who thinks she knows exactly how I should live my life and what I should do with my inheritance. She's made my life miserable."

He ranted on for several more moments before it dawned on him that their only response was identical wide-eyed, open-mouthed stares. Caleb winced. Clearly, he'd said more than he'd intended. Well, it was past time he told them about the money anyway.

"So let me get this straight," Eli said, raising a hand. "You have rich relatives on your mother's side, and even though one of them married a poor man, your grandfather, he later cashed in on a silver mine and became a wealthy man in his own right. And your biggest problem is how to spend your money. I don't exactly see the misery in that."

Caleb didn't have a ready response. Eli was right—and with that stern expression he looked so much like Amos Calhoun that a wave of homesickness hit Caleb.

But home was gone. And so was his father. Yet he did have another chance at family, if he didn't make a complete mess of this.

Lowering his head, Caleb struggled with what to say next. Finally he looked at them. "From what you've said, I know I probably grew up a little different than you two."

Eli and Nathaniel exchanged a glance, although it was Eli who responded. "If you can call sleeping under porches and eating out of the trash 'a little different,' then I reckon you're right."

There was no self-pity in Eli's voice, only a calm acceptance. But Caleb felt as if he'd been punched in the gut. "I'm sorry," he said quietly. "I didn't realize."

Nathaniel shrugged. "We don't dwell on our childhood, and we don't normally talk about it. The important thing is that we survived it."

Caleb dropped down into the chair again. "Wasn't there anyone to help you out? Maternal relatives? Friends?"

"If there was anybody on our mother's side of the family, we never knew about it," Nathaniel said. "We were so young that we didn't pay any attention to what might've been talked about around us."

Caleb hesitated for a moment and then plowed on. "If you don't mind me asking, what happened to your mother?"

Eli leaned back in his chair, clasped his hands behind his head and stared at the ceiling. "Mama died when the house we were living in, near a little community called Taylor's Crossing, caught fire. Nathaniel and I had been down to the creek to get a bucket of water for her—it took both of us to carry it. We were supposed to come right back..." His words trailed off, and Nathaniel took up the story.

"I took it in my head to play around while we were there,"

Nathaniel said. "I was trying to jump from rock to rock, and I ended up falling in. Eli had to drag me out, and then we were both wet. We sat in the sun a while trying to dry off so we wouldn't be in trouble."

Eli's Adam's apple bobbed up and down, and his voice had gone husky. "When we returned to the house, it was in flames. We tried to get in. We were screaming for Mama, trying desperately to reach her, but it was no use."

Caleb stared at the floor. He'd been devastated when his own mother died, and he'd been older and still had his father. He couldn't even imagine what Elijah and Nathaniel had been through. "What did you do?" he asked.

"We ran to the nearest neighbor's house, which wasn't near at all, and told him what had happened," Nathaniel said. "The man said he'd take care of everything. Told us to stay put. After that, things are kind of a blur."

Eli straightened in his chair. "When the man returned, he told us the Indians were responsible for the fire. And that Mama had died. He said we were going to live with him."

"So you stayed there?"

His brothers exchanged a glance again, an uneasy one this time, and some sort of unspoken message was relayed.

"No," Eli said. "That man was meaner than a snake. We moved on."

"Moved on? By yourselves?"

"Yep."

Although Caleb tried to get them to open up, to tell him more, they wouldn't. Finally, he stopped asking questions. No matter how badly he wanted to, he couldn't change their childhood. But he could be a part of their lives now, from this point forward. *Should he offer them money?* Caleb suspected he'd end up with a fat lip if he did.

"I'll send Aunt Victoria a telegram and ask her to stay put for a while," he said instead. "I'll let her know I'm coming to see her as soon as I can. She probably won't know anything helpful, but it can't hurt to ask."

Eli nodded his satisfaction, then rose and stretched. "Nathaniel and I are going fishing. You wanna come along?"

Caleb hesitated. *Did they really want him, or were they being polite?*

Nathaniel added his own invitation. "Yeah, I kinda like the idea of having a little brother to tag along after us."

Caleb couldn't stop the grin from spreading across his face, and then he laughed out loud when Eli shot Nathaniel a look beneath lowered brows. "I've experienced that little brother thing," Eli drawled. "It's not always that much fun."

With a good-natured grin, Nathaniel slapped his older brother on the back. "And now there are two of us."

"I'd like to go along," Caleb told them. "You got an extra fishing pole?"

Eli picked up his hat. "No, but it won't take but a minute to rig one up."

As they left the jail, Caleb thought about the sorrow and shadows in his brothers' eyes as they'd talked about their childhood. The night he'd met them they'd admitted to making some questionable decisions. He wanted to know more, but he wasn't about to ask specifically about that.

Lord only knew what would've happened to him if the situations had been reversed. He realized with a start that the phrase, "Lord only knows" was actually the truth.

Did anyone really ever know what they would do in the same circumstances?

***

Caleb stretched and yawned. He'd grown far too comfortable on this creek bank. If he didn't watch out he'd be asleep soon.

Since the Brazos was still flowing too swiftly for decent fishing, Eli had directed them to this shady spot on a little creek. It had proved perfect. All three of them had spent the last couple of hours laughing, talking, and catching more fish than they could eat.

"How about sharing these with the Hortons and their boarders?" Caleb asked now.

With a glance at his stringer of fish, Nathaniel nodded. "Sounds good to me."

Eli grunted an agreement before adding, "Better snag a few more, just in case."

An hour later the Calhoun brothers stepped up on the back porch of the boarding house. "You better go make sure it's all right with Mrs. Horton before we start cleaning the fish," Eli said.

Caleb entered the back door, not surprised to find Abby and Irene Horton already bustling back and forth between the pantry and the kitchen. He explained about their afternoon's catch, and was pleased by their enthusiastic response.

"That sounds wonderful," Mrs. Horton said. "It's been a while since we've had anything like that."

Caleb nodded. "Good. We'll get to work cleaning them out back."

"I agree with Mama," Abby said. "Fish sounds delicious. Let us know when you're done out there, and we'll fry them up."

"Actually, if you don't mind us working in your kitchen, I thought maybe we'd do the cooking," Caleb said. "You got cornmeal?"

Surprise flickered across her face. "Yes. But are you sure you don't at least want some help?"

"Believe me, in the Rangers, if you want to eat, you better know how to cook. We take turns when there's more than one of us, and nobody ever complains." Caleb grinned. "Of course, that could be because a complaint means it's automatically your turn next time. I've choked down rattlesnake meat, turtle eggs, lots of hardtack and jerky, and a time or two, even less appetizing fare. Including the hoe cake I told you about."

Abby smiled at that, and then sobered. "I never thought about the working conditions for a job like yours."

He shrugged. "It gets rough at times, although everybody usually makes up for lost time once we hit a town..."

Abby tilted her head, those huge blue eyes staring at him as she soaked in every word, and a wave of shame swept through him when he remembered exactly what "making up for lost time" had sometimes entailed.

Even though there were good, decent men in law enforcement, there were plenty of hell-raisers, too. Caleb had known some of them, kept company with them for awhile. He'd soon tired of most of their escapades and exploits, and been downright appalled by others, but he sincerely hoped Abby never knew about some of the things he'd seen and done.

That self-revelation was followed by confusion. Caleb had always considered himself honest to a fault, even about his own faults and sins. Yet he realized that he didn't want Abby to know anything about the seamier side of life at all. He never, ever wanted her to look at him in disappointment. *Why in the world should that matter?*

Their gaze connected again, and a wave of longing for something he didn't even understand hit him, nearly pulling him under.

Caleb shook his head, much as he had to shake off the water after rescuing Henry. Yet he still felt like he was drowning. And there was no one to rescue him.

"You were saying? Caleb?"

He'd stopped talking in mid-sentence. "Oh, nothing important," he said. "I'd better get busy, or we'll never have these done in time for supper."

Abby gathered things he would need, including the largest cast iron skillet they had, and the lard.

"I've already started a potato salad," she told him, "and I have some cornbread prepared."

"That sounds good," he said.

"Do you need a knife?"

"Nope, have that taken care of—I never travel anywhere without mine. Imagine my brothers are the same."

She nodded. "I hope Eli and Nathaniel like spice cake, that's what we're having for dessert."

"I don't know about them, but I love it. You sure you have room for everybody? We don't mind eating on the back porch."

Her mouth dropped open. "You will do no such thing. There'll be plenty of room at the table. The surveyors are gone. Even if they weren't, we would squeeze everyone in."

After they'd cleaned the fish, Abby brought them soap and a towel, and the brothers washed up outside at the pump.

They then trooped inside and got to work. Mrs. Horton's manners lacked the shine and polish of a Boston socialite, but there was such warmth and welcome in her voice that it made the hostesses from back east seem the backward ones.

"Sheriff, it's so good to see you. And Dr. Nathaniel. Come on in."

As they set to work, Caleb was intrigued to see that Eli and Nathaniel knew their way around a kitchen, too. Even though the Calhoun brothers didn't work together as well as Irene Horton and Abby, they managed to get the job done. Of course, it helped that the side dishes and desserts had already been prepared.

Despite the size of the kitchen, when the other diners arrived, the room was near to bursting at the seams. Although Eli spoke with everyone, Caleb noticed him tug on his shirt collar a few times, and look longingly at the back door. Nathaniel seemed more comfortable, but not entirely at ease. *What were they accustomed to?* Probably not many large family style dinners in their past.

Everyone seemed to enjoy the food, and the conversation, but

Caleb found himself watching and listening to Abby more than he liked. And apparently more than Jenna liked. His old friend glared at him across the table.

Caleb's thoughts were interrupted by the voice of Bliss drifting in from the back porch. "Sounds like somebody's having a party and forgot to invite me."

Irene Horton jumped to her feet, and pushed the screen door open. "Come on in, Deputy Walker."

"Thank you, ma'am. And please call me Bliss."

"Would you like something to eat?" Mrs. Horton added. "We have plenty."

"Don't mind if I do," Bliss said. "I'm hungry enough to eat boiled buzzard eggs."

Eli shook his head. "You out socializing, Bliss, or do you have something on your mind?"

"I need some help over at the saloon."

Eli's brow's rose. "What's going on?"

"Bartender wants us to break up a pool game."

Putting his fork down, Eli asked, "Something Big John can't handle?"

Bliss shrugged his stooped shoulders. "The fellows involved are drunk"—he paused to take a piece of fish from the platter—"and still in the saddle."

Eli pushed back his chair. "You're telling me they're inside the saloon on horseback?"

Bliss chewed and swallowed. "Yep."

"Trying to play pool?"

The deputy took another bite, chewed, and after swallowing said, "Yep, and it's starting to get a little ugly in there."

Caleb laughed until his shoulders shook, while Eli glowered at him. "If you think this is so funny, maybe you should come along and help."

"I'd be glad to," Caleb said.

Nathaniel placed his napkin on the table and stood. "I'd better get to the office. If there's a fight you'll probably be bringing me fellows to stitch up." He thanked the Hortons for their hospitality as he left.

Eli stood and said his goodbyes to the family and the boarders as well.

Caleb pushed back his chair and followed Eli to the door. He glanced back at Abby. He hated to be rude. "Sorry to rush off this way."

She waved him on. "That's okay, duty calls. I understand. Thank you for the fish—it was delicious. Having someone else prepare it was even better yet."

Her gratitude warmed him. "You're welcome. Believe it or not, I was even planning on doing the dishes."

She smiled. "Sure you were."

Her smile warmed him even more thoroughly than her gratitude had, and his complicated, convoluted feelings for Abigail Horton occupied his thoughts as he trailed after Eli—right up until he stepped through the door of the saloon and a chair sailed past his head.

Caleb ducked, and surveyed the full-blown brawl that Bliss had called "a little ugly." Furniture was overturned. Broken bottles and glasses, as well as cards, dice and several hats, littered the floor. The sound was deafening. Men were slugging each other as they shouted, slipped and slid through all of it. And yet no one was shooting. Caleb was puzzled by that until he noticed that no one was armed. Obviously Big John Finley was one of those saloon owners that collected guns at the door. *Good.*

Another quick glance around the room revealed several people scrambling for cover behind the bar, and a young man sitting alone at a corner table, seemingly oblivious to the uproar around him. He held a drink in one hand and battered derby hat in the other. When someone bumped into him, causing his spectacles to tilt, the young man finally got up and out of the way, before disappearing through the back door. Something about him pulled at Caleb's mind, but before he could figure out what, Eli captured his attention.

Eli had already yanked two men off their mounts and was heading for the other two, so Caleb decided the first order of business was to get the four terrified horses out of the building.

He grabbed the reins of a gray gelding, soothing the frightened animal as best he could. The horse reared once—legs flailing—and almost took out a chandelier. Caleb held on, running his hand down the animal's quivering neck, as the candles in the punched-tin sconces swayed wildly above them. "Easy now, everything's going to be okay."

Once outside, he tied the horse to a hitching post several spaces down from the saloon—out of harm's way.

Although spooked, the animal didn't seem to be injured, so Caleb hurried back inside. On the next go around, dodging flying debris with every step, he managed to nab two horses at once and was surprised to see a beautiful black-and-white piebald following along behind as they headed for the door. "Smart fella," he said, as he led them all outside.

After securing them, Caleb barreled back into the saloon, ready to start corralling the humans, but was distracted by the sight of Eli knocking two men's heads together. One moment they were cussing and trying to kill each other—and Eli—and the next moment they were crumpled at his feet.

Eli stepped over them and moved on. He wasn't even winded. It dawned on Caleb that his brother could've easily killed him that first day, even without the Colt. It also occurred to him that this was the attitude and demeanor he'd been aiming for—he'd been trying to emulate a brother he hadn't even known.

Caleb was shaking his head over that when Bliss ambled over, nimbly side-stepping two men that tumbled by slugging what little sense they had out of each other.

"So what started all this?" Caleb shouted.

Bliss shrugged and leaned in so he could be heard with less effort. "All I know is that some drovers hit town with full pockets and empty heads. Drank too much, bragged too much, bet too much. Ended up with this."

Caleb nodded, and then noticed several women in their feathers and finery leaning on the stair rail above. He couldn't help but laugh at their disappointed expressions. They knew as well as he did that most of these fellows were on their way to jail or the doctor's office when this was over.

He stopped laughing when a fist shot out of nowhere, connected with his jaw and snapped his head back. Bliss ducked and grabbed a chair in the same movement, then brought it down across the other man's head. The old deputy stepped aside to let the brawler fall.

"You okay?" he asked Caleb.

Wincing and rubbing his jaw, Caleb grinned. "I'm fine."

Caleb glanced down to make sure his badge was visible, and then dove into the brawl with one of Captain Parnell's many warnings echoing in his ears, *"Don't start anything. But if somebody else does, feel free to finish it up."*

Chapter Seventeen

JENNA WAS AWAKE when Abby entered the bedroom after cleaning the kitchen and finishing her evening chores. The girl's presence didn't bother Abby as it once had. While Jenna still wasn't exactly pleasant company, she treated Robby well, and that meant a lot. She'd not mentioned her wedding plans again, thankfully. Jenna still made the odd demand or request for help from time-to-time, although she didn't seem offended when Abby told her no.

Yet tonight, there was a melancholy mood about Jenna as she stared at the ceiling and sighed heavily.

Abby turned down the lamp and changed into her gown. Should she ask if everything was all right? Jenna spoke before Abby could decide.

"Have you ever been in love?" Jenna asked.

"Not really. What about you?"

"Yes."

Abby thought about asking "With whom?" but was strangely reluctant to know. "I guess Henry is the closest thing to a beau I've ever had," Abby admitted. "We've been close forever. He..." She hesitated, uncertain how much to say.

"He loves you, and the feelings aren't mutual," Jenna guessed.

"Right." Abby climbed into bed and adjusted her pillow. "I've never felt romantic about him. He's proposed to me numerous times, but I can't accept. It would be unfair. He deserves someone who will love him with all her heart."

"I've always been a little in love with Caleb," Jenna confessed. "He was always so much fun. Really wild and crazy."

"He certainly seemed different when I met him," Abby said. "Reserved or stoic would be an apt description." *Except for that kiss.*

"I think the military had something to do with his current demeanor," Jenna said. "Believe me, he was different when we were younger." After a moment, she added, "I always assumed we'd be married."

Abby's breath caught in her throat. "Di...did he propose to you?"

"No."

Caleb had told her the truth. "Why did you pretend he had?"

Jenna's voice sounded small in the darkness. "Because I needed someone. I was scared. After my Papa died, I realized how alone I really was. I was always surrounded by people, yet I knew that if I disappeared no one would really care. So I got up one morning and decided to sell everything and go."

"Why seek out Caleb?"

"Because he's the most good-hearted person I've ever known. I knew if I could get to him, even if he didn't marry me, he wouldn't turn his back on me. I hoped he'd change his mind and want to plan a future together. Unfortunately, that hasn't happened."

Compassion tugged at Abby's heart. "Someone will come along."

"I suppose," Jenna said, with a decided lack of enthusiasm. "It's just all so confusing. I know Caleb won't abandon me, but I wish we could go back to the way things used to be. Everyone loved being around him back then, especially children and old people. I don't miss everything though," she added. "That boy would start a fight at the drop of a hat."

Since Caleb had told her how impulsive he was, that piece of information didn't surprise Abby.

"Although one of his worst altercations was my fault," Jenna said with a trace of laughter.

"Let me guess. He defended your honor and got himself beat-up by one of your suitors?"

Jenna chuckled. "No, he got himself beat-up by me."

Abby turned toward the other girl in the darkness. "What?"

"My grandma always told me to be very careful around boys," Jenna said. "That once they got what they wanted from a girl, they'd be gone."

Having heard similar remarks from her mother, Abby merely responded with a murmur.

"Then one day, Caleb asked me for a cookie."

Still confused, Abby prompted, "And?"

"I nearly beat him to death to keep him away from it," Jenna said. "He wanted something from me, and I was scared he'd disappear once he got that cookie."

Both girls laughed uncontrollably for a few minutes. When they quieted, Jenna said, "Don't worry. Except for a few kisses years ago, Caleb never asked me for anything else."

Abby groaned. "Am I that obvious?"

"Yes. Although if it makes you feel better, I don't think Caleb has a clue how you feel about him. He seems pretty oblivious about that sort of thing."

"Thank you. For some reason that does bring me comfort. Although to be honest, I'm not sure myself how I feel." *If Jenna had guessed, then it wouldn't be long before Caleb did. How humiliating.* "I'm surprised he hasn't married yet," Abby admitted.

"Believe me, it's not for lack of opportunity," Jenna said. "Caleb's had women throwing themselves at his feet since he was old enough to shave. He's never seemed interested in any one in particular, though. He's left a trail of broken hearts."

Even as Abby's heart sank, she vowed it wouldn't be broken. When Caleb Calhoun left Moccasin Rock, her heart would be intact.

She adjusted her pillow and closed her eyes as Jenna quieted. Abby was startled to realize she'd enjoyed talking to her. Perhaps with a little time and effort, they might even become friends.

Just as Abby began to drift off, Jenna spoke up again. "Will you try to be a little quieter when you get up in the morning? I'd like to sleep later than the crack of dawn. Your being such an early riser has been very trying for me."

Okay, so friendship might take a *lot* of time and effort.

***

Caleb flexed his jaw, relieved that he was able to open and close his mouth with minimal pain. At least he'd be able to drink his coffee.

"So what happened to you?" Henry asked. Both men sat in the kitchen of the Horton boarding house, and for once Henry seemed more curious than hostile. Caleb didn't mind satisfying his curiosity.

"Skirmish over at Finley's Saloon. Turned into an all-out brawl."

"Looks like you got popped pretty hard," Henry said, with a trace of a smirk.

Caleb shrugged. "I did. Thankfully, other than this all I got were some scraped knuckles. Eli and Bliss both escaped serious injury, too. Some of the drovers weren't as lucky. A couple of them are over at the doctor's office, some in jail."

"Sounds like a wild night," Henry said.

Caleb nodded. He was glad that everything had calmed down around town, but now he wasn't sure what was going on around here. Abby was acting strangely—entirely different than she had the night before at supper.

When he'd slipped in from the saloon, he'd heard her and Jenna laughing. Yet Abby seemed to be in a more somber mood today, ignoring both him and Henry.

She was peeling and slicing peaches, moving around the kitchen in a flurry of activity, and never even once glancing in his direction. For some reason it bothered Caleb. He was supposed to be leaving her alone, not the other way around.

Caleb settled back in his chair. Even though it was early, the room was already hotter than blue blazes. It was much cooler in the parlor, where Miss Culpepper, Preacher and Mrs. Horton were gathered. And yet here he and Henry sat.

Abby moved into the pantry and pulled up the door to the root cellar. Caleb jumped to his feet. "Can I bring something up for you?"

"No, thank you."

Caleb plopped back into his chair. "Sometimes I wish I'd never come to this town," he muttered.

"I wish you hadn't either," Henry said with a brisk nod.

Caleb laughed while Henry continued to glare at him.

Then, as if the hostility was too much effort, Henry gave him a sheepish grin. "I understand. Sometimes I wish I'd never come here either," he said.

"Weren't you born here?"

Henry shrugged. "So maybe I wish my parents had never come here."

Both men's attention shifted to Abby as she returned with a few more peaches, then peeled them and then began rolling out a pie crust.

"We're both lying," Caleb whispered.

Henry's only response was a disgusted grunt.

Abby wiped her hand on a rag and then disappeared into the pantry again.

Caleb jumped when Jenna appeared in his line of sight and smacked her hand down on the table. He hadn't even seen her enter the room. Good thing she hadn't been aiming to shoot him. Henry was staring up at her wide-eyed, as well.

"I am sick and tired of you two mooning over that girl," Jenna leaned in and hissed.

Caleb opened his mouth to respond, but Henry beat him to the punch. "I am not mooning over her," he said. "I don't even know for sure exactly what that means, but I know I'm not doing it."

Jenna rolled her eyes. "Yes, you are. You follow her around like a pathetic little puppy dog, waiting for her to give you a pat on the head." Caleb watched, fascinated, as red crept up Henry's neck.

The young man looked up at Jenna and narrowed his eyes. "I don't think I like you," he said.

Jenna snorted. "I won't be shedding any tears over that," she assured him. "It's about time someone told you the truth. I heard that you've proposed to her over and over again. What's the matter with you?"

Henry's mouth gaped open, and then closed, several times, reminding Caleb of a fish. He actually felt sorry for the fellow. *Come on, defend yourself.*

"I love her and I want to marry her," Henry said. "What else am I supposed to do?"

Jenna, hands on hips, leveled a scornful look at him. "How about you get a little starch in your backbone? How about you let her know that she's not the only fish in the sea?"

Her choice of words was so close to what Caleb had been thinking that he couldn't stop a grin. He raised his cup to cover it just as Jenna whirled around to him. He put the cup down and waited. Caleb was accustomed to her directness.

"And you," she said. "I know good-and-well you've seen your share of pretty girls." She jerked a thumb in Henry's direction. "Not like this rube here. You have no excuses for your behavior."

"Now, Jenna," Caleb said. "I'm not smitten like Henry is. I just happen to enjoy a pretty girl's company. There's no way you're going to rile me as easily as you did him, so you might as well hush up."

"I'm not trying to rile you," she said. "I'm seriously wondering what is wrong with you two. How can you…" She clamped her mouth shut as Abby stepped back into the room.

Jenna turned to Henry. "Come on. You and I have some talking to do."

Caleb was stunned when Henry stood and followed Jenna from the room.

"What was that all about?" Abby asked, brows raised.

Caleb shrugged. He wasn't going to tell her what they'd been discussing, and he had no idea what Jenna had planned for Henry.

He watched as Abby deftly lifted the pie crust and placed it in a pan, and then spun it in a circle as she used a fork to crimp the edges.

Once the crust was in the oven, Abby washed her hands and then picked up a basket with fabric in it, and headed for the table. He stood and pulled her chair back.

"Thank you," she said, barely glancing at him. She pulled a needle and thread from the basket and began hemming a hand-kerchief. She worked steadily, at turns seemingly bothered by his presence, other times ignoring him completely.

Caleb didn't mind bothering her, but he discovered that he didn't much care for being ignored. "When you're done with that hankie, will you make me one?" he asked. "Only bigger, so I can mop up my tears when you treat me like this."

Her startled gaze flew to his and her fingers stilled. Then she smiled. She bent her head over her work, busy again. At least he'd gotten her attention. Unfortunately, he'd also rattled her. On the next stitch, the needle pierced both cloth and skin.

"Ouch," she said, dropping everything.

Caleb took her hand in his, turning it so he could examine her finger. "Sorry, that was my fault. It doesn't look too bad, though. Only a flesh wound. You'll live."

He winked at her, and then without a second thought, pressed her finger to his lips. She froze, eyes wide. Caleb returned the look for several heartbeats—each faster than the last—before leaning toward her. Heat spiraled through his stomach as he drew closer. No matter how much he lectured himself about what was right, or what was best, he needed to feel those lips beneath his. Now.

Suddenly Abby blinked and jerked her hand away. Caleb deliberately assumed his reserved expression as he pushed back from the table. Hiding—he hoped—the frustration roiling inside him. He strode from the room without another word.

Obviously, Abby wasn't interested in a kiss from him. That was fine, and better for both their sakes. What had possessed him to do something so all-fired stupid anyway? He was a lawman. He had better things to do than kiss a hurt finger. *Like shoot somebody!* Growling and muttering under his breath, he stormed down the hall and out the front door.

Chapter Eighteen

A S SOON AS the screen door slammed, Abby wilted in her chair. She hadn't meant to hurt Caleb's feelings. She'd realized that he was holding her rough, work-worn hand and had reacted without thinking.

Yet vanity was the least of her problems. The man had touched her fingers and she'd felt it clear to her toes. He'd leaned in close enough for her to smell his shaving soap and to see that his green eyes had darkened. She'd thought for a moment that he was going to kiss her. And she wouldn't have objected.

This time she hadn't been caught by surprise. And she'd been around him enough to know a little about his flaws…and yet… she would've kissed him back.

She placed a trembling hand to her lips and waited for her heart to settle down, acknowledging the truth. She was falling for Caleb Calhoun, a man who was determined to put her father behind bars. A man who had women chasing after him. *A man who left behind a trail of broken hearts.*

Her treacherous train of thought ground to a halt as Reverend Wainright ambled into the kitchen.

"You wouldn't happen to have a pot of coffee going, would you?"

Hiding her shattered composure behind a smile, Abby rose

from the chair and made an attempt to pull herself together. "As a matter of fact, I do have coffee ready. You make yourself comfortable and I'll have it for you in a moment. I need to remove a pie crust from the stove first."

Preacher settled down at the table, murmuring his thanks. He looked up in surprise when she placed a piece of cake in front of him, along with the coffee.

"Here you go, a little something to hold you over until supper. I'll have pie ready soon, too."

"Thank you, Abby. That's kind of you."

As Preacher picked up his fork, she noticed that his movements were slower than usual, his hands a little shaky.

"You feeling okay?"

He swallowed before answering her, and even that seemed to take effort. "I'm fine. Just a little worn out."

Preacher rubbed his hand across his jaw, the growth of several days' whiskers rasping against his fingers. He'd been clean-shaven during the revival. Were the whiskers a return to his normal look? Or was he too tired to shave? And why was he tired to begin with?

"Is there anything I can do?"

"Nothing you can do unless you got a recipe that'll turn me from an old crow back into a spring chicken," he said.

She smiled at him. "I don't have anything like that. The mercantile has some tonics and other medications, though. I'll be glad to go and get something. Or maybe I should call Dr. Nathaniel Calhoun."

He waved both offers away. "No, I'll be all right with some rest. Thank you, though."

Abby ran a rag across the table top. "Where are you headed from here?"

"I have an open invitation to stay with a young pastor and his family at Slocum's Prairie," he said. "I may go visit there while the weather's still good."

"No more revivals?"

"I'm not sure yet. I'm leaving that up to God. When it's quittin' time, I believe he'll let me know."

They chatted for a while, none of it important, but there was something that Abby wanted to discuss with him, something that had been bothering her. She sat down at the table.

"Preacher, I regret my remarks to Jenna. The ones you overheard." She floundered for a moment. "About not caring whether she went to church, I mean. I shouldn't have lashed out at her."

He shrugged. "I really didn't give it a great deal of thought." Preacher placed his fork beside his plate and gave her his full attention. "I might've phrased it a bit differently than you did. But I don't fault you for putting your foot down. There's a big difference in turning the other cheek and letting someone walk all over you. Sorta like that woman at church that lit into your mother."

Abby sighed. "I've got to admit that Mrs. Dunlop stunned me for a moment, but at least she was acting true to form. What she says usually rolls right off me. For some reason Jenna Nolan vexes me even more every time she opens her mouth. Still, I didn't mean what I said about not caring if she ever went to church."

"I suspected that," Preacher said. The compassion in his brown eyes seemed to invite her to unburden herself.

"It's as if she deliberately provokes me," Abby said.

Preacher nodded. "Her behavior is a bit unusual, and also seems contradictory at times. It's my observation—only as a bystander, you understand—that Miss Jenna doesn't exactly shy away from confrontations with anyone."

"Maybe so," Abby said. "Yet it feels more personal with me."

"You think she's partial to a certain lawman?"

Abby lifted one shoulder and glanced away. "Yes, so she says."

"The same one you've taken a liking to?"

Oh no, had everyone noticed? Abby drew in a deep breath, ready to deny it, and then she let everything—the breath, her frustration and the truth—out in a rush. "Yes, but 'taken a liking to' sure sounds more simple than what's going on in my head." *And heart.*

She wanted to change the subject, certain that an old man, especially a preacher, wouldn't have a clue about matters of the heart. Even if he did, she didn't want to burden him while he was feeling poorly.

Then she remembered her last conversation with Jenna, and how vulnerable the other woman had seemed. "In fairness, I should mention that Jenna's not all bad."

The preacher nodded. "See there, you've hit on one of the most interesting things about life. Most people aren't."

Abby propped her elbows on the table. "It sure makes it difficult to know how to treat her," she admitted.

"The Bible gives us instructions on how to act with other folks," Preacher said, "although walking that line between heavenly direction and earthly reality can be a bit tricky at times. It says in Romans, *'If it be possible, as much as lieth in you, live peaceably with all men.'* And in Matthew it says, *'Love thy neighbor as thyself.'* Yet it's all easier said than done when folks are acting contrary."

Abby straightened. "Well, I'm going to give it my best effort."

"Good," Preacher said. Then he studied her for a moment, his expression thoughtful. "God also gives us instincts when things aren't quite right. Be compassionate and caring, but if your gut tells you something's wrong, then listen. I'm not saying there's anyone beyond God's grace, but He's the only one who can help some folks."

Preacher suddenly seemed almost desperate for her to understand. Was he warning her about someone in particular? Was he talking about her father? Abby longed to tell him the whole story, yet she couldn't risk it. And she knew the truth of Preacher's words. The things her father said about the leader of the Latham gang ran through her mind. Shooting people and leaving them to die with no more thought than he'd give to killing an insect. It made her shudder. She wasn't naïve; she knew there was evil in the world.

"Thank you, Preacher." She laid her own hand atop one of his wrinkled ones. "I'll take care."

He patted her hand. "Good. Because often you've got to look beyond what people are saying, and look at what they're doing. That'll usually tell you what you need to know."

Abby nodded. "The adage is true; actions do speak louder than words."

"Exactly." He looked thoughtful as he took a bite of cake, chewed and swallowed. "Then again, sometimes people are plain difficult to figure."

"I'm not sure what you mean."

"What are your impressions of Miss Culpepper?"

Abby's mouth dropped open in surprise. "Why she's a lov... lovely woman."

Preacher looked at her, one brow raised.

"She's whiny," Abby blurted. Then regretted it immediately. "But she's sickly, which she can't help."

"That's what I'm talking about," he said. "The woman says she's sick. Does she act sick?"

Abby thought about all the times that Miss Culpepper bustled into a room, full of vim and vigor. How she pitched in around the house, despite their protests, with increasing frequency. Involving herself, enthusiastically, in daily activities. "No, she doesn't act ill at all," Abby said in amazement. "Are you saying she's pretending?"

"Not necessarily. I'm saying her actions aren't matching her words. Could be any number of reasons for that, of course."

She stared at him, curious. "All right, is Jenna's behavior supposed to be telling me something different than her words?"

He shrugged. "I'm not sure," he admitted. "If I had my guess about that girl, I'd say she was about eat-up with loneliness."

Abby nodded. "She's said as much to me."

"I thought so," he said softly.

Preacher finished his cake and coffee, and shortly afterward returned to his room for a nap. After he was gone, Abby mulled over his words. He was right about Jenna, was he also right about Miss Culpepper? Maybe so. But he was wrong about her father.

Then a chilling thought struck Abby.

Had he been warning her about Caleb Calhoun instead?

***

The echo of her shoes hitting the boardwalk accompanied the chant reverberating through Abby's mind, *"Where are you Marshal Adair?"*

She'd slipped away from the house long enough to check in at the telegraph office, but hadn't even crossed the building's threshold before Mr. Moore looked at her and shook his head. The man knew by now that she was expecting a message, although he didn't know from whom.

After leaving there, Abby walked the two blocks to Martin's Mercantile for a few things, including a tin of tea leaves, and some throat lozenges for Miss Culpepper.

As Silas gathered the items, he motioned to a crate he'd just opened. "Got some lemons in," he told her. "They won't last long. You want me to package some up for you?"

"Yes, thank you, Silas. I bet the boarders would love some lemonade."

She paid for her purchases and was headed home when the sounds of a commotion spilled out from the alley. Judging by the high-pitched name-calling, it was young boys, and not particularly alarming. She paused only when she heard a familiar, deep voice. "What's going on here?"

Caleb Calhoun. Abby hadn't seen him since he'd stormed out of the kitchen the day before.

The next voice she heard was Robby's. Alarmed, Abby scurried around the side of the building and then stopped short. Four boys stood there, two bigger ones, looking none the worse for wear, and two smaller boys, Jamie Wilson and Robby, with shirttails pulled loose and hair mussed. Robby also had a bloody nose.

"I want an answer," Caleb said to the boys after a nod in Abby's direction. "What's going on?"

Since he was handling the situation, Abby remained silent, although she did slip her brother a handkerchief.

The creak and rumble of a wagon drew the boys' attention to the other end of the alley, but Abby was focused on Robby—breathing so hard his chest was jerking as he swiped at his nose. He glanced at her, but it was Caleb he addressed. "It was nothing."

Jamie darted one quick look at Robby, and then a nervous glance at the two bigger boys. "That's right," he agreed. "Nothing."

It was obvious to Abby that some sort of male code of conduct was preventing them from telling whatever was really happening.

She waited to see what Caleb would do.

"Nothing, huh?"

One of the older boys spoke up. "Only having a little fun."

Caleb pinned him with a glare. "Seems to me that your idea of fun might differ a little from theirs," he said with a nod in the direction of the younger boys.

Robby's breathing had calmed, although his story didn't change. "Just having a little friendly talk," he insisted.

"Well, I'm afraid this discussion will have to wait," Caleb said after a moment. "I've got something I need your help with."

Robby's eyes widened. "You need help from me?"

Caleb nodded. "Can you take a message to the livery stable?"

"Yes, sir." Robby's expression was so serious as he listened to Caleb's message—obviously nothing important—that Abby bit her lip to keep from grinning.

Robby and Jamie trotted off toward the stable immediately, and Caleb turned his attention to the older boys. They didn't seem near as cocky as they had a moment ago.

"I'm assuming that my young friends will be able to complete their tasks without fear of further assault," he said softly.

"Yes, sir," one of the boys mumbled as he looked down and kicked at the dirt a couple of times. The other boy swallowed hard but couldn't seem to speak.

Caleb finally nodded to them. "Good. Now get out of here."

Both boys beat a hasty retreat.

As the sound of their footsteps receded, Abby turned to Caleb. "Thank you for that."

"You're welcome. I wasn't really sure what to do at first. I wanted to take those bigger boys and knock their heads together. Then I figured they'd only catch up with Robby and Jamie later and start in again."

"I think you're right."

"This way, maybe they'll realize that I'm keeping an eye on the younger ones, without my having to say it and embarrass anyone."

"I appreciate you taking that into consideration."

Silence hung between them for a moment. Then they both spoke at once.

"Look, I'm sorry," he said.

"I'm sorry if…" she said.

They both stopped, and then laughed.

"Do you have to go straight home?" Caleb asked.

Surprised, it took a moment for Abby to respond. "No. Why?"

"I thought we might go for a walk. Not far, just around town."

"O…okay." *It's only a walk, people do it all the time. It means nothing. You will not act like a ninny in this man's presence. You will not be another broken heart he leaves behind.*

"I wanted to get to know you a little better," Caleb said. "You told me you wanted to travel, now tell me something else about yourself."

Abby suspected he would eventually work the conversation around to her father. Until then, what could she possibly tell him?

That she knew a dozen different ways to cook potatoes? Anything she could speak knowledgeably about related to cooking and cleaning. She was so dull that she felt herself diminishing right before his eyes. And yet he really seemed interested. She hugged that knowledge to her heart as they set out.

There wasn't much to see in Moccasin Rock. They lingered for a while in front of the burned-out hotel—like most everyone in town had done at one point or another—both remarking on how fortunate it was that the fire hadn't spread. They also stopped at the site that had been selected for the new courthouse. The current building, a two-room log cabin, had been sufficient for many years, now something bigger was needed.

"The way I understand it, the surveyors will begin work on this project as soon as they're done with the bridge work," Abby said. "The new building will be built of sandstone, and if everything goes as planned, the new courthouse will also house the jail. There's been some talk in recent years of moving the county seat to Fair Haven. Folks here don't want that to happen. That's part of the push for all these improvements to Moccasin Rock."

"Fair Haven is a much bigger town, so I see the logic there," Caleb said. "But isn't that Claiborne County? I thought this was Yates County."

"It is." Abby shrugged. "That's part of the problem. But nothing's come of it yet, except a lot of talk. The old-timers say that's all it'll ever be."

Caleb asked a few questions about the bridge, and the new courthouse, and even more about the surveyors. Abby told him what she knew, which wasn't much.

They paused a moment in front of the window of the *Moccasin Rock Gazette*, watching Luther Tillman set type for the next edition. They then stopped by the livery stable so that Caleb could clear up any confusion that Eagan Smith might have about the hastily-concocted message Robby had delivered.

Afterwards they made a brief stop by the mercantile where Caleb picked up a tin of boot polish. "I wasn't planning on being in Moccasin Rock for long," he explained, "so about all I had with me was a razor, toothbrush and some clothes."

Caleb then asked if she needed anything, and Abby pointed to the brown paper package in her arms. "I've done my shopping for the day."

Although she thought about it later, many times, Abby could never quite recall how they ended up at the jail, or how she ended up in Caleb's arms. One minute they were talking—speculating on where Eli and Bliss might be—and the next he was taking the package from her and laying it on Eli's desk. And suddenly she couldn't even breathe, let alone speak.

Her heart was racing when Caleb drew her close and lowered his head. Although his eyes were shut, Abby waited until the last second to close hers. *The man was beautiful.*

Caleb moved his lips slowly over hers, and Abby made an involuntary little sound and practically melted into him. At her reaction, he tightened the embrace and deepened the kiss. When he lifted his head his green eyes had darkened to near black and his voice was a husky rasp.

"I should've asked *this* before I did *that*," he said, "but is it all right if I kiss you?"

"It's a little late now," Abby whispered, "however my answer would've been, 'It depends.'"

Caleb raised his brows. "On what?"

"Did you do that because you felt sorry for me?"

A grin spread across his face. "No. I did it because I felt sorry for myself." Before she could ask what he meant, Caleb said, "I've wanted to do that for a while now."

Heat filled her face, but she didn't turn away. In fact, she took the opportunity to study him as she'd yearned to. After several moments under her scrutiny, he began to squirm a little.

"Everything okay?" he asked.

"Yes. This is something I've wanted to do for a while." She drew her fingers across his jaw. "What's this little scar here?"

He glanced away. "Oh. That happened years ago in military school."

"How?"

Shrugging, he said, "A group of cadets were picking on this scrawny kid and I told them to stop it or they'd be sorry."

"So what happened?"

"They turned on me. Said that I was too..." He paused, his expression grim, and she mentally filled in the blanks: too nosy, too bossy?

"Too what?" she prompted.

"Pretty," he mumbled, "and they were going to do something about that."

Abby gasped. "So they attacked you?"

Caleb shook his head. "No, I attacked them."

"Just you, against a whole group?"

He nodded. "Luckily, between the way I defended myself, and the fact that I earned a few battle scars of my own that day, I was treated with more respect after that." He rubbed a hand along his jaw. "As I've mentioned before, I've had a tendency to act before I think a thing through. However, military school, military service and the Rangers have helped me rein that in a lot. I try to look and act the part of a dedicated lawman." He shrugged self-consciously, as if he expected her to find that amusing.

"There's nothing wrong with wanting to be good at what you do."

"It really is important to me," he said. "I'm not quite as hardened as some, though."

She thought of Sheriff Calhoun. "You mean like your brother?"

He drew her close again. "Yeah, but I really don't want to discuss Eli right this minute."

"No? What do you want to talk about?"

"I don't want to talk at all," he said as he tightened his arms around her.

Abby's heart thudded against her ribs as Caleb lowered his head for another kiss. *Or was it his heart she felt?*

He'd barely brushed her lips with his, when a mocking voice called out, "I see you took my advice—keep the daughter in sight, and do whatever it takes to get her to talk. With such a pretty girl, it wasn't much of a chore, now was it?"

Abby stiffened, going cold inside, and then turned her head toward the voice. A man she didn't know stood near the door. Humiliation and anger battled inside her as she tried to push away from Caleb. He refused to let her go.

"What do you want, Becker?" Caleb's voice was a low growl as he addressed the man without looking at him.

"I came by to see if you had any news about our missing outlaw. I feared you might be hanging around here wasting time, but I see you're hard at work."

"You'd better get outta here," Caleb ground out, "because as soon as I let go of Abby, my hands are going to be wrapped around your neck."

"I'm going," the other man said with a nervous laugh. "Keep up the good work."

A muscle twitched in Caleb's jaw.

"Who was that man?" Abby hissed as she struggled to break free.

Caleb closed his eyes with a groan, and then opened them with a sigh. "That's Garrison Becker," he replied. "A stock holder in the B&H Railroad. The Latham gang cost him a fortune and he's taken a personal interest in seeing your father brought to justice."

Abby looked into his eyes, her stomach sinking as she understood the true meaning of his brief explanation. She tried to pull away again, but Caleb held her firm.

"Please Abby, let me explain."

"It doesn't appear as if there's much explanation needed," she said. Her voice trembled and she made an effort to control it. "You stayed and pretended an interest in me so I would lead you to my father."

"Perhaps the staying part is accurate, but I never had to pretend to like you."

"Whatever you say," she snapped. "Now let go of me this instant or I will scream so loudly that every man in Moccasin Rock will come running. Hopefully all of them armed to kill."

He dropped her arm and stepped back.

The last thing she heard him say was, "It's not what you think."

But that was a lie. Preacher *had* been warning her about someone. If only she had listened.

Chapter Nineteen

AS SOON AS Abby bolted away, Caleb set off in search of Becker. He found the man, along with the banker, Mason Hawthorne, having a meal at Bony Joe's.

Looking neither right nor left as he entered, Caleb strode toward them. Becker glanced up, did a double take and dropped his fork. He appeared poised for flight, and Caleb was bound and determined to give him the boost he needed to make that happen.

Caleb got within a few feet of the table when something blocked his vision. He tried to dodge it, but whatever it was moved with him. Muttering a curse, he looked up into the determined eyes of Eli.

"Afraid I can't let you do this," his brother said.

"You don't have any say in it," Caleb snapped. "Besides, I don't intend to kill him. I only want to have a few words with him."

Eli flicked a glance at Caleb's clenched hands. "I have a feeling you plan on letting your fists do the talking."

Others in the café stared. Caleb lowered his voice. "I guarantee you, he deserves worse than what I've got in mind."

"Maybe so," Eli said, "but in your current mood, you're liable to do something you're gonna regret. At least wait until you've had a chance to cool off."

"You don't understand what he did," Caleb insisted.

"You're right, I don't." Eli gestured to a table on the other side of the room where Nathaniel sat. "So why don't you explain it to the two of us while we have a bite to eat."

"Don't want to interrupt," Caleb said, trying once again to move past his brother. Nathaniel motioned him over at the same moment Eli gave him a little shove toward their table.

"Join us," Eli growled. "I insist."

Caleb grew more frustrated by the second until Eli added in an undertone, "By the way, money bags, you're paying."

Caleb reluctantly smiled, some of the fight going out of him as he followed Eli to the table.

Within a few minutes Caleb had his temper under control and was grateful for Eli's interference. Taking a deep breath, he told them what Becker had said, and how angry, hurt and embarrassed Abby had been. His brothers stared at the other man across the room, looking almost as upset as Caleb had been.

"Still, it's my fault," Caleb admitted. "I'm the one that put her there, to be held up to ridicule."

Eli shrugged. "Doesn't excuse what Becker did."

"No, it doesn't," Nathaniel agreed.

Even though he wasn't hungry, Caleb let himself be coaxed into having a cup of coffee and a slice of pie—making mental note of the fact that neither was as good as what Abigail Horton made.

They were finishing up when Becker and Hawthorne rose from their own table. Becker hurried straight outside. Hawthorne made his way over to the Calhouns. Eli introduced him to Nathaniel.

"Garrison Becker told me what happened," Hawthorne said as he smoothed his beard. "I know he lacks judgment and tact, but he didn't mean the girl any harm."

When the men at the table stared at him without comment, he changed the subject.

"I can see we disagree on that, so how about you bring me up to date on the search."

"Have a seat," Eli said. "Not much to tell, though."

"Eli's right," Caleb said after the other man was seated. "I've discovered nothing helpful by watching the family. As far as I can tell Irene Horton rarely leaves the house. She goes to church, and she's been to the store a couple of times. Other than that, the only time she left was to take food to a neighbor who's ill. I was suspicious of that, but it really was what she was doing. In fact, since her hands were full, she asked me to carry a cake for her."

Hawthorne nodded thoughtfully. "What about the daughter?"

"Abigail Horton leaves almost as infrequently as her mother." He started to mention Abby's berry picking trip with Henry, then decided against it. No sense causing undue trouble for either of them.

"Except for church and a few trips to the telegraph office and the mercantile, Abby's almost always at the boarding house," Caleb said.

Hawthorne's gaze sharpened. "The telegraph office?"

"Yes, I asked the operator what she wanted, and all he would say is that she was waiting on a message. He didn't know who it was from, though."

"She's never sent a telegram?"

"Nope, I asked that, too."

As Hawthorne stood to leave, he gave Caleb a hard look. "I disagree with Mr. Becker on any number of things, including how one conducts himself in front of a lady. However, I'm in complete agreement with him about one thing. Bob Horton, alias Webb Latham, must be brought to justice. I'm running out of patience."

As Caleb headed toward the boarding house later, he couldn't shake the foreboding that filled him. Abby was angry with him now, and she'd be devastated when he dragged her father from Moccasin Rock in handcuffs. *Maybe Bob Horton had managed to slip away and would be captured by some other lawman, in some other town.* Caleb was surprised by how much the idea appealed to him.

He wasn't sure if it was thoughts of Abby, or the pie from Bony Joe's, but he had a knot in his gut. Maybe he should move on now. Eli could keep an eye on things and notify him if anything happened.

What more could he do here?

Before he made it to the house, Nathaniel caught up with him. "Someone came in right after you left and told us there's been another sighting of Bob Horton down by the river. Eli said to meet him at the livery stable."

That answered that question.

When Caleb reached the livery, Eagan Smith was already saddling the buckskin for him, while Eli saddled his own horse. Caleb took over for Eagan, and listened as Eli filled him in on the area they'd be searching—one of the more remote spots in the cedar breaks above the river.

"Didn't we already go over that area more than once?" Caleb asked as he tightened the cinch.

Eli nodded. "Yep, obviously we missed him. Or he moved in after we moved out." He tossed Caleb a rifle—a Springfield Trapdoor. "Probably won't need it," Eli said, as they mounted up and headed out, "but since we don't know exactly what we're riding into, best be prepared. Bliss went into Fair Haven this morning, so it'll just be the two of us. That old coot will be sorry he missed all the excitement."

Caleb smiled. "I imagine he will."

They rode in silence, but as they neared the search area, a thought occurred to Caleb. "So who spotted Bob?"

"A farmer who'd taken the ferry to Boone Springs yesterday. On the return trip today, he decided not to wait for the ferry, and crossed over at Rocky Ford. His horse stumbled, and he was nearly swept from the saddle."

Caleb glanced over in time to see a grin cross Eli's face. "And?"

"The farmer said he began shouting and *praying* real loud, and that's when he noticed someone darting through the scrub and brush higher up on this side of the river. He was surprised that although the man looked in his direction, he didn't even slow down. Farmer said the fellow seemed to be running scared. That's when he remembered the missing outlaw."

"Well, if it is Bob Horton he saw, I don't think we'll have any trouble bringing him in," Caleb said.

"Why's that?"

"Because Bob doesn't have a gun, and—"

The crack of rifle fire brought an abrupt halt to his explanation.

"Well, he found one somewhere," Eli shouted as they both dove for cover—Eli doing a rolling dismount from the saddle while returning fire, and Caleb more or less falling.

Even as they grabbed their rifles and urged the panicked horses back up the trail out of harm's way, and sought shelter themselves, Caleb was trying to make sense of what he'd just seen Eli do.

Never—in all his time in the military or the Texas Rangers—had he seen anybody draw and fire with that kind of speed, especially while on the move.

Caleb's thoughts came to a grinding halt when it dawned on him that Eli had switched to a rifle and was still returning fire.

"What are you doing?" Caleb hissed.

Eli frowned at him. "When someone shoots at me, I shoot back."

They were both crouched behind a scrubby tree line by this point, not far from the abandoned cabin they'd discovered during an earlier search. Bob must be holed-up there. Caleb scooted closer to Eli.

"Hold your fire," he said. "Bob's stopped shooting. I want to bring him in alive, if it's possible." His stomach lurched at the thought of hauling Bob's body back into town.

Eli was still frowning, although he lowered the rifle. "You thinking about his daughter?"

Caleb nodded. "And Mrs. Horton and Robby. Bob going to

prison will be hard on them, but not as hard as having to bury him, for real this time. Let me try to talk him into surrendering."

Eli shrugged and lowered his gun.

"Besides," Caleb said, "maybe he doesn't know who he's shooting at. There are a lot of folks that want him dead. He's probably scared. Let me talk to him."

Eli motioned for him to proceed.

"This is Ranger Calhoun," Caleb shouted in the direction of the cabin. "You need to give yourself up. If you make us come in there after you, it's not going to end well."

There was no response, but also no gunfire.

Encouraged, Caleb raised up a little. "Just step outta there, we're not going to shoot you."

A volley of rifle fire—off target, though still too close for comfort—was the only response.

"For an outlaw, he sure is an awful shot," Eli muttered as he shouldered his own rifle again.

There were several more shots from Bob when suddenly they heard frantic scrambling sounds and a few muffled curses.

When the commotion quieted as abruptly as it began, Caleb and Eli exchanged glances. Caleb shrugged at the question in his brother's eyes. He had no idea what was going on.

Glancing in the direction of the cabin again, he caught a flash of color. A blue shirt. Bob had stepped outside.

Caleb motioned for Eli to wait, and then shifted around until he got a clear view of the gun...and the arm of the man holding it. Whatever had caused the outlaw to venture out of the cabin, it had rattled him enough to make him careless. Caleb could put an end to this, without putting an end to Bob.

"I'm going to shoot the gun out of his hand," Caleb whispered.

Eli's brows rose, but he didn't speak.

Although he didn't have the speed that Eli had, Caleb was an excellent marksman. He never missed when it mattered. And this mattered. Bob wouldn't be happy if he were wounded. But at least he wouldn't be dead. With a knot in his gut bigger than before, Caleb squeezed the trigger.

A grunt of pain, followed by a thud, told Caleb he'd hit his mark. He and Eli waited several minutes before cautiously approaching the cabin—and the crumpled figure lying face down in front of it.

Dread filled Caleb. "Don't you dare be dead," he muttered. Reaching down, he eased the outlaw's body over—and found himself staring into the angry eyes of one of the surveyors. The one with the "nothing personal" dislike for lawmen.

Caleb grinned. "Well, hello, Cecil."

***

"I wasn't even trying to kill you," the irate surveyor insisted when they reached the jail. "I only wanted y'all to move on. I was willing to wait it out, holed-up in that cabin, until I saw the snake." Shuddering, he added, "I figured I'd rather take my chances outside than have venom coursing through my veins."

Caleb laughed as he grabbed the key to the cell door. "I almost hate to tell you this, but that wasn't even a poisonous snake."

Cecil's curses filled the air as Caleb guided him inside the cell and over to a cot. "Now, sit down and be still," Caleb told him, "before your arm starts bleeding again. Eli should be back with the doctor any minute."

Once they'd figured out it wasn't Bob Horton the farmer had spotted, it hadn't taken Caleb and Eli long to figure out why Cecil had been shooting at them. The hapless thief hadn't realized they were looking for someone else, and had panicked at being caught hiding some silver he'd pilfered from an unsuspecting Moccasin Rock resident.

Between his fear of dying, either from snake bite or gunshot, or being arrested, the overwrought crook had babbled enough to also incriminate himself in several other crimes. Including the recent petty thefts from the mercantile and the saloon.

"I'll go talk to his friends," Caleb said when Eli returned with Nathaniel, "and see if they knew what he was up to. He's been a busy boy." *That may explain the fancy gold letter opener in their room.*

"Sounds good," Eli said.

The other surveyors seemed genuinely shocked at the news of their friend's arrest. Yet after some thought they admitted he'd probably been responsible for troubles they'd had in many of the areas they'd worked.

Caleb escorted the two of them to the jail to talk to Eli, and then left. His brother could sort it all out. Caleb had to talk to Abigail Horton. And it couldn't wait.

Unfortunately, Abby managed to avoid him at every turn that evening. Even pleading a headache and retiring to her room before supper. Miss Culpepper eagerly volunteered to help Mrs. Horton in the kitchen.

In his room later, Caleb debated on whether to write a note and slip it under her door. *What if Jenna got it first? That could cause more trouble.* He would give Abby some time. Surely he could make her see reason eventually.

Caleb was surprised to realize that it wasn't only forgiveness he was after. He was almost desperate to make Abby actually *like* him again. And he wasn't even sure why. Should he tell her that he had money? That he could take her anywhere she wanted to go?

No. In his heart, Caleb knew money wouldn't sway a girl like Abby. Plus, she wouldn't go anywhere with a man who wasn't her husband. And he wasn't ready for that.

Chapter Twenty

I T WAS THE next day before Caleb caught up with Abby again. She stood in the kitchen with a rare expression of defeat on her face, and a large wicker basket overflowing with wet clothes balanced on her left hip.

Preacher sat at the table sipping coffee. Caleb joined him there, although his attention remained fixed on Abby. *She normally seemed so competent and in control.*

Gathering his nerve, he expressed his concern. "Everything okay, Abby?"

She stared at him, her mouth compressed into a tight line and storm clouds brewing in her blue eyes. "I'm a little behind in my chores," she snapped. "I couldn't sleep last night, and then I overslept this morning." She didn't say, "And it's your fault," yet he heard the words loud-and-clear.

He pushed to his feet, anxious to make amends. "Is there anything I can do to help?"

Without another word, she dropped the basket onto a nearby chair, picked up a knife from the counter, slapped it on the table and then crossed over to the pantry. She returned with a large graniteware pan overflowing with potatoes and placed it on the table in front of him.

Caleb blinked at her. *What did she want him to do?*

"You asked what you could do to help," Abby said. "Peeling potatoes would help me a great deal."

Caleb dropped back down in his chair.

"I'll be back to get the peels later," she said. "I cook them up for the chickens."

He gave her a hesitant nod, reluctant to say anything else.

Preacher seemed to be battling a smile as he glanced up at Abby. "Do you have another knife?"

"Sure," she said, in a much softer tone. As she handed it to the man, she leaned in and whispered something. It sounded to Caleb like she said, "Please, don't overdo." *What was that all about?*

Both men got to the task immediately, sharing a companionable silence as they worked. Caleb's glance strayed often to Abby as she bustled in and out of the kitchen—her cheeks pink from the heat, and strands of her hair escaping the braid that hung down her back. She truly was one of the prettiest women he'd ever seen. He'd known other pretty women, yet there was something special about this one, no two ways around it.

"I'll be out at the clothesline for a while," she said. While not exactly friendly, her voice sounded warmer than earlier.

Caleb stopped working, gripping a potato in one hand and the knife in the other, as he watched her leave.

He realized with a start that the old preacher was studying him. Caleb returned his attention to the task at hand. Settling in for the long haul, he took off his gun belt and placed it on the table. Preacher's gaze followed his movements, and then honed in on the Remington.

"Would it make you feel better if I moved that?" Caleb asked.

Preacher's white eyebrows rose. "Why would it?"

"Well, you know. You being a man of the cloth. I wouldn't want to make you uncomfortable."

Preacher laughed for several moments before finally replying, "I was only thinking what a nice little gun that was."

A Remington 44-40 was a nice little gun?

Preacher put down his own knife, and pulled back the long, black coat he always wore. He then plunked an old Colt dragoon on the table.

Caleb let out a low whistle between his teeth.

"Weighs about four-and-a-half pounds," Preacher said.

Leaning in for a closer look, Caleb said, "I'm surprised you can carry that thing."

The old man grinned. "I do list to the right occasionally. I've carried a gun with me since I started preaching. Most of the time back then, it stayed in my saddle holster. Since trains replaced my original mode of transportation, I've taken to toting one."

"So you were a circuit-riding preacher?"

"Yep. For a number of years. Although later I struck out for wilder territory and did some preaching on my own."

"Did you ever marry?" Caleb asked, as he watched a peel curling around the blade of the knife.

"I did. And we had a beautiful baby girl."

"Where are they now? Do you see them often?"

"The good Lord saw fit to take them home a good many years ago."

Caleb's hands stilled. He looked up. "Home?"

Preacher nodded. "Little Sarah died when she tumbled from the wagon while we were traveling with several other families. A wheel struck her before anybody could get to her." He swallowed hard, several times, before he spoke again. "Since we were miles from a cemetery, we buried her there, beside the trail."

Caleb stared at him in stunned silence. "I'm sorry." Though the words seemed inadequate, they were all he had to offer.

Preacher acknowledged them with a nod. "My wife, Ella, never recovered from the loss." He, too, stopped working for a moment, a faraway look in his eyes. "Her grief made her weak, I suppose. She caught a sickness that swept through the next community we stopped in. Other folks recovered, but my Ella was low already, and that took her all the way down. When I pulled out of there, I left another piece of my heart behind. I know they're in heaven, though. I'll see them again."

In response to Caleb's continued silence, Preacher asked, "What's the matter?"

"You're a man of God. How could all that happen to you?"

Preacher's eyebrows rose. "Did you think that nothing bad happened to Christians?"

"I honestly don't know what I thought," Caleb admitted. "But how can you still love God when He...took it all away? He left you all alone."

The old man sighed. "I wasn't alone. God was right there with me, every step of the way. I don't know how I would've made it otherwise."

Caleb shook his head in amazement. "So you weren't angry? It didn't hurt?"

Preacher's brown eyes darkened, an expression of pain flashing across his face. "Oh, it hurt. Still does." He drew in a breath. "But it says in the Bible that it rains on the just and the unjust. Bad things happen. God answers our prayers; only sometimes he doesn't answer them in the way we want."

When Caleb didn't respond, Preacher picked up the conversational slack. "Are you a church-going fellow?"

Caleb suspected the man already knew the answer to that, so he responded honestly. "No, the times I've gone, it's left me feeling sorta empty."

The preacher was listening, whether out of politeness or genuine interest Caleb couldn't say, yet for some reason he wanted to tell him more.

"It seemed like some folks were there to participate in ritual and ceremony and were only going through the motions," Caleb said. He struggled to explain his feelings. "And then there were some who seemed so…good—like they weren't living in the same world as me, wouldn't have the same problems. Like they understood every single word that was being said, and even the hymns made them cry. I wasn't getting that at all. I felt bewildered and outta place."

Preacher studied him a moment before picking up another potato. "You suppose some of those folks were going through something personal, and just happened to be in a public place?"

Caleb shrugged. "I guess so. But I've seen religious people do some horrible things to each other. Wasn't interested in being part of that."

The preacher dropped the potato and put up his hand. "Let me ask you something. Have you ever met a fellow lawman who occasionally broke the law? Or a crooked storekeeper who put his thumb on the scale?"

"Yes, to both."

"Do you automatically avoid or distrust people of those professions now?"

"No, of course not." Caleb wanted to be offended. Where was the deep theological discussion? This old man was speaking to him like he was a child. Yet for some reason he wasn't bothered by it.

Although Preacher set to work again, his attention remained on Caleb. "Do you think that God judged you based on what the people in the other pews were thinking, feeling or doing?"

Caleb shook his head. "Hadn't really thought about it like that, but no, I don't."

The old man sighed. "Son, being a Christian is a personal thing. Between you and Jesus. It says in the Bible to believe on the Lord Jesus Christ and *thou* shalt be saved. It doesn't say that all the folks around you get a say-so in that. Or that you go through any great rigmarole for it to happen."

Caleb let that sink in.

Preacher gestured toward his old revolver. "Most of my services were done without ceremony of any kind. Only a gun, my Bible, and whatever shade tree, brush arbor or tabernacle that could be found. I'm not much on ceremonial type stuff, either. However, there isn't anything wrong with it—as long as everything that's said and done is pointing people toward Jesus. If it's not, then no wonder it left you feeling empty."

"It did for a fact," Caleb said. "I guess that's hard for somebody like you to understand."

Preacher snorted. "I've had my problems. But Jesus has a way of filling up those empty places in your life—and your heart—if you let him. Of course, what happened to me wasn't the same thing you're talking about necessarily. I was in bad shape, though."

The old man laid the knife down, picked up his coffee cup, took a sip, and then resumed his reminiscing. "Like I mentioned, I knew God was with me when my wife and child died, but I was still a young man...facing a long life without them. For a while there, I wished I'd died, too. One day I was having a particularly difficult struggle with that. I hadn't been sleeping or eating, and I honestly didn't care what happened to me. One of the older women of the community brought me some food. She stayed and talked to me, encouraged me to eat, and it seemed as if my life mattered more to her than it did to me. She cared, and that meant something to me. Afterwards, I got to thinking about what would've happened if the deaths had been the other way around."

"The other way around?"

Preacher nodded as he picked up another potato. "What if God had taken me first? And Ella and Sarah had been left to fend for themselves. If they had lived and I hadn't, I like to think that God would've placed someone in their path to help. Since that's not the way it happened, I got to thinking about what God wanted from me. One thing I felt, clear down to my bones, was that He wanted me to go on preaching the Gospel. And secondly, I decided that maybe he meant for me to do some stepping."

"Stepping?"

"Stepping in, stepping up. Helping others. Ever since that time, I've had a special place in my heart for those who've lost a spouse or a child, and even more so to help in those cases where a father might be missing. For whatever reason."

Caleb remembered Preacher's comments on the stairs the night they'd met. He hadn't stayed to cause trouble.

"You stayed here to look after Abby?"

The old man shrugged. "Seemed the thing to do."

That bothered Caleb in ways he didn't even understand. "I wouldn't have hurt her," he said softly.

"Maybe not on purpose," Preacher agreed, "but there's more than one way to hurt somebody." He glanced over his shoulder to make sure they were still alone. "It worried me that she seemed so sheltered and naïve."

Abby was both of those things, and Caleb had known it all along, too. Regret and confusion fought for a prominent position in his thoughts. He laid the knife down and leaned back in his chair. "I don't know what to do," he said. "She's not the type of girl that a fellow trifles with—"

Preacher's voice was firm. "No, she's not."

Caleb flinched. "Yet I can't seem to stay away from her," he admitted. With all the tangled thoughts and emotions running through his mind, Caleb was startled by his next words. "How did you know when it was time to settle down? When you knew you'd met the right girl?"

"Well, it wasn't like it is nowadays," Preacher acknowledged. "We lived in a small village, not many choices. But I loved my Ella with all my heart. I always figured God put her there just for me."

Giving voice to his earlier thoughts, Caleb said, "Abby is one of the prettiest women I've ever seen, yet it's more than that."

"Good," Preacher grunted. "It's not wise to court a woman based on her looks."

Caleb nodded. "Agreed. If I was only interested in a pretty face, there's always Jenna." He groaned when he realized how that sounded. And he'd said it to a preacher.

"I'm sorry, sir."

Preacher went right on peeling potatoes. "Don't fret, son. I wasn't born an old man. Or a preacher."

Caleb smiled. "What I said really isn't fair to Jenna either. Our friendship is…difficult to explain. But that's all it is, friendship."

"No need to explain. All I was trying to say is look beyond the physical, and look beyond the present."

"I understand the physical, but what do you mean about the present?"

"Before you ask for a woman's hand, you need to ask yourself some hard questions."

"Such as?"

"Such as, will you still find her lovely, and lovable, when she's big with child? Or when her youth has faded? If you can't see that happening, then you need to leave her be. Because some man will love her and want her, no matter what the future brings."

An image of Abigail Horton, a baby in her arms and a child clinging to her skirt flashed through Caleb's mind. And the realization that it didn't scare him was enough to shake him up.

"It says in the Bible that a virtuous woman is worth far more than rubies," Preacher said. "Just something to keep in mind."

Caleb stood as Abby returned.

"Goodness, you two make good hands," she teased as she gathered the potato peels. "If y'all ever decide to give up on your current occupations I'll put in a good word for you over at Bony Joe's."

"Thanks, but I think I'll stick to preaching," the old man drawled.

Smiling, Abby swept out again.

"Well, her disposition sure improved in a hurry," Caleb grumbled. "I'm not sure I'll ever understand women."

"I'm not about to step off into a discussion like that," Preacher said. "Although from my own experience, I will say that at times a woman, even one that loves you, can be downright disagreeable and outta sorts, and…"

He paused, and Caleb waited for the words of wisdom that would follow. "And, what?" he prompted after a moment.

"And nine times out of ten, it'll be *your* fault."

Caleb laughed. He had no trouble believing that.

Chapter Twenty-One

ABBY FLICKED A fingertip to the bottom of the flat iron, and then laid it aside. Still hot enough. She spread one of Robby's shirts over the wide oak plank to which she'd pinned an old blanket and a fresh, clean sheet. She then adjusted the board, which was propped upon the backs of two chairs, until it was in the position she needed.

Looking up at the sound of footsteps, Abby smiled at Henry as he rounded the corner of the house. "Hello."

"Hey, Abby. It was so quiet up front I figured I'd find you back here."

"It was too hot to do this in the house." She stilled as a thought occurred. "Is something wrong with my father?" Just as he'd promised, Henry had continued to make regular visits to the cave.

"No, that's not why I'm here. Although to tell you the truth he does seem to be going a little stir-crazy."

"I can imagine," Abby said. "I'd hope to go see him today, but Mama's going next door in a few minutes. Mr. Henderson is still sick, so she's pitching in to help there. I need to stick around here."

Henry nodded.

"So what did you want to see me about?" Henry hadn't proposed in a while. Hopefully he'd given that up and they could have a nice conversation.

"Actually, it wasn't you I wanted to see. I was hoping that Robby might want to work with me today. I'll pay him. One of our hands quit and I need a little temporary help."

"Taking Robby is fine by me. You'd better check with Mama, though. Why don't you step inside and ask her."

Jenna Nolan, nibbling on a cookie and looking bored, poked her head out the screen door. "I'll go ask Mrs. Horton if you want me to. She was upstairs when I came down."

Henry nodded. "Thanks. I'd appreciate that."

"You're welcome." Jenna popped the rest of the cookie in her mouth and closed the screen.

When the sounds of her footsteps receded, Abby turned to Henry. "Do you think she heard us talking about my father?" she whispered.

Henry immediately set her mind at ease. "No, Jenna would've jumped right into the conversation if she had."

"That's probably true." Abby touched the bottom of the iron with the tip of her finger again.

"Still hot?" Henry asked.

"No, but I've got another one heating on the stove."

"I'll get it for you." He took the cool one from her, bolted into the kitchen and was back with the hot one before she could protest. Abby placed it on the end of the board.

"Thanks, Henry." She stretched and rubbed at a sore spot on her back before resuming her chore. "What are you delivering today?"

"Load of watermelon. Bringing them in from the field and then on to the train station. They'll be selling most of them in Fair Haven."

The screen door opened and Robby raced out ahead of Jenna. "Hey, Henry. Mama said I could go!"

"She also said to put your shoes on," Jenna reminded him.

Robby grumbled, and returned to the house. "I'll be right back," he said over his shoulder to Henry. "Please don't leave without me."

"I won't," Henry said with a smile. He turned to Abby. "Glad he's so eager. It's hard work."

"I don't think that will matter," Abby said. "He loves being outside. This will give him something to do." *And keep him out of trouble.* She'd finally gotten Robby to confide in her about the altercation with the bigger boys and had been dismayed to discover that he'd been defending their father's honor. How badly would he have been hurt if Caleb hadn't stopped the fight?

Jenna ambled over to the ironing board. "You missed a wrinkle," she told Abby, pointing to the tail of the shirt.

Abby drew in a deep breath, not sure if she was gathering air to scream or cry, when Jenna spoke again. This time though, her words were directed at Henry.

"Would you mind if I go with you?"

Brown eyes wide, Henry stared at her. "And do what?"

Jenna shrugged. "Keep you company. Tell you interesting stories about Colorado." She grinned. "Maybe let you know when you've missed a melon in the patch."

Laughing, Henry glanced at Abby, and then shrugged. "Sure, why not?"

Abby understood that Henry was trying to help her by taking Jenna away for a while. Yet she had no explanation for Jenna's desire to go. For some reason, the girl had been very attentive to Henry recently.

"You might want to change into some old clothes," Henry said to Jenna. "It'd be a shame to mess up a dress that pretty."

Jenna shrugged. "I don't have any old clothes."

Robby flew through the door again, yelling, "I'm ready," and the three of them trooped toward Henry's wagon in a flurry of goodbyes.

"I've got plenty of old clothes to loan you," Abby mumbled

as she resumed ironing. She hadn't wanted to go with them, yet for some reason she wasn't happy being left behind. She had the peace and quiet she often wished for, but instead of being relaxing, it seemed unsettling.

Miss Culpepper had announced at breakfast that she was taking the train to Fair Haven. Abby had asked if she needed someone to accompany her, but the older woman had insisted on going alone. The surveyors were off somewhere working, Preacher was napping, and Caleb and Eli had taken the ferry to Boone Springs to search for her father.

She'd seen very little of Caleb since he'd peeled potatoes for her several days earlier. Was he avoiding her, or fully occupied with the search for her father? Both possibilities bothered her. Caleb had apologized again, though, about the encounter with Mr. Becker. He'd cornered her in the kitchen one evening, and had seemed so sincere, hat in hand, genuine dismay in his eyes, that she'd forgiven him.

Still, things didn't feel the same as they had before the incident.

In fact, Caleb seemed more and more uneasy and frustrated as the days passed with no sign of the fugitive, while Abby grew more anxious. She longed to confide in Caleb, yet she owed her allegiance to her father, first and foremost.

The sound of the front door closing echoed through the house. Her mother had left for the neighbor's. When the stray dog trotted up the back steps and curled up near her feet a few minutes later, she was actually glad for the company.

"How did you manage to time that right?" she asked him. "And how long do you think it'll be before Mama catches you in Robby's room?" The pup yawned and wagged his tail.

After getting him some food, Abby continued on with her ironing. When finished, she took the crisply pressed garments inside and put them away in the appropriate wardrobes. She left Miss Culpepper's dress on a peg attached to the outside of her door—an arrangement the woman had requested right after moving in. Abby found the set-up rather odd, but so was Miss Culpepper. The older woman had simply stated that she valued her privacy, and she would clean her own room. That was fine by Abby.

After finishing upstairs, Abby dusted the parlor, scrubbed the kitchen floor and the downstairs hallway, and finished cooking the evening meal before the harvesting trio returned.

"Thought y'all might want this for after supper," Henry said as he placed a watermelon on the table.

"Thank you," Abby told him. "Sounds good. Join us?"

"Sure. I'd better wash up, though. I'm pretty grubby."

Robby was just as dirty, yet Jenna appeared nearly as pristine as she had when they left.

Abby suspected the girl had stayed in the wagon all day, so she was surprised to hear Robby proclaim, "Jenna's the best."

Although amused by her little brother's infatuation, she felt a stab of something different when Henry added, "She really is a lot of fun."

I could be fun, too, if I never had to do a lick of work. Abby was surprised by her own shrewish thoughts.

"After supper Jenna's going to teach me how to make a kite," Robby added.

"That's wonderful," Abby said, "now go wash up."

Abby was prepared to step in and help Robby if Jenna let him down—not that she knew how to make a kite. But the other girl was true to her word. After the meal was over, and the other diners had moved to the parlor, Jenna asked for some flour.

Abby stared at her in shock. "You're going to cook?"

Jenna seemed equally incredulous at that thought. "No, it's for the kite. I need about a quarter cup of flour, and some water. And a bowl to mix it in."

"Oh." Abby brought Jenna the flour, and tried not to appear too interested as the other girl added the water and stirred it into a paste. Jenna made additional requests, from Robby and Mrs. Horton, resulting in large pieces of paper, sticks, strings and strips of cloth scattered across the table.

Despite her initial feigned disinterest, Abby couldn't resist watching the process, and was as caught-up in the excitement as everyone else by the time the kite was complete.

"It's getting late," her mother said, "we should wait until tomorrow for the maiden voyage."

Robby looked at her, disappointment on his face. "There's still some daylight, Mama. Please let me try. I'll never ask you for another thing…at least not this week."

Irene Horton smiled and ruffled his hair. "All right, let's see what you can do."

Everyone stepped outside as Robby—an intense, purposeful look on his face—ran down the middle of the road, string in hand, kite dragging, then bobbing along behind him.

Abby held her breath as a gust of wind took hold, and the simple, homemade contraption bounced a couple of times and then sailed through the air. Those on the porch cheered and applauded.

Abby noticed that Henry, standing in the front yard, was looking at something else—a smile curving his lips. She followed the direction of his gaze…straight to Jenna. The girl stood in the road, whooping and hollering with every bit as much enthusiasm as Robby. Then Jenna reached down, hiked her dress up past her ankles and ran after him. Instead of being scandalized, Henry's smile widened. Abby shook her head.

After they'd all gone inside for the night, Abby walked in to find Miss Culpepper talking to Robby in the parlor. "I picked these up for you in Fair Haven today," the woman said as she handed him a leather pouch.

Robby eagerly untied the bag, tipped it, and let the colorful glass marbles fill his hand before dropping them back inside. His expression when he looked at Miss Culpepper was a reflection of

Abby's confusion. He wasn't sure why she'd given him the gift, or if he should accept it.

"Don't worry," the woman said, "I asked your mother if it would be okay."

That brought a smile to Robby's face. "Thank you," he said, and then offered her a hesitant hug. She returned it with a good deal more enthusiasm, smiling as he pulled back and hurried up the stairs.

The woman's smile faded when she caught sight of Abby. "If you'll excuse me, I'm headed up to bed," Miss Culpepper said softly. "It's been a long day."

"Of course," Abby murmured, "I'll see you tomorrow."

Alone again, she sighed, not at all sure what was happening in her own home. Miss Culpepper's behavior seemed a bit odder every day. Henry was smitten with Jenna, whether he realized it yet or not, and Caleb Calhoun still hadn't returned.

And most worrisome of all…she missed Caleb so much that it hurt.

Chapter Twenty-Two

THE NEXT MORNING, Abby returned from the garden to find Caleb sitting with Preacher at one end of the long kitchen table. *He's back.*

Both men stood to their feet when they spotted her. Abby motioned them back down, and was reassured when Caleb greeted her as he always had. Obviously, he wasn't avoiding her...and he hadn't found her father. Both of those things made her ridiculously happy.

"Don't let me interrupt," she said, "please go on back to what you were doing."

They resumed their discussion as Preacher flipped open his old Bible. A little later, she looked up to find Caleb staring off into the distance. Deep in thought. Abby wanted to give them privacy, but she had chores to do. The two men didn't seem to mind, though, or even notice her at times. She overheard some of their conversation, and knew they discussed everything from the baby in the manger, to the broken body on the cross, and the barren tomb. Repentance. And forgiveness.

The next day they were deep in discussion on the front porch. Later that afternoon, she walked into the parlor and found them praying together. She stepped back out, curiously moved by the sight.

Caleb seemed almost shy as he approached her later in the yard, hat in hand.

"I wanted to tell you that I accepted Jesus as my Savior," he said, "and I'll be baptized along with the others who were saved during the revival—the river's been too high until now. I was hoping that you and your family could be there."

Her throat tightened. "Oh, Caleb, we wouldn't miss it for the world. I'm so happy for you."

"Thank you, Abby." He looked down at his hat for a moment, then back at her. "I don't know if I can put into words exactly how I feel, but Preacher told me that Jesus has a way of filling up the empty places in your heart, and your life, if you let Him. I can already tell he's right."

Tears burned her eyes. "That's wonderful. When will the baptismal service be held?"

"Preacher said he checked with Pastor Brown, and they decided on this coming Sunday—as long as it doesn't rain again."

"Are you nervous?" she asked.

He grinned. "Nope, I've already plunged myself into the Brazos once, might as well have another go at it."

***

The following Sunday there seemed to be more people lining the banks of the Brazos than there were citizens of Moccasin Rock. Just as with revivals, a baptismal service was an occasion that some considered soul-stirring, and others considered entertainment. Abby admitted to herself that she was of both camps.

They were far enough from the bluff—having chosen a portion of the river where the bank was more easily accessed—that she wasn't worried about anyone finding the cave, yet she couldn't help glancing in that direction from time-to-time.

There were both men and women scheduled for baptism, nine in all.

Pastor Wilkie Brown and Reverend Wainright waded out about hip deep. Although the current wasn't moving swiftly, it seemed to Abby as if the older man was having trouble keeping his balance. She watched anxiously until he got his footing. She sure had become fond of the man. Originally, he'd planned on leaving right after the revival, and Pastor Brown would've handled the baptisms alone. *Why had Preacher stayed?* Whatever the reason, Abby was glad he had.

She was too far away to hear the actual words, yet Abby knew what Pastor Brown was saying. The words and even the cadence were familiar enough that she could silently recite them along with him. One after the other, he baptized each convert and sent them, dripping, shivering and smiling, back to their waiting families.

A small canvas tent had been erected near a grove of trees for the ladies to change their clothing, and a tarpaulin had been thrown over a couple of tree branches on the opposite side of the grove for the men.

There would be a potluck dinner when the service was complete, with each woman of the church having brought enough food for their own family, plus extra to share.

Abby held her breath as Caleb stepped into the water and waded out. He exchanged a few words with Pastor Brown, and then turned toward the older man. Then they bowed their heads and prayed. Preacher had one arm around Caleb's back when he looked up and began to speak.

Unlike Pastor Brown's softly spoken words, Preacher's voice bounced across the water and carried through the crowd. "Upon thy profession of faith, I baptize thee, Caleb Calhoun, now my brother, in the name of the Father, the Son and the Holy Ghost."

He whispered something, and Caleb reached out and took hold of Preacher's arm. The old man lowered him backwards into the water, his voice ringing out even louder now.

"Buried in the likeness of His death," then pulling Caleb up as he solemnly intoned, "Raised in the likeness of His resurrection." Caleb came up sputtering, and scrubbed his hands across his face.

All three men made their way toward the riverbank. After a brief greeting with the boarding house residents, both Preacher and Pastor Brown left to change clothes. Caleb remained.

Jenna, although quieter than usual, immediately pushed herself forward and hugged Caleb with her customary enthusiasm.

Eli and Nathaniel's expressions were hard to read, although they both stepped up and shook Caleb's hand. He allowed that, and then abruptly pulled them both into a hug. Abby's throat tightened at the sight of them. They might not have known each other for long, but clearly there was a bond there.

Abby watched as her mother and the others, including Henry, took turns at offering their congratulations to Caleb. Then it was only her.

"I'm so very happy for you, Caleb."

"Thank you, Abby. That means a lot to me."

He leaned toward her, as if to draw her into a hug, and then glanced down at his wet clothing. He took her hand instead, pressing it between both of his. For once, Abby wished she was as spontaneous and carefree as Jenna. She longed to throw her arms around him, even if it meant drenching her best dress.

At that moment, a shrill whistle pierced the air. They turned to where the others had gathered. "If you'll bow your heads," Pastor Brown said, "we'll have a word of prayer before the meal."

After the prayer ended, Abby and Caleb headed toward the others. "I guess I'd better change in to something dry before I eat," Caleb told her.

Abby nodded and turned toward the makeshift tables fully loaded with food, while he veered toward the trees. Abby spotted Jenna and Henry, heads bent toward one another as they filled their plates. They then walked toward a blanket where some of the young people in town had gathered. As Abby drew closer to them, she heard Jenna telling Henry to take her arm.

Good heavens. Abby knew Jenna was a bossy girl, but this was taking it to extremes. Strangely, Henry didn't seem to mind. He balanced his plate on his left hand and slipped his right hand around Jenna's elbow.

Abby frowned. *If she hurts him, she'll have to deal with me.*

She realized with a start that although she was concerned about her old friend, she wasn't nearly as upset as she'd been when she'd seen Jenna clinging to Caleb the first time.

Shaken, Abby admitted the truth to herself. The odds of her heart being intact when Caleb Calhoun left town were getting slimmer each day.

Chapter Twenty-Three

STANDING AT THE kitchen counter slicing a coffee cake, Abby struggled with the anxiety that seemed to build daily. It had been more than three weeks since her father had sought refuge in the cave, and nearly that long since Abby had seen him.

Thankfully, Henry Barnett continued to take provisions to him as needed. Henry had also smuggled a note back to Mrs. Horton, from her husband, assuring her that he was alive and well. Abby had watched her mother read the note and smile, and, to Abby's relief, she'd asked no questions. But her father couldn't remain hidden forever. *Where are you, Marshall Adair?*

Abby wanted to confide in Caleb, yet she knew that until she could prove her father's innocence, she'd be putting the ranger in an impossible position. So she kept her silence, and her secrets.

Layering the cake slices on a platter, Abby glanced down as a blur of black and white fur streaked by, headed for the back door. Robby followed at a more sedate pace, hands in his pockets, whistling a carefree tune—the picture of innocence.

Abby was startled when her mother, standing at the stove tending a pan of bacon, addressed Robby without turning around. "That dog needs a bath if he's going to keep sleeping up there with you."

Her son stopped in his tracks, mouth open. "W…when do you want me to give him one?" he finally asked.

"There's a tub on the back porch. Please see to it right after breakfast."

"Yes, ma'am." Robby beamed a smile in Abby's direction as he pulled back a chair at the table.

"What are you going to name him?" Abby whispered.

"Prince," Robby answered promptly. "Don't you think that's a perfect name?"

Abby thought "Rags" would be more suitable for the little fellow, though she would gladly call him by the more regal moniker if it made her brother happy.

"I think it's a fine name," she told him.

Grabbing a stack of plates from the cupboard, Abby welcomed each of the boarders as they arrived for breakfast. The table was full in minutes.

Mrs. Horton added her greetings as she placed the bacon and a basket of biscuits on the table. "Let me grab a jar of peach preserves before we get started," she said.

Abby nodded, although her thoughts were elsewhere. *How long had Mama known about the dog? What else does she know?* A resounding crash made her forget everything.

"Mama!" Abby was running toward the pantry before the word left her mouth. The sounds of scraping chair legs and cutlery clanging against plates told her that the others were close on her heels. Just inside the pantry door, she stumbled.

The stepstool, one leg broken off at an angle, had been upended. The crumpled figure of her mother lay beside it. Even in the dim light, Abby could see the blood flowing from the gash on her forehead.

The others crowded into the small space as Abby dropped to her knees.

"Move back," she said, "I can't see anything." Panic lent a

sharper edge to her voice than she'd intended, but everyone stepped out of the way and back into the kitchen. She patted her mother's cheek. "Mama, can you hear me?"

There was no answer, no reaction at all—not even a twitch of discomfort nor a groan of pain.

She grasped her mother's shoulders, not sure what to do next.

Caleb stepped in. "Here, let me," he said gently. He picked Irene Horton up and carried her into the kitchen before glancing back at Abby. "Where do you want me to take her?"

The sight of her mother's arms hanging limply at her sides brought a piercing pain to Abby's chest. "To the doctor," she said.

"I've already sent Robby for the doctor," Miss Culpepper said briskly. "Hopefully he'll be here any minute. Please take her to her room, Ranger Calhoun. She'll be more comfortable there, and she and the doctor will have some privacy."

Even through her fear, Abby was aware of how differently Miss Culpepper was behaving. Clearly concerned, yet oddly in control. That was something to dwell on later. Right now Abby had more important things to worry about. She ran ahead of Caleb, opening doors and clearing a path. "Please, finish your meal," she called out to the others.

Everyone except Miss Culpepper expressed their concern and then returned to the table as Abby asked. The older woman marched resolutely along behind Caleb, and a glimpse back at her determined expression told Abby that it would take more time than she had to make her remain behind with the others.

Once inside the bedroom, Caleb placed Irene Horton on the bed. "I'll go down and wait for Nathaniel." He took Abby's hand and squeezed it. "I'll send him up here as soon as he arrives."

"Thank you, Caleb."

She and Miss Culpepper waited—Abby holding a cloth to her mother's head to stop the bleeding, while Miss Culpepper appeared to be praying.

As Dr. Nathaniel entered, Abby was taken aback to hear Miss Culpepper mumbling, "No, no, not again," before going back to her prayers.

Her mind already numb with worry, Abby couldn't make sense of that. She turned instead to greet the doctor.

"Thank you for coming. I'm sorry to trouble you."

"No trouble at all," Nathaniel said, as he moved to Irene Horton's bedside and opened the black leather bag he'd brought along. "Can you tell me what happened?"

Abby told him what little she knew as he examined the wound to her mother's head. He stilled when the patient flinched and pulled back further into the pillow. He smiled at Abby. "That's a good sign."

Though Irene Horton's eyes remained closed, she moaned again when Nathaniel touched her head, seemingly in pain and annoyance, and the sound was as sweet as any choir to Abby. She was so caught up in her relief, that it took a moment for her to notice that Miss Culpepper had collapsed into the nearest chair, hands to her face, shoulders shaking as she sobbed. Whatever the source of her distress, it was getting worse. Abby didn't have time for the histrionics.

Voice firm, she addressed the older woman. "Perhaps you should go to your room and lie down."

Miss Culpepper shook her head, her gaze riveted to the bed as she fished a handkerchief from her pocket. "No. As soon as she's awake, I need to talk to Mrs. Horton, in private."

Abby wasn't about to leave her mother alone with a woman who was acting so strangely. "I'm afraid that's not possible," she said, arms crossed.

Dr. Nathaniel flashed them both an uneasy glance as he continued to clean Mrs. Horton's wound. She stirred again as he began securing a bandage to her head. Suddenly her eyes popped opened and her voice broke the strained silence.

"Goodness, what happened?"

Abby explained about the accident as Nathaniel wrapped a strip of gauze around her head to hold the bandage in place.

"I'm so sorry to have caused all this fuss," Irene said when he stepped back. "I knew that stepstool was wobbly and I should've tended to it."

"Don't worry about that," Abby said. "I'll get someone to repair the stool."

Her mother mumbled a thank you, and then grasped at Abby's arm. "Who's taking care of everything in the kitchen?"

"All the diners had to do was eat their meal, Mama. I'm sure they'll be okay." She started to add, "Jenna's there" but that would make her mother worry more. "I'll check on everything in a bit."

As he packed up his bag, Nathaniel Calhoun asked her mother a few random questions to be sure she was okay mentally, Abby realized, before taking his leave. "You seem to be perfectly fine, all things considered," he told her at the door, "but get some rest, and send word for me immediately if you begin to feel worse."

After he was gone, Miss Culpepper pinned Abby with an almost desperate look. "Will you please let me speak to your mother alone?"

Abby glanced at her mother and explained about Miss Culpepper's request. "What do you want me to do?" she asked.

"I'd rather you stay," Irene Horton said, with an uncertain glance at their boarder.

Miss Culpepper's shoulders slumped as she looked at Abby. "All right, although I'm sure you're not going to like what you're about to hear."

***

"It's not easy for me to talk about," the older woman said, "but I was assaulted when I was only sixteen." She swallowed several times before speaking again. "At the time, I thought it was the worst thing that could ever happen to me." Her voice broke. "Until nine months later when they took my baby away."

Abby dropped down to the edge of her mother's bed. That was not what she'd expected to hear, at all. She waited in silence, her heart heavy, as the older woman attempted to regain her composure.

"Although I had no prospects for marriage, I wanted to keep my dau…daughter so badly," Miss Culpepper said. "I begged my father. He wouldn't hear of it. It just wasn't done. My mother was dead, so there was no one to intercede on my behalf."

Irene Horton pressed a hand to her mouth as tears gathered in her eyes. Like Abby, she listened in silence.

All three women turned as Nathaniel tapped on the doorframe and stepped back into the room. "I'm sorry," he said, after a sweeping glance at all of them. "I forgot to leave something for the pain." He handed Abby a piece of paper that had been folded into a pouch. "All you need to do is stir this powder into a glass of water. If you need anything else, just send for me."

"Thank you," Abby said.

After he'd gone again, Miss Culpepper resumed her story. "I know Papa thought it was for the best. He told me so. The baby deserved a better life than I could give her. They wouldn't even let me hold the child, although I got a glimpse of her. Reddish-brown hair, a little button nose. The prettiest child I'd ever seen."

Irene Horton made a sniffling sound, and Abby got up and crossed over to the bureau to get her a handkerchief. Her mother wiped her eyes and nose when Abby handed it to her, but her attention was riveted on the older woman. "Did they tell you where they took …your baby?"

Miss Culpepper nodded. "Father told me that they'd given her to a family that would love and cherish her. Those people were headed to Wisconsin."

Goosebumps ran up Abby's arms.

"Once the baby was gone, my father thought I'd bounce right back to the daughter he knew, but I never got over it. I truly grieved. Father didn't understand that, and our relationship was never the same. To be honest, I didn't understand it either," she added softly. "It's still a mystery to me how the maternal bond can be so strong in someone so young. I know this sounds strange, but my arms actually ached to hold…my baby."

"You never married and had other children?" Irene asked.

Miss Culpepper shook her head. "No. I stayed at home and tended to my father. He had a debilitating illness in his later years. I couldn't leave him. And there was nowhere for me to go anyway."

Irene twisted the handkerchief in her hands. "So why are you here?" she whispered.

Abby suspected they both knew, yet she held her breath in anticipation of the answer.

"Because after years of searching, and praying that my child was still alive, I was told that she was running a boarding house in Moccasin Rock, Texas.

A deep sob escaped Irene Horton, and it was a moment before she could speak. "How do you know for sure that I'm the child you gave up?"

Miss Culpepper's voice shook when she responded. "I did not give you up, you were taken from me. But in answer to your question, when my father died a few years ago, I found an old letter when I cleaned out his desk. It was from a man named Douglas Marsden."

Abby knew that name was significant, even before her mother gasped.

"He assured my father that baby Irene was doing well, growing up happy and healthy, and that their little family was settled in Peshtigo, Wisconsin."

Abby fought back tears of her own. Little Irene Marsden had not lived a happy life.

"That was true at one time," Irene told the other woman, "but my mama and papa both died. I was placed in an orphanage. Until I met and married Bob, I had no family at all."

Miss Culpepper nodded. "I discovered that eventually. As soon as I had access to my father's money, I hired Pinkerton agents to find out what happened to you. It took a while, but they finally tracked you to Green Bay, and from there on to the orphanage. Unfortunately, a fire had destroyed the records for that part of the state. I kept hiring agents, and corresponding with people in nearby communities. Clergymen, judges, anyone I thought might know something. I wasn't certain where you'd ended up until earlier this year." She leaned back in her chair as if exhausted. "When they confirmed your whereabouts, I headed to Texas."

Irene's eyes widened. "Why didn't you tell me who you were when you first arrived?"

"I was trying to decide how to do that when I discovered that your husband had passed away." She paused. "Of course, it seems now that he didn't. But at the time I didn't think you could handle another major disruption in your life."

"Why didn't you tell me later?"

"Do you remember when I first got here? How I took ill?"

Irene nodded. "You came down with a cough and chills."

"Yes, and you fussed over me," Miss Culpepper said. "I was able to spend time with you, and it meant the world to me. I didn't know how to be a mother, yet that nurturing spirit runs deep in you—whether it's with your own children, or even a stranger. As long as I needed you I knew you'd be more inclined to let me stay. So even after I recovered, I pretended to be sickly. Although not everyone cared for me"—she glanced at Abby—"and there were times that I was afraid of being sent packing, I cherished whatever time I could get with you."

Abby pressed a hand to her chest, but it didn't ease the ache there.

"I've wanted to tell you, so many times," Miss Culpepper added on a shaky breath. "I tried to involve myself in whatever you were doing so we would have more opportunities to talk, but I could never figure out how to bring it up. I thought several times about leaving my door unlocked, and letting you discover some of the letters and telegrams I'd received regarding your whereabouts—and take my chances that you'd welcome me into your life. Yet every time, I got scared and decided to wait a little longer. In case this time with you was all I had, I wanted to make it last. When I saw you lying there earlier, and I thought I might lose you again, I decided I would tell you the truth as soon as I could, no matter what the consequences."

Abby swiped at her eyes. So much made sense now, including Miss Culpepper's frequent offers to help in the kitchen, and her reaction during the confrontation with Mrs. Dunlop at the church. *She was protecting her child.*

"So what do we do now?" Irene Horton asked in a whisper.

"Long term, I'm not sure," Miss Culpepper said. "But right this minute, if you have no objection, I'd like to hug my baby."

Abby watched as her mother nodded and Miss Culpepper approached the bed—wrapping her arms around the sobbing woman as she murmured soothing words.

With one last glance over her shoulder, Abby slipped from the room—leaving them to a reunion many years in the making.

Chapter Twenty-Four

CALEB WAITED IN the parlor, not sure what was happening to the Horton family. Nathaniel had told him that Irene Horton would be okay, but they were sorting through some family issues. *And that Abby might need him.* He didn't even question how Nathaniel knew that Abby's needs mattered to him.

Now Caleb stood at the foot of the stairs, one arm on the newel post, anxious to see what was happening. The house was quiet. Too quiet.

After finishing breakfast, Jenna had taken charge of Robby and they were off on a walk somewhere to keep the boy from worrying about his mother. The surveyors had gone to Boone Springs. He wasn't sure where Preacher had gone.

Caleb straightened when he heard a door open upstairs. Abby descended the stairs, tears streaming down her face, and walked straight into his arms.

"Hey, now," he soothed as he guided her head to his shoulder. "What's this all about? Nathaniel said your mother wasn't badly hurt."

"She's fine, it's…" Abby shook her head, unable to finish her sentence. Caleb led her to the sofa and pulled her close, holding her until she felt like going on. He then listened with mounting incredulity as she filled him in on what happened.

"And I've treated Miss Culpepper so badly," Abby added. "She was scared, and worried about how we'd react, and about whether she'd be accepted, and I didn't even try to get along with her."

"Oh, darlin', I never once heard you say anything unkind to her."

Abby sniffed. "Maybe not, but I was thinking all sorts of unkind things. Instead of giving her the benefit of the doubt, and trying to determine what was really going on, I kept her at arm's-length. No matter what was happening I could've been nicer to her."

Caleb wanted to take away her pain, yet he didn't have a clue what to say. He tightened his arms around her. He also wanted to kiss her—but she was distraught, defenseless. It didn't seem right.

So he held her until she quieted, then placed a finger under her chin and tilted her face up. He brushed the tears from her cheeks with his thumbs. At his gentle touch, something flared in Abby's eyes, something that knocked the breath out of him.

He wasn't the only one who wanted a kiss.

Caleb dropped his hands and held perfectly still as Abby placed her lips lightly on his. He'd certainly been kissed by more skilled women. Abby seemed uncertain and shy—even a little awkward.

And it was the sweetest, most intoxicating thing he'd ever experienced.

It left Caleb thunderstruck. He'd been concerned about Abby growing too attached to him. Now he understood with startling clarity that it was his heart in jeopardy.

He returned the kiss, lest she think he wasn't interested at all, but he kept it light. If he responded like he wanted to, it would scare her half to death.

Caleb then pulled back, and encouraged her to tell him more about her mother and grandmother. They talked for a while, and with no apparent clue to the confusion in his mind and the turmoil in his heart, Abby thanked Caleb for his support and headed upstairs.

She stopped on the bottom step. "Thank you, Caleb, for saying exactly what I needed to hear."

He gave her a little smile. "No problem. Glad I could help." Caleb had actually said very little, mostly that everything would be okay. He hoped it was true.

Caleb watched until she was out of sight. What should he do? Could he be the kind of man she needed and deserved? If not, he couldn't let those kisses happen again.

Maybe he should just run as far and as fast as he could. For both their sakes. *Please God, help me to know what to do.*

***

Caleb had planned on getting out of the house early the next morning, and staying gone until he had his thoughts untangled. But Abby asked him for a favor as soon as he entered the kitchen.

"Do you mind checking in on Preacher and see if he wants breakfast?" she asked. "I'm worried about him, but I'm making gravy and I don't dare leave it."

"Worried?"

"He's normally an early-riser," she said over her shoulder from in front of the stove, "and I haven't seen him yet today. And not much for the past few days. He's hardly eaten anything lately. I'm concerned that he's feeling poorly."

"I'll see what's going on," Caleb said, already heading for the door. Now that he thought about it, he hadn't seen Preacher much in the last few days either.

Upstairs, he tapped lightly at the old man's door, and then opened it when he bade him enter. Caleb's first thought when he stepped inside was that it was too quiet.

Not that one old man would normally make a lot of noise, but there was a stillness in the shadows that seemed unnatural, and the oddest sense of expectancy…of waiting.

Caleb shook off that fanciful notion as he approached the bed, but an icy dread filled him at his first glimpse of Preacher. The man's skin was ashen, and his brown eyes were flat and lifeless.

Trying not to show his alarm, Caleb addressed him in a calm voice. "Abby was wondering if you're coming down to breakfast."

"No," the old man rasped. "I'm plum tuckered out. Think I may stay here in bed for a bit."

"Are you ill?"

"Could be, I guess. Been feeling run down for awhile."

"I'll get Nathaniel to come and look you over," Caleb said.

"No need," Preacher muttered, and then closed his eyes again.

Caleb left, easing the door shut behind him, and hurried down the stairs.

"What's wrong?" Abby asked as soon as she saw his face.

"He's sick."

Abby removed the gravy from the stove. "I'll go get Dr. Nathaniel."

Caleb shook his head. "Preacher said there's no need. But I'm worried. Will you see if you can talk him into it?"

"Of course." She headed for the stairs with a purposeful stride, Caleb right behind her. She tapped on the door, and they waited a moment before entering.

"Preacher?" she called out. "Caleb says you're sick but you don't want the doctor."

"He's right, on both counts." The voice wasn't as deep as normal, although the humor was still evident. "I'm ready to go home, Abby."

Caleb took a deep breath. Preacher was only homesick. That was something he could deal with. "Where do you want to go? I'll help you get there. Someplace here in Texas you used to live?"

When the old man closed his eyes without answering, Caleb

turned to Abby. "Help me gather his things," he told her. "I'll take him home personally."

She touched his sleeve. "Caleb, Preacher wasn't talking about going someplace he used to live. He's ready for *God* to take him home."

Caleb stared at her in disbelief. "He's giving up? He's ready to die?"

Preacher's eyes flickered open. "I'm not looking forward to death, but I sure am looking forward to Heaven." A coughing spell wracked his thin frame. He spoke again as soon as it passed. "I believe God's telling me I've finally reached the quittin' point. I'm not about to stop listening to him now. Angels have been propping me up in the pulpit for a while anyway. It's time."

Preacher closed his eyes again, and then turned his face toward the wall. A helpless feeling washed over Caleb. "What can I do?" he asked Abby.

Her brow furrowed with worry. "Will you go for Dr. Nathaniel anyway?" she whispered.

"Of course." If he were in a bigger city, Caleb would've used his money to bring in the best doctor to be had. He didn't know much about his brother Nathaniel, or his qualifications, but he knew he was a good man. And for better or worse, he was all Moccasin Rock had to offer.

Nathaniel's office was housed in a single-story board and batten structure not far from the jail. It included living quarters in the back. The whole place needed a coat of paint, although it was immaculately clean.

Caleb pounded on the back door, realizing he'd interrupted his brother's breakfast when Nathaniel opened it holding a napkin.

When Caleb explained what was going on, Nathaniel agreed to see Preacher at once. "Give me a moment to wash up, and to leave a note on the door saying where I'll be."

Back at the boarding house, Nathaniel was alone with the

patient for about ten minutes before joining the others in the hall. "I'm afraid there's nothing I can do," he said, compassion in his eyes.

Caleb drew in a breath. "Nothing? What's wrong with him?"

"From what I can tell, he's simply worn out. His body is slowly shutting down. I've seen this sort of thing before. He's decided it's time to go, and so he will." He placed a hand on Caleb's shoulder. "I'll stick around in case you need me. In the meantime, he wants to talk to you."

"Of course."

Once inside the room again, Caleb stood near the bed, uncertain what to do. He'd spent as much time as possible with his father during his last hours but....

"Have a seat," Preacher said, as if this were a social call.

The room was furnished similarly to Caleb's, so he grabbed the only chair and placed it next to the bed. He settled down, intending to stay until the old man was gone, or ran him out. Whichever came first.

Since Preacher's sense of humor seemed to be intact, Caleb decided to retain a light-hearted attitude, too.

"It's kinda unfair of you to go when I still have so many questions for you," Caleb said. "I'm saved now, but I'm uncertain as to how I'm supposed to go forward. I don't know exactly what I should do."

Preacher opened his eyes, staring at the ceiling instead of Caleb. "Study the Bible, go to church, and treat folks like you want to be treated."

Caleb sighed. "I'm willing to give it my best shot, although I can't imagine ever being as good as some people."

"I thought we'd been all over that," Preacher muttered. "It says in the Bible, in Ephesians, *For by grace are ye saved through faith; and that not of yourselves: it is the gift of God: Not of works, lest any man should boast.*"

Preacher cleared his throat, and Caleb battled a smile. The old man might be down, but he wasn't out yet.

"You can't be good enough," Preacher continued. "We have all sinned and fallen short of the glory of God. Every single one of us. There's only One who's perfect. And it ain't you."

Caleb chuckled softly.

The old man looked him in the eye. "Son, asking Jesus into your heart doesn't make you perfect. It doesn't even make you close. It should make you want to try harder to act right, though."

"I will try," Caleb said, "although I'm afraid that some things will be a lot harder than others."

Despite the warmth of the room, Preacher tugged at the blanket, pulling it closer to his chin. "You worried about your job?"

Caleb nodded. "Some."

"I got to admit that lawmen have a rougher row to hoe than most people," Preacher said. "You have to make some tough decisions, sometimes in the blink of an eye. You need to remember that you're doing it to protect others, folks who didn't choose a life of crime. People have free will; they can choose between doing good or evil. And for those who make the wrong choices, there are consequences."

They were silent for awhile. *What was Preacher thinking?* Was he thinking about all the sermons? All the people who'd sat in front of him while he tried desperately to reach them with God's word? To tell them about Jesus. Caleb had been the last of many.

All of a sudden he was overwhelmed by that thought. "I can't believe that after so many years of you doing this, that it all ends here, with me," Caleb said.

Preacher sighed. "It's not an ending. It's a new beginning."

"Beginning?"

He pointed up. "Me there, you here."

Pure panic flashed through Caleb. "You're saying I should be a preacher?"

The old man gave him a tired smile. "No. I'm saying that you'll get a chance to share the gospel from time to time. Don't hesitate."

Caleb choked down his fears. "I won't," he whispered.

Preacher drifted off to sleep a few minutes later. Abby and Caleb took turns sitting with him throughout the day, although he didn't seem to know they were there. Nathaniel slipped in often to see if he could be of help, but there really wasn't much that could be done.

Sometime in the middle of the night, Preacher roused for a moment and reached out a hand. Caleb took it, surprised by the old man's strength. His heart was heavy when the grip fell slack a few minutes later.

Caleb had been present when other folks died, yet for some reason this one hit him almost as hard as his father's passing.

He sat there a moment. *Should he offer up a prayer?* What in the world could someone like him say to God, about someone like Preacher?

Then he remembered something that Preacher had said during one of their long conversations. "The words don't have to be fancy, son. Just tell God what's on your mind and in your heart."

So he did.

***

A few days later, Caleb thumbed through Preacher's old Bible, swallowing past a lump in his throat when he saw the dedication. *To my beloved husband, Hamilton. From your loving wife, Ella.*

Reverend Hamilton Wainright had been laid to rest in the little graveyard behind the Moccasin Rock church. His funeral was well-attended, though only a handful of those gathered had known him. The man had spent his life traveling and preaching—first from settlement to settlement, and then town to town—making a lasting impression, but few lasting friendships.

Caleb and Abby were now sorting through the meager belongings he left behind.

"Preacher told me he had no family left," Caleb said. "I'm not sure what to do with his things."

"While you were gone to get Nathaniel, Preacher told me he wanted you to have them," Abby said as she blinked back tears. "Specifically his gun and Bible."

Caleb nodded, but didn't say anything. He didn't have words. He would cherish both items. Preacher had underlined favorite passages and scribbled notes in the margins of the Bible. Caleb planned to read every word. There was no real family history recorded in the Bible though, only a date of birth for Sarah Wainright, and then, only a few years later, that of her death. Then, under that, another death date, for Ella Wainright.

Preacher's wife and daughter had died so long ago. *How had he kept going?* How had he left them behind and kept moving on alone?

Caleb stilled as he remembered what Preacher had told him, "I didn't go alone. I had God with me every step of the way." Caleb understood that now, in ways he never could've before.

No matter what path lay ahead of him in life, he'd never walk it alone.

Chapter Twenty-Five

THE NEXT COUPLE of days were rain-drenched dreary ones, which fit Caleb's mood. A pall had been cast with the old man's death, and none of the Horton house residents seemed to know how to act or what to do.

In addition to grieving, Caleb was fighting a sense of impending doom regarding Bob Horton. The man had been missing for nearly a month now. Yet he was still spotted in the area occasionally. *Where could he be hiding?*

If Caleb didn't find the outlaw soon, his time with the Rangers was probably over, and if he did find him, his time with Abby might be coming to an end.

Caleb still wasn't sure exactly what he wanted to happen with her, but he couldn't imagine riding out of Moccasin Rock and never seeing that pretty face again.

His musings came to a halt when Henry entered the kitchen in a state of excitement that was hard to miss.

"I have the most wonderful news," Henry said.

Abby stared up at him, eyes wide. "What?"

Henry looked around, as if realizing for the first time that they weren't alone, and that he'd interrupted supper. "I'm so sorry. I got a little carried away." He hesitated a moment, his gaze lighting on an empty chair. "Where's Jenna?" he blurted.

Caleb looked at him in surprise. *What did he want with Jenna?*

Abby didn't appear to think the question an odd one. "She volunteered to take some food to the Hendersons. She should be back soon. Have a seat and I'll fill you a plate. We've got ham, green beans and mashed potatoes."

Mrs. Horton and the others echoed the invitation.

"Thank you, that sounds great," Henry said, "but I'm too excited to eat." He glanced around the room again, before adding, "I'll wait out on the porch. Abby, will you join me when you're done?"

Abby chuckled. "Please excuse me, everyone. I'd better see what this is all about."

She was still laughing as she followed him down the hall and out to the front porch. Caleb wasn't sure what was going on, couldn't even hazard a guess. Then a thought occurred. Had Henry found Bob Horton? What would that have to do with Jenna?

"Will you excuse me?" He addressed his remark to the other diners in general, and didn't stay long enough to see if anyone responded.

Caleb was in the parlor before his conscience caught up with him. He slowed. Eavesdropping wasn't something he was proud of, although it might save him a lot of aggravation and searching. Henry and Abby had already stepped out onto the front porch, so Caleb crept toward the door.

"It turns out my parents have saved nearly every cent they've ever made," Henry was saying. "I'm not rich by some people's standards. But I've got money, Abby. Mama and Papa are moving into town to live with Mama's sister. They're turning everything, including the house, over to me."

"Henry, that's wonderful. I'm so happy for you."

"This means I can do whatever I want. I won't need to spend money on building my own house."

"You can open your own business," Abby said with excitement in her voice. "You've talked about that before. What do you want to do?"

"I'm not sure," Henry said. "Now that I have options, I'm a little shocked to discover that I don't mind carrying on with the farm. The big difference is that I can hire more help, I won't be tied to the place all the time."

"So you had no idea about the money?" Abby sounded breathless, and Caleb's heart gave a strange little lurch.

"Not a clue," Henry said. "This also means I can travel some, Abby."

Caleb held his breath. He hadn't been sure what he wanted until right this very minute. Now it was all so clear. He wanted Abby. *Forever.*

For the next several moments their voices dropped so low he couldn't make out what was being said. When he heard Henry saying goodbye, Caleb turned and hurried upstairs—but one big question trailed right along with him.

Had he waited too late to tell Abby how he felt?

***

The row of stitches wasn't straight, then again neither were Abby's thoughts. Sighing, she took her sewing scissors from the basket, snipped the thread and started over. If only she could handle her thoughts as easily.

She didn't need to look up to know that Caleb Calhoun was staring at her from across the parlor. Although Jenna chattered away to both of them, Caleb had been studying Abby for the past hour. He'd been behaving most peculiarly—opening his mouth every now and then, like he wanted to say something, and then closing it again.

It was a relief when footsteps sounded on the porch. "Come in," Abby called, smiling. It was probably Henry coming to share his latest thoughts about being wealthy. The boy had already spent the money ten times over and he'd only learned about it yesterday. Abby couldn't wait to see what he'd decided on now. She almost laughed at how Jenna perked up. Obviously, she thought it was Henry as well.

When the screen door opened, Abby sobered immediately. The man standing in front of them was definitely not Henry. Or anyone else she knew. This man was older, and dressed in rumpled, baggy clothing. His shoulders stooped, and tufts of gray hair stuck out from under a grubby hat.

Jenna sank back against the sofa cushions, and a prickle of unease crept up Abby's spine. She wasn't worried about being accosted with Caleb here, yet there was something about the man that put her nerves on edge. Despite his bedraggled appearance, his eyes were alert, his gaze sweeping the room and landing briefly on both women, and coming back to Caleb more than once.

The man removed the hat and held it loosely in one hand while bowing to the women.

"Can I help you?" Abby asked, trying to remain friendly in case he was a down-on-his-luck individual who needed help.

"I'm looking for Miss Abigail Horton."

Her mouth dropped open. "I'm Abby. Who are you?"

"I'm a peddler, thought you might be interested in some sewing notions."

"I'm not interested. Thank you for stopping by," Abby said, dismissing him with a brisk nod.

The stranger didn't leave. Instead, he stepped further into the room, and looked her directly in the eyes. "If you don't need needles and thread, I've got other items that might interest you."

Glancing at Caleb for reassurance, Abby placed her sewing back in the basket. "No, but thank you."

She stood when the man stepped back toward the door, as did Caleb, whose wary expression matched her thoughts.

"Well, thank you kindly anyway," the man said. "Before I go, would you mind if I drew some water from your pump out back? My dog, Ol' Blue, has been running loose while I've made the rounds around town, and I'd like to offer him a drink before we head out."

Abby froze. *Old Blue's running loose.* This was the man her father was counting on to save his life? It couldn't be. As she searched for words, he spoke again.

"Miss Abigail?"

Abby gave him one more searching look, and then pushed her concerns aside. "Yes, of course, take all the water you need. Before you go though, I've decided I would like to discuss some sewing notions with you. Why don't you come along to the kitchen with me?"

"Yes'm. Happy to."

A startled expression crossed Caleb's face. He stood and followed them from the room.

Abby turned and waved him back. "I'll only be a moment."

He narrowed his eyes and continued to follow.

"Caleb, please."

He stopped, but Abby could feel him watching as she and the peddler made their way down the hall.

In the kitchen Abby motioned for the man to have a seat at the table. She'd figure out what to tell the others later. Right now she had more important things to tend to. Shutting the door, she whirled to face him. "Who are you?"

The man remained standing, straighter than he had in the parlor. Nothing timid about him now. When he spoke, his voice had changed as well.

"I'm Jim Adair. Didn't you send me a telegram?"

Abby gaped at him, stunned. "Yes," she finally managed to say. "Although you're not exactly who I was expecting."

Laughing, he reached into a pocket of the baggy trousers and pulled out a badge. "I wasn't sure what I was walking into," he admitted as he showed it to her. "I thought I'd check things out first. I don't have any sewing notions, by the way. Nor a dog. However

I do have some questions about why I got a message that could've only come from Bob Horton." He tucked the badge away again. His expression sobered. "Since I know for a fact that he was killed some months ago."

She shook her head, but didn't get a chance to explain before he spoke again.

"No need to tell me differently. Not only is he dead, his death was my fault."

"How was it your fault?" Abby asked.

"Because he was determined to help me with a problem, and I didn't do enough to stop him. I let an inexperienced man walk right into something that got him killed." Regret darkened his eyes. "I should've locked him up." He gave a little shake of his head. "Since that message you sent was one only he and I knew about, I figured I'd better see what you needed."

"We have a lot to talk about," Abby said. "Why don't you sit down, and I'll bring you a cup of coffee."

He nodded, and lowered himself into one of the chairs. She still wasn't convinced this man was her father's friend. She had a few more questions.

She placed the cup in front of him, and then took a seat on the other side of the table. "When did you meet my father?"

He took a sip of the hot brew, and then shook his head. "Can't remember."

Abby tensed, ready to fly through the door and scream for Caleb, until the man added, "I've known him from the time we were both young pups."

She relaxed. "What about that telegram I sent you—what does that sentence mean?"

"Blue was a hound that belonged to a man that lived up the road. The old man kept the dog inside every night—" he gave a soft laugh—"until one night when he didn't. Your father and I were having ourselves a feast in that man's apple orchard when old Blue treed us."

Abby laughed, imagining her father at that age.

"After that, we paid a little more attention to where that dog slept, and the phrase 'Old Blue's running loose tonight' eventually became a code for something's wrong. I'm glad he shared that story with you."

"He didn't tell me what it meant, only that I should send it to you."

"I'm glad that he did," Jim said. "My guilt will follow me forever, but if I can help his family out, I'll feel a little better. Now, what can I do for you?"

"That's what I'm trying to tell you; there's no need to feel guilty. My father's alive. He gave me that code recently."

Jim Adair's gaze sharpened. He sat the coffee cup down. "Perhaps you'd better tell me everything."

He was out of his chair before she got halfway through her story. He began to pace back and forth as she talked. When she got to the part about sending the telegram he stopped her. "Take me to Bob. We'll get this straightened out."

A great weight lifted from Abby. "He's hiding out down by the bluffs on the Brazos River. I'll take you there right now."

"Do we need horses?"

Abby shook her head. "If we had horses, it would be faster, but I always walk out there. It's not far."

He nodded, then looked down at his grubby apparel. "I left my real clothes at the train station. These things are so loose I might lose them if I have to make any sudden moves. And I need my gun belt. I'll grab my things and change and clean up a little. Can I do that here?"

"Yes, of course," Abby said. "I'll be ready to go as soon as you are."

Jim Adair left through the back door to the alley, and Abby sank into the chair, covered her face with her hands and began to cry. Someone was taking over. The marshal would get everything straightened out. *Thank you, God.*

Abby jumped when a hand touched her shoulder. She looked up at Robby's concerned eyes.

"Is everything okay, Abby?"

She hugged him, and he didn't jerk away. "Everything's wonderful," she told him. "That man was Marshal Adair. We're going to the river to bring Daddy home."

Robby didn't seem at all reassured. "If everything's good, why are you crying?"

"Believe me, these are happy tears."

He still seemed skeptical, but after giving her a reassuring pat on the arm, he left, with his canine companion close on his heels. Robby was probably on his way to tell the Wilson kids his Daddy was coming home.

Abby wanted to tell her mother, too, but she might decide to accompany them to the cave. Abby wanted her father to have a chance to clean up first, and surprise his wife. Mama might be angry for a bit, but she'd come around as soon as she realized that they could all live together as a family again.

Abby dried her eyes and went to pump water in a basin for the marshal. *Just a little longer, Mama, and this nightmare will all be over.*

***

Caleb stood near the corner of the house and watched the peddler leave through the back door. He followed. Nearing the alley, the man stopped, stooped down and appeared to be pulling up his sock.

Caleb stepped forward and placed a hand on the man's back. "You and I need to have a little talk," Caleb said. "You're going to tell me exactly what you and Abigail Horton talked about."

When the man straightened, he was pulling something from his pocket. Caleb went for his gun.

The man stilled, and then spoke—in a voice completely different than he'd used in the parlor. "I wouldn't suggest that, son. You're about to bite off a whole lot more than you can chew."

Caleb didn't know the man, but he knew the tone. Authority. This was someone who was used to getting exactly what he asked for. Caleb didn't plan to be an exception.

"Who are you?" he asked as he moved his hand away from his holster.

The man had fished a badge from one of his big, droopy pockets, and now pulled out a .41 Colt Thunderer. "My name's Jim Adair. I'm a U.S. Marshal."

Caleb didn't even try to hide his astonishment. "A marshal? What are you doing here?"

"I had a little business with Abigail Horton."

"What kind of business?"

"I'm not at liberty to say at this time."

All at once, Caleb knew. This was about Bob Horton. Anger swept through him. "Look, if you know where her father is, you need to tell me. I'm the Texas Ranger who was bringing him in when he managed to escape. It's my job, my future, on the line."

The marshal's hard expression didn't waver as he glanced at Caleb's badge. "I'm aware of who you are, but there's more going on here than you know about. I'll answer any questions you have in due time."

Caleb growled. "Abby's known where he was all along, hasn't she? I can't believe this."

"I'm sorry." The soft, hesitant voice came from behind him.

He swung around to face Abby, although he couldn't speak yet.

The marshal glanced back and forth between the two of them. "I'll get my things and be right back," he told Abby.

She nodded. Caleb waited for her to say something, anything, after the man left, yet she simply stood there, twisting a corner of her apron around her finger.

When he spoke it was impossible to keep the hurt from his voice. "I thought we were friends." *And more.* "You were only stringing me along." *Kiss the big, dumb ranger and he won't notice anything else.*

"Oh, Caleb. It wasn't like that, at all. Please don't be upset."

"I have a right to be angry." He shook his head. "You had the nerve to act so offended when you found out I was supposed to be keeping an eye on you."

She ducked her head. "Yes, I did, didn't I? I'm sorry for that, too. I guess we were both doing what we had to do. I wasn't deliberately trying to cause you trouble; I was trying to help my father. When I explain, I think you'll see that I—"

Caleb turned away, heading down the alley. "I'm not interested in your explanations. Share it with the marshal."

He had to cool down before he tried to explain any of this to Eli or Captain Parnell. Or before he got Marshal Adair and Abby to answer some questions. *And he would get some answers from that girl.*

He was still fuming when he spotted Henry Barnett several blocks away, trying to load a packed burlap bag onto the back of a mule. The ornery critter wasn't having any of it. Every time Henry would approach with the bag, the mule would sidestep.

It was almost comical, and ordinarily would have been enough to make Caleb laugh. But in his current frame of mind he couldn't. He was about to step forward and offer to hold on to the mule, when Henry glanced over his shoulder in the opposite direction. It was behavior that Caleb had seen before. Henry was nervous. Worried about being seen. Why?

Anticipating that Henry would glance in his direction as well, Caleb stepped behind the corner of a building just in time.

The animal brayed again, and Henry let his frustration ring out loud and clear. "I don't intend to haul all this stuff out to the river on my own. Even if it takes all day, you're the one who's toting it. If you don't behave, I'm selling you to…"

His voice lowered and Caleb missed the end of the threat, but he was more intrigued by the first part anyway. *The river?*

On a hunch, Caleb followed as Henry began leading the mule

toward the edge of town. The animal was making so much noise that it was no problem to creep along for a ways undetected.

It didn't take long for him to figure out exactly where Henry was headed.

Chapter Twenty-Six

HALF-RUNNING, ABBY WAS several feet ahead of Marshall Adair as they raced up the trail and neared the cave. She glanced up and stumbled to a stop.

In a scene eerily reminiscent of their first meeting, Caleb Calhoun stood beside her father. He hadn't snapped the handcuffs on yet, but he looked every bit as stern and forbidding as he had that first night.

Her stomach lurched. "Caleb, no!"

Henry stood nearby, shoulders drooping.

Abby darted toward Caleb, but the marshal grabbed her arm. "Wait. Let me handle this."

"Nothing to handle," Caleb said. "I've got a prisoner to transport."

"There's something you don't understand," Jim Adair said.

"There's a lot I don't understand," Caleb snapped. "All I know is that I've got a captain, a banker and a railroad executive breathing down my neck. And I'm taking this man to Austin." He stopped to glare at Henry. "I may arrest him, too, for harboring a fugitive."

Henry paled, though his only reaction was a quick, telling glance at Abby.

Bob Horton had taken one look at Jim Adair, and his shoulders relaxed. "You did it, Abby."

Smiling, Bob then addressed the marshal, "Hello, Jim. Thanks for coming. I figured maybe you could send somebody. I didn't know you'd travel all this way."

Ignoring Caleb Calhoun, Jim Adair stepped forward and grasped Bob's hand, shaking it and thumping him on the back with his other hand. "I was out of town and didn't get your message right away. And even then, I didn't understand it. I thought you were a goner, old friend."

Despite Caleb's protests to the contrary, he was clearly interested in what was going on. Abby noticed that he kept one hand on her father's arm, yet he didn't try to restrain him with the cuffs. He glanced back and forth between Bob Horton and Jim Adair as they spoke.

"I've made a big mess of things," Bob admitted.

"We'll get it all straightened out," the marshal promised.

As they talked, Abby shifted around the little circle, pleading with Caleb, and then watching and listening as Marshal Adair tried to explain the situation. Every few seconds her father burst in with a bit of the story, as did Henry.

It was a confusing situation for Abby, and she knew everything that had transpired. She couldn't imagine what was going through Caleb's mind. But surely he could see that her father shouldn't be arrested.

Abby was directly in front of the mouth of the cave when someone grabbed her. She was startled more than scared...until she felt the knife at her throat.

She turned her head as far as she could, and looked into the frightened eyes of the last member of the Latham gang—Nash. She hadn't even considered what would become of him.

At her cry of alarm, all eyes turned in her direction.

"No!"

Abby wasn't sure which man shouted it, but it was a guttural sound.

"Is this the other member of the gang?" Jim asked.

Her father nodded, and the fear in his eyes brought tears to her own. "Yes, that's Nash Latham," he said.

Henry's fists were clenched, but he looked as if he might faint before he could use them.

At first glance, Jim Adair and Caleb, both with guns drawn, were more in control of their emotions. Although there was a muscle jerking in Caleb's jaw.

"Let her go, or I will shoot you where you stand," Caleb said through clenched teeth.

Nash tightened his grip and Abby gasped. "You won't," Nash said, "because you could miss me and hit her."

"I don't miss." There was no bravado in Caleb's comment, only quiet assurance. "I may not be the fastest gun around, but I'm willing to bet I'm the most accurate. If you harm her, you'll never see another sunrise."

Nash's breath was coming in choppy little spasms and his hands were shaking. The knife shifted against Abby's throat and her quivering knees nearly buckled.

"I don't care," Nash said. "Better to die here and now than to go to jail. My old man spent years in the pen. He couldn't stand being cooped up. Made him cr...crazy. I've got the same problem. I've barely been able to stand this cave, but at least I could come and go."

Caleb's gaze sharpened. "You were at the saloon during the brawl."

Nash ignored the comment, but increased the pressure on Abby's throat. "I'm not going to be locked up. Ever."

Her father stepped forward, hands out, pleading with the outlaw. "Nash, I know you're not a bad person at heart. If it wasn't for you, I'd be dead."

"That's true, I tried to take care of everything," Nash agreed, "but I'm not smart. I never have been. The only reason the gang let me tag along was because Webb was my brother. I was so sad when Webb died."

Nash was swallowing convulsively now, and despite her own plight, compassion filled Abby. "He always told me what to do," Nash said. "When he was gone, the others didn't even care what happened to me or you. They were ready to toss you out and let the animals have you."

"I know," her father said. "I wasn't unconscious all the time."

"I couldn't leave you like that. I was tired of death. I don't want to hurt your daughter now. But I'm not going to jail."

"No matter what anyone else said, you are smart, Nash." Bob Horton's tone was soothing. "Not only did you keep me alive, you managed to rescue me when I was captured by the law. That was real smart of you to send the telegram and use the badge to get me out of there. You could've run while you had the chance. Why didn't you?"

"I didn't send a telegram, and I only took you out of there because I needed you," the young man said, his voice breaking. "I really didn't know what else to do. I watched Webb all those years, seeing how he did things. He could sneak in and out of a town, even a room, and nobody would even notice. Unless he wanted them to. I watched, and no one paid me any mind. I learned a lot. I learned how to survive on my own...but I didn't want to."

Nash had been inching back as they talked, upwards and away from the others. Taking her with him. Abby wasn't the only one who noticed. Every man tracked each step they took. Nash had to be getting close to the top of the bluff. Should she kick him? And take her chances that he'd be so startled that he'd drop the knife? Or would he jerk back and slice her throat? *Please, God, show me what to do.*

Before she could make any move, the sound of horses' hooves thundered toward them. Two riders dismounted on the trail below and came charging forward—Eli Calhoun and that odious railroad executive, Mr. Becker.

Eli assessed the situation quickly and drew his gun.

"How did *you* know Bob was here?" Caleb asked, clearly astonished.

"I didn't," Eli told him. "Robby came to the jail and said he was worried about Abby. Said she was crying and heading to the river with a stranger named Marshall. He told me where to look for her. The boy tried to find you and Henry first. Glad he came to me. I told him to go on home and I'd see what was going on." He paused for a moment. "So what is going on?"

As a new round of explanations began Abby was as distracted by the new arrivals as the others were, and grateful to her brother— obviously nothing got past Robby. Then she noticed that Nash had relaxed his grip on her. He didn't drop his arm, yet there was a subtle change in his stance, even his breathing. Instead of being more frightened by the additional gun aimed his way, he actually seemed calmer.

"Mr. Becker, I'm so glad to see you," Nash blurted. "Please, get me outta here."

The railroad executive paled, and then cast a nervous glance around at the others. "I don't know what you're talking about, young man."

"B...but Webb always said you'd take care of everything if we got in trouble," Nash stuttered.

"I've never seen this man in my life," Becker said. "Now, don't just stand there, somebody shoot him!"

It took Abby a moment to put all the pieces together—and probably Henry, too, based on his expression—but in the blink of an eye Marshal Adair had jerked Becker's hands behind him, and Eli stuck a gun under the man's chin.

Everyone's attention shifted to Becker, even Nash and Abby's, as the man cursed and threatened everyone within hearing distance.

"Well, I guess we know who was tipping the gang off," Marshal Adair said. "Collecting insurance and part of the stolen loot, too, huh?"

"You idiot," Becker spat at Nash. "I had everything under control. I sent a telegram arranging for Bob Horton to spend the night in Moccasin Rock. I'd arranged for him to disappear later...for good. But you had to go and get him before I could." Becker then turned his attention to Jim Adair and began trying to bribe his way out of trouble.

During that distraction, Caleb holstered his gun and moved in closer to Abby and Nash. He addressed the young man now in a low, almost casual tone. Caleb seemed so calm that he calmed Abby.

"I need you to understand something," Caleb told Nash, "and this is man-to-man. I'm not letting you leave here with the woman I love."

Love? While Abby was still reeling from that declaration, Caleb spoke again. His tone still quiet, almost conversational. "I don't think you want to hurt her, but if you do, even by accident, I will follow you, dog your footsteps for the rest of your days. You'll never close your eyes again without seeing my face. Do you understand what I'm telling you?"

Nash swallowed hard, took one more step up and back...and lost his balance. In a heart-stopping moment, Abby realized they were now sliding down the other side of the bluff—and still he clung to her. She fought to free herself, as well as stop the downward momentum. She was vaguely aware of the sting of rocks against her palms as she slid, and her knees slamming into the ground, then a dizzying downward spiral.

Suddenly she was free—she wasn't sure if he'd let her go, or if she'd wrenched loose. She saw the glint of the knife's blade as it bounced along beside her. If only she could stop sliding, she could start clawing and climbing her way back up. But she couldn't stop.

She heard voices shouting out her name, and Nash's terrified scream. *Or was it her own?* Then there was nothing but sky as she hurtled toward the river. She drew in a deep breath and hit the water with such force that it stunned her. By the time she could move again, her lungs felt as if they were bursting. She kicked, trying to push herself up, but one foot was trapped in her petticoat, and the water sucked at her clothes, pulling her further under.

Someone grabbed her, yanking her toward the surface. Nash! She struggled with all her might, until the need for air overrode her fear. She let herself be dragged upward. When she broke the surface, Abby opened her mouth, gulping for air, and at the same time began twisting and pulling away from the arm that clutched at her.

"I got you, Abby. Everything's okay."

"Caleb!"

"Yes, d…darlin'." He too was gasping for air, holding her with one arm and trying to work his way toward the bank with the other. She let herself go limp, although her heart still pounded as he pulled her with him. After what seemed an eternity, her legs finally scraped against the riverbed. They stumbled, separated and righted themselves. As soon as they were both on their feet, he pulled her into his arms again.

Abby clung to him. "Thank you, Caleb."

She could hear others racing toward them around the base of the bluff. They only had a moment alone, but he made the most of it.

"I've never been more scared in my life," he said, his voice ragged. He kissed her once. Hard and fast. A few moments later they were joined by Eli, Henry and her father. Caleb stepped away from her. Everyone was talking at once. She could see Jim Adair up on the bluff, and Garrison Becker with his arms behind his back. Thankfully, he hadn't managed to escape in all the chaos.

"Did any of y'all see what happened to the outlaw?" Caleb asked, wiping water from his eyes.

"He went in near the same spot Abby did, but he never resurfaced," Eli said. "We got down here as fast as we could." He looked Caleb over. "I guess we coulda taken the shortcut like you did. Although I might've taken off my gun belt first."

Caleb glanced down at the water dripping from his gun and

holster, and shrugged. "I didn't stop to think about it," he admitted. "However, I hope that's my last drenching in the Brazos."

It dawned on Abby that Caleb hadn't taken the trail around the base of the bluff, or tried to navigate the steep side from which she'd tumbled. He had jumped from the top. She stepped closer and squeezed his hand. He gently returned the pressure before she stepped away.

Abby shoved strands of wet hair away from her face. Now that it was all over, her teeth were chattering and she was shaking. Was it from experiencing the knife at her throat, or the fall, or the water… or Caleb's declaration of love? She wasn't sure.

Then doubt hit her. *Had he meant it?* Or was it only a means of negotiating with Nash?

Before she could ponder that further, Eli pointed toward the river where Nash's hat floated downstream.

"After I get Becker to the jail, I'll come back here and search for him," Eli said.

Caleb nodded. "I'll stick around and start looking now."

"I'll bring you back some dry duds, a dry gun and your horse," Eli said. Then he shook his head. "How did you manage to survive before you met me?"

Abby smiled at Caleb's disgruntled expression. Then she sneezed.

"Come on," her father said, "let's get you home." Before they left, he turned to Caleb. "Hopefully, I won't be seeing much of you from now on, so let me thank you now for saving my daughter's life. Nothing personal, I have no complaints about the way you treated me, but I'm ready for my life to get back to normal."

"You're welcome, Sir," was all Caleb said.

As she followed the others to the trail, Abby turned for one last look at the ranger. *Did you mean what you said?*

Chapter Twenty-Seven

THERE WERE SO many people milling in and out of the Horton Boarding House that Caleb was beginning to think he'd never get a moment alone with Abby.

Once word spread that Bob Horton had returned again, Moccasin Rock folk began showing up in a steady stream to hear his story.

Caleb suspected Bob had already tired of talking about his adventure, yet the man kept welcoming his friends and neighbors, and patiently answering their questions. Mrs. Dunlop even dropped by, bringing baked goods, although she didn't stay long.

Finding the kitchen nearly empty for the moment, Caleb leaned in close to Abby as she sliced a pound cake.

"I can't believe you went to Henry for help, and not me," he whispered.

Abby turned those big blue eyes up to him. "Oh, Caleb. What would you have been able to do? You couldn't have helped me."

Probably true, but still it hurt.

"So what happens now?" Abby asked as she spread the cake slices out on a platter. She didn't look at him this time. Was she referring to the two of them or to the situation with her father? Caleb chose to answer the easier of the two.

"I'm taking Garrison Becker to Austin. It might take a while to sort everything out. There'll be an investigation and a trial. One thing is clear though—your father is free. He's sharing what information he has, and Jim Adair is vouching for him."

Her shoulders relaxed. "That's wonderful. Did you see any sign of Nash?"

Caleb shook his head. "No, there's a possibility that he never made it out of the river. If that's the case, his body will wash up somewhere eventually." He paused a moment before his next remark. "I really hate what happened. I know he was confused. I wish it would've turned out better."

Abby only nodded, but the haunted look that crossed her face spoke of her regrets as well.

Caleb closed his eyes against a sudden vision of Abby hurtling toward the river. "I'm grateful that it didn't turn out worse," he said.

She shivered. "Thank you, again."

"I'm so glad I was there."

"Me, too."

"We're pulling out first thing in the morning," Caleb added, "and I'm spending the night at the jail to watch over Becker."

She stared at him then, not asking any questions, but her expression was troubled. Before he could say anything to reassure her, Miss Culpepper came in.

The older woman beamed at Abby. "Your father is such an interesting man."

"Yes, he is, Miss…" Abby paused at the same moment that Caleb noticed the mixture of hope and hurt that flashed across the older woman's face. *How strange this must be for them.*

Abby started over. "Yes, he is, Grandmother."

The two women exchanged a smile, and then began chatting about Bob Horton's return. Even though Caleb was truly glad to see their relationship evolving, he was anxious for time alone with

Abby. There was so much he wanted to tell her, and he didn't know how to say most of it.

When several other people wandered into the kitchen, Caleb knew it would all have to wait. He grabbed Abby's arm and tugged her toward the door. "I'll be back as soon as I can," he whispered.

"I'll be here," Abby said. She then squeezed his hand and gave him a tremulous smile before turning to the guests.

With one last lingering look at her, Caleb headed to the jail. He'd hated to be so vague about his return, but in addition to the work involving Becker, he also planned to spend some time with his Aunt Victoria. He had to find out what she knew about his father.

*****

Aunt Victoria sat in front of the tea service in her suite at the Trinity Hotel in Austin, her back rigid, her shoulders straight.

She'd changed since the last time Caleb had seen her. Her hair was whiter, the lines around her mouth and eyes were more pronounced, and there was a slight tremor in her hands. Yet she was still as formidable as ever.

Caleb had just asked her to tell him everything she knew about his father, and her lips had flattened into a thin line.

"I'll admit I never cared for Amos Calhoun," she finally said. "I thought your mother could have done better."

Caleb opened his mouth, ready as always to defend his father.

She stopped him with a wave of her hand. "I understand. That's not the issue at the moment."

"No, it's not. Please, tell me what you know about my father's past."

She leveled a determined green-eyed gaze at him. "What's this all about?"

Caleb had inherited that same eye color—and that same determination—from this side of the family. He could be every bit as stubborn as she was. And yet he didn't want to sit here all day arguing. Might as well tell her.

Leaning back in his chair, he explained. "Recently, I had occasion to stop in a small town called Moccasin Rock," he said, "and was stunned to discover that I have two brothers living there."

Instead of being intrigued, Aunt Victoria seemed annoyed. "Impossible," she snapped as she picked up her tea cup.

"No, I assure you it is possible. Eli, the older of the two, looks more like Daddy than Daddy did."

Now he had her attention. "What did you say his name was?"

"Elijah. The other one is named Nathaniel."

The trembling of her hand worsened. She sat her cup down. "So they really are alive," she whispered.

Caleb stared at her, stunned. "You knew about them?"

"Yes, your father spoke of them often."

He shook his head. "To everyone except me," he said.

"And now you feel betrayed."

It was a statement, not a question, yet Caleb answered anyway. "Of course, I do."

Standing, he began to pace, anger building with each step. "And I need some answers. Why did he leave his wife and sons and start a whole other life, and another family, in Colorado?"

"Please be still," Victoria said primly, gesturing toward a chair. "You remind me of a caged animal."

Caleb stopped pacing and perched on the chair's edge—whatever it took to keep her talking.

She picked up her cup again and took a sip of tea before continuing. "I really don't know much, only that long before he met your mother, or even moved to Colorado, your father was a farmer here in Texas. At one point, he and his family were having a particularly difficult time making ends meet and he decided to collect on a debt owed him by someone living in another state."

"A debt? What kind of debt? From whom?"

She shook her head. "He never provided any details, at least not to me. Your mother may have known."

"Mama never said a word to me if she did. Then again, she never talked to me about any of this."

"She may have decided it was your father's story to tell," Victoria said. "Unfortunately, that story was a tragic one. Amos was gone from his home for a good long while—I'm not sure if he was successful in collecting the debt or not—and returned to Texas only to discover that his wife and sons had died in a fire."

What? "His wife died," Caleb said. "His sons were very much alive. They hoped for years that he'd return. What made him think they were dead?"

"According to your father, a neighbor told him that he'd seen smoke, and hurried over to see if he could help. When he arrived the place was fully engulfed in flames. Even though he tried to help, Amos Calhoun's whole family had been trapped inside. They'd all perished."

"That's not what happened," Caleb said. "Eli and Nathaniel weren't even in the house. Why would the man say something like that?"

"Maybe the neighbor thought they were dead. Whatever the reason, that's what your father was told. He blamed himself; he was a broken man. Then, later, after he'd remarried and after you were born, he chanced to happen upon an old acquaintance in Denver. The man mentioned something about running across one of Amos's sons in San Angelo. Although your father was devastated by the reminder of what he'd lost, he calmly assured the man that he was mistaken."

"But it wasn't a mistake," Caleb said softly.

"Apparently not. Somehow the man finally told him enough to persuade him that he really had seen one of the Calhoun boys." She sipped her tea, expression grim. "That began a desperate search that would last the rest of Amos Calhoun's life."

Caleb closed his eyes for a moment. *How helpless his father must've felt.*

Victoria cleared her throat. "I must say, although I didn't care for your father, I believe he truly cared for his family. He searched diligently for them. And for your mother's sake, I assisted in any way I could."

He looked at her. "You financed the search?"

"No, your mother had plenty of money from your grandmother. All I did was put your father in touch with the right people. Unfortunately, it was all for naught. As far as I know, Amos Calhoun never had a clue where his sons ended up. To be honest, I never believed the rumor. I thought they were dead."

"Why didn't he ever tell me?" Caleb said, almost to himself.

"He wanted to," Victoria said. "But he kept holding out, hoping that someday he'd be able to tell you exactly where they were. And, to put it bluntly, he was ashamed. He felt guilty for not knowing, instinctively, that his children were alive. And also for leaving them to start with. Sending you off to military school was one of the most difficult decisions he ever made, or so he said. Although your mother and I were able to convince him it was the right thing to do, he lived for those times you were home."

Caleb hung his head. As much as he'd hated it, and balked at the time, he knew now that his mother and aunt had made the right decision. *But what a sacrifice his father had made.*

"Eventually the search for his older sons became an obsession," Victoria said. "He was still searching for them right up until he became incoherent."

"I think maybe he tried to tell me about them at the end," Caleb said, "although I didn't have a clue what he was talking about."

They sat in silence for several moments.

"Tell me about your brothers," she said.

Caleb shared what he knew, which wasn't much.

Victoria nodded with approval when he mentioned that one was a physician, and winced a little at learning the other was a lawman.

Eventually, as he'd known she would, she worked the conversation around to him and his chosen profession.

"Have you given any more thought to settling down, doing something more productive with your life?"

He leaned back in the chair. "Nope, I'm pretty happy where I am."

"Caleb—"

He cut her off. "I'm not trying to be rude Aunt Victoria, but you're wasting your breath. Although while I'm here, I will tell you that I do have plans for the money."

Preacher's words had come back to him time and again recently. *I figured He wanted me to do some stepping. Stepping in and stepping up, helping people.* Even though Caleb couldn't help in the same way Preacher had, he planned to do what he could.

"What sort of investment did you have in mind?" Victoria asked.

"I have no intention of investing it. I plan to give it away."

She let out a gasp and pressed a hand to her chest. "Caleb, you sound as if you're ready to dash out into the street and start handing out stacks of cash to the first strangers you stumble across. At least let me set up some sort of charitable fund."

He could give her that much. "Fine. I want the funds dispensed through churches."

She stared at him, brows raised. "Churches?"

"Yes."

She sank back against the sofa, allowing herself to slump for the first time in his memory. "You've changed, Caleb."

He nodded briskly. "More than you can imagine. And I'll tell you all about it, soon. For now, I've got something I need to tend to back in Moccasin Rock first."

He was astonished to see her eyes fill with tears.

"Caleb, although you have been fortunate enough to find additional family members to enrich your life, please remember that *you* are all I have left."

Caleb winced as guilt washed over him.

"Am I really all that dreadful?" she asked softly.

He shook his head. "No. I'm sorry, Aunt Victoria. I promise to come see you soon. And I do have one piece of news that might cheer you. I'm planning to be married."

"To...Miss Nolan?" She actually looked pained, and he choked back a laugh. His aunt had never cared for Jenna, and had gone out of her way to avoid the unruly girl.

He shook his head. "No, her name is Abigail."

Victoria's eyebrows lifted. "Who are her people?"

Should he tell her he'd met Abby while handcuffed to her father? No, perhaps he'd pushed her far enough for one day.

"You've never heard of them," he said. "But they're good folks."

She started in with a barrage of questions. He stopped her in mid-sentence. "That's all I can say for now. But, if you promise to be nice, I'll bring Abby to meet you."

She gave him a smile. "I'd like that."

Caleb hugged her then, something he hadn't done in years, and told her he loved her, which he'd never done before. He was surprised to realize he meant it.

Chapter Twenty-Eight

BACK IN MOCCASIN Rock, Caleb dropped by the boarding house first, anxious to see Abby. He found only Mr. and Mrs. Horton—both busy in the kitchen. They were laughing together when he walked in and sobered immediately when they spotted him.

Despite her worried expression, Irene Horton greeted him warmly, while her husband tensed. "Is something wrong?" Bob asked with a frown.

"Nope, everything's fine," Caleb assured him. "I was wondering if you could rent me a room again."

"Why, of course," Irene said. "Your old room is still available."

Bob Horton's shoulders relaxed. "I forgot that you have family here," he said.

Caleb nodded. He wanted to talk to Bob about his daughter, but he'd better make sure Abby was interested in his offer of marriage first. "I guess I'll take my things on upstairs. Is Abby up there?"

Irene's face lit up at the question, while Bob merely looked confused. "No, she had some errands to run. Why?"

"I had something I wanted to ask her."

As Caleb left, he heard Irene Horton whispering to her husband. Hopefully the man would be accepting of the idea that Caleb wanted to become a part of his family.

After leaving his suitcase in the room, Caleb headed out to let his brothers know what he'd learned while in Austin. It wasn't much, but hopefully it would bring them some peace.

Eli was sitting at his desk sorting through some wanted posters when Caleb pushed open the jail house door. "Where's Nathaniel?" he asked.

"Well, hello to you, too," Eli said.

Caleb grinned. "Sorry, it's just that I wanted to tell y'all what Aunt Victoria said."

Eli tossed the posters aside. "Why didn't you say so? I think Nathaniel's at his office."

Nathaniel was at his office, and wasn't busy, so Caleb filled them in on the little he'd learned.

They both stared at him when he'd finished speaking, Nathaniel sitting at his desk, and Eli leaning against the doorway. Neither said a word. Caleb was beginning to wonder if they'd heard him at all when Eli finally spoke. "He never intended to leave us for good?"

Caleb shook his head. "No."

"And he tried to find us."

"Yes, according to Aunt Victoria, he searched for years. Even when it became physically impossible, he kept on hiring detectives. I guess there are things we'll never know—like who told him y'all were dead to start with—but I feel certain that Amos Calhoun loved his sons. All three of us. Just out of curiosity," he added, "did you ever live in San Angelo?"

Nathaniel turned to stare out the window without comment. Eli provided a husky, "Yes," but no further details. They both suddenly seemed uneasy. And unwilling to talk. At least to him.

Caleb hoped someday they'd confide in him, in the meantime, he'd leave them be.

"If you gentlemen will excuse me, I'm off to the boarding house to see my favorite lady. I have something important to ask her."

Eli smiled. "Glad to hear it."

"If you're talking about Abigail Horton, she's not there," Nathaniel said.

"How do you know?"

Nathaniel pointed out the window. "Because I saw her headed down the street a few minutes ago."

"Oh. Thanks," Caleb pulled open the door.

He was stopped by a question from Eli. "Where's your gun?"

"I left it with Eagan Smith when I went to Austin. Bliss told me Eagan doubled as a gunsmith around here."

Eli nodded. "The man knows horses and guns."

"After the soaking the Remington took in the Brazos, I wanted to make sure it was in good working order," Caleb said. "The grip didn't feel quite right."

"You've been walking around unarmed?" There was concern and disapproval in Eli's voice.

"No, big brother, I took Preacher's old dragoon with me. I'm tired of hauling that thing around. I left it at the boarding house. After I find Abby, I'll pick my gun up from Eagan."

Whistling softly as he shut the door, Caleb headed in the direction Nathaniel had pointed. He was on the opposite side of the street when he spotted Abby leaving Martin's Mercantile. He called to her, and she turned and waved—a huge smile spreading across her face as he started toward her.

Caleb was halfway across the street when he heard someone shout at him. A prickle of unease lifted the hairs on the back of his neck. Time seemed to slow as he turned in the direction of the voice.

A young man stood in the middle of the street with a gun in his hand. *Nash Latham.*

"I can't stand it," Nash cried out, his voice and his gun hand shaking. "Knowing that you're looking for me, hunting me down, is making me crazy. This is gonna end right here, right now, one way or the other."

From the corner of his eye, Caleb saw Abby moving toward him. He kept his attention on the gun as he shouted at her. "Stay back, Abby." *Please, God, make her listen to me.*

She halted, and Caleb drew in a steadying breath. "There's no reason to do this," he called out to Nash. "I'm not even armed. We can talk this through."

Nash's only response was to steady the gun with his other hand.

Despite the icy pin pricks of fear jabbing at him, sweat popped up on Caleb's brow. Either Nash was too far gone to reason with, or the young outlaw was more like his brother, Webb, than he'd realized.

Abby was screaming and moving again, and Caleb caught a glimpse of Eli barreling down the boardwalk. Nash glanced in their direction. Caleb's heart stopped for a moment. *Stay back*, he silently implored them.

In desperation he stepped toward Nash, attempting to divert his attention. "I'm the one you're after," he shouted. "I'll say the same thing I said last time. You hurt anyone I love and I'll hunt you down."

The ploy worked. Nash's gaze swung back to Caleb as he pulled the hammer back.

Caleb sensed, more than heard, the angry and panic-stricken reaction of Abby and Eli, and was only vaguely aware of the bedlam breaking out around him as bystanders dove for cover. His focus had narrowed to the end of Nash's gun.

As Caleb's own heartbeat pounded in his ears, he raised his hands.

Just as gunfire erupted, someone shoved Caleb, hard. He tumbled sideways and got up spitting dirt. People were screaming and running in every direction.

Who had pushed him? Caleb looked to the middle of the street and saw Henry Barnett laying face up, blood covering the front of his shirt. The bullet that was meant for him had found another target. A glance in the other direction revealed Eli, gun in hand, and Nash Latham on the ground.

Caleb rushed toward Henry at the same moment Abby did, both kicking up dirt as they ran. Pushing past curious bystanders now filling the street, they dropped to their knees by the wounded man's side.

Henry's eyes flickered open when Abby said his name, but it was Caleb he addressed.

"You kept me from dying in the river, and I've re…returned the favor," he said, his voice a raspy whisper. "We're even now."

"Even?" Caleb was as perplexed as he was furious. "That's the most idiotic thing I've ever heard. Was your pride important enough to be killed over?"

Henry groaned. "To be honest, I didn't mean to actually get shot. I was only trying to push you out of the way."

"But why?"

"I told you I didn't want to see you hurt. I also did it for Abby— figured she'd be miserable without you."

Before Caleb could reply, Nathaniel rushed up. Abby placed her hand on Henry's face as Nathaniel knelt down and ripped the wounded man's shirt open.

Abby's voice shook as she brushed Henry's hair back from his brow. "Don't you dare die on me." She paused for a moment, biting her bottom lip, before whispering, "What would I do without you?"

Henry reached for her hand, then his eyes rolled back as he lost consciousness.

"Help me get him to my office," Nathaniel said to Caleb. "I need to remove that bullet."

Caleb prayed as they lifted Henry and carried him inside. *Please, God, don't let him die.* As Nathaniel began working on Henry, Caleb rushed back outside and into the street, ready to attack Nash with his bare hands if he was still alive. He wasn't.

Caleb's steps faltered when he saw Eli standing over the young outlaw's body. "I'm sorry I didn't get him before he got to Henry," Eli said as Caleb neared.

There was a depth of sorrow and weariness in his brother's eyes that Caleb had not seen before.

"I'm grateful that you stopped him," Caleb said, "but I'm sorry that it was necessary. All of this is my fault."

Eli ran a hand over his eyes. "No, it's not. He made his choices. And he wasn't the first I shot, although I sure wouldn't mind if he was the last." He turned away and headed toward the undertaker's.

A crowd had gathered outside Nathaniel's office, and Caleb herded all the concerned bystanders back across the street. When two older people implored him to let them through, he discovered they were Henry's parents. Caleb apologized and escorted them into the waiting area.

Abby was sitting inside wringing her hands. She looked up at him, tears on her face, and then jumped to her feet to embrace the elderly couple. Within minutes they were all on their knees praying. Caleb left to go help Eli, offering up his own prayers every step of the way.

He stopped when he remembered Abby's earlier statement. She'd said to Henry, *"What would I do without you?"* Those words went straight to Caleb's heart now and echoed in his mind. *Abby loved Henry.* And Henry had been willing to take a bullet if it would make Abby's life better. Why hadn't he seen it sooner? *They belong together.*

The surge of emotion was nearly unbearable, but he drew in a deep breath and pushed everything from his mind. Henry's survival was all that mattered right now.

After Nash's body was in the undertaker's office, Caleb and Eli washed up and started toward Nathaniel's.

For once, Caleb was glad that Eli wasn't much on conversation.

There was no way he could communicate the depth of his heartache right now. He didn't even know how to explain it to himself, let alone someone else.

After Nathaniel operated on Henry, he tried to convince everyone, even the young man's parents to go on home.

"Your son won't know you're here," Nathaniel told them, "so you might as well get some rest."

Although they resisted, the couple looked as if they were about to drop in their tracks. Abby was finally able to convince them to go. "Why don't I go home with you," she said, "and keep you company tonight? I'm sure that Dr. Nathaniel will send word out to us if we're needed."

"I will," Nathaniel agreed. "You leaving now is in Henry's best interest in the long run. He's going to need you to be well-rested."

Caleb and Abby exchanged one quick look before she was gone, but there was no time for words. In a way Caleb was relieved. He didn't know what to say anyway.

"Do you mind if I stay here tonight?" Caleb asked after everyone else was gone. "In case you, or Henry, need me."

"Of course you can stay," Nathaniel said. "I've got everything under control right now. Why don't you go on back to the bedroom and get some rest. I'll let you know if we need anything."

"I appreciate it."

But Caleb couldn't sleep. After several hours of tossing and turning, he rummaged through the items on Nathaniel's bureau until he found a piece of paper and a pencil. He sat down to write the hardest words he'd ever written. He returned to the examination room where his brother was bent over the patient.

"What's the verdict?" Caleb asked.

Nathaniel straightened. "He'll make it. I'll have to watch for signs of infection, but it's looking good so far. I've got him sedated right now. You should be able to thank him sometime tomorrow."

"Do me a favor?"

"Of course."

"Will you thank him for me?"

Nathaniel hesitated. "Sure. But why?"

"Now that I know he's going to be all right, I'm headed back to Austin for a while." Caleb placed the note he'd written on Nathaniel's desk. "Will you see that Abby gets that?"

Nathaniel frowned. "Sure. When will you return?"

Caleb swallowed, hard. "I don't know." He did. *When it doesn't hurt to see Abby with Henry Barnett.*

Neither spoke again until Eli came in a few minutes later. Nathaniel looked up from tending Henry long enough to catch Eli's attention.

"Our baby brother is leaving."

Caleb grinned. He'd sure miss these men. And everyone else in Moccasin Rock, for that matter.

"Why?" Eli asked.

Caleb shrugged.

"You taking Abby Horton with you?"

"No."

Eli's brow rose. "I thought you were going to ask her to marry you?"

Caleb struggled for a casual reply. "Things change."

"I think you're making a mistake running off," Eli said.

"It won't be the first mistake I've made," Caleb confessed. Both brothers were staring at him now. He leveled with them. "Look, Abby deserves happiness. I realized earlier that she shares a life-long, likely unbreakable, bond with Henry." He jerked a thumb in the wounded man's direction. "As much as I love her, she loves him."

Eli's brows drew together. "I believe you're mistaken on that. I think she's been pretty sweet on you since you got here."

"I thought so, too," Caleb admitted. "I suppose it was simple infatuation. I was something new and different."

"I agree with Eli," Nathaniel said. "Even if we're wrong, you could stay here and try to change her mind."

Caleb shook his head. "No. I won't stand in the way of her happiness. I'm not going to fight for a future that's not mine. And as much as it pains me to say this, I think she'll be better off with him."

Eli continued to scowl at him. "Do what you gotta do, I guess. Don't stay away forever, though. We spent a lot of years waiting for another Calhoun to show up. We didn't get the one we intended, but you'll do."

Caleb gave them the best version of a carefree smile he could muster, said his goodbyes and headed to the boarding house. He was relieved when the doorknob turned easily. Someone had left it unlocked for him. Trying not to wake anyone, he crept upstairs for the suitcase he hadn't unpacked.

He was in and out in minutes. Standing at the edge of the yard, Caleb glanced over his shoulder at the old house. A lot had happened since the night he'd first set foot in the place. And a lot had changed. Mostly him.

Chapter Twenty-Nine

ABBY EASED OPEN the door to the doctor's office, hoping not to wake the patient. She paused at the sight of Nathaniel, asleep, head bent over his desk.

She'd caught a ride into town with one of the Barnett's farm hands, and had made arrangements with another of the hands to bring the couple in to see their son as soon as they were up and around. She hadn't wanted to wake them early, but she couldn't wait any longer to check on Henry.

She approached him now, her heart heavy with dread. *Please, Lord, let him be okay.*

Henry stirred and opened his eyes as she neared. She took his hand in hers. "How are you feeling?"

He grinned at her and then groaned. "Like somebody shot me."

She swallowed a sob. "Henry, you sweet, crazy man. I don't understand why you did what you did, but I'll be grateful for the rest of my life."

"I saw the sheriff rushing in," Henry said, closing his eyes, "and I was afraid it was too late. Since you seem to be pretty partial to the man that was about to be gunned down, I figured I'd better do something."

Abby clung to his hand, too touched to speak for a moment.

"So tell me what I can do for you," she said after she regained her composure.

"Can you tell Jenna I want to see her?"

Abby smiled. "I've noticed you've become a little preoccupied with that particular lady."

Although still paler than normal, Henry's face took on a little color as he glanced up at her. "It started out with her wanting to help me," he confessed, "by making you jealous. Then somewhere along the way, I actually went and fell for the girl."

She squeezed his hand. "I'm so happy for you, Henry."

Neither had noticed Nathaniel awaken until he joined them.

"If I overheard you correctly," Nathaniel said, "and interpreted it correctly, there's something between you and Miss Nolan?"

"Yep," Henry said. "And if you tell me I'm going to live, I'm about to ask that girl to be my wife."

"You'll live."

Henry smiled. "Good. Thank you, Doc."

"That explains why I had to insist that Miss Nolan leave here a few hours ago and get some sleep," Nathaniel said.

"Jenna was here?" Henry's eyelids were drooping, and his voice heavy, but Abby could tell he was pleased.

Nathaniel nodded. "She tapped on the door, asking about you. I told her you were okay. However, she insisted she wouldn't sleep a wink until she saw you with her own eyes. She stayed for about an hour before I made her go." Nathaniel shook his head. "Miss Nolan can be a bit stubborn and…forceful."

Henry and Abby both smiled.

"I can't wait to tell Caleb," Abby said.

Nathaniel cleared his throat, glanced at her, and then looked away.

A chill slid down Abby's spine. *Something was wrong.*

"I'm sorry," Nathaniel said, "but Caleb's gone again."

Gone? "When will he be back?"

"From the way he was talking, it's doubtful that it'll be anytime soon."

Abby's breath caught in her throat. "Why?" she whispered.

He motioned her over to his desk, away from Henry, and handed her a piece of paper. "He left you a note."

She dropped into Nathaniel's chair and unfolded the paper with trembling fingers. *"Abby, I'm moving on, but I hope and pray you and Henry will find much happiness together. I'm grateful to Henry for my life, and I'll always be grateful to you and Preacher for making me understand what was missing from that life in the first place. I hope you get a chance to travel, and see all of the lovely places you've dreamed of. Have a good life, Abby. Years from now, when you remember those who loved you, please count me among them. Caleb."*

Her throat ached and tears blurred the words. Nathaniel was staring at her.

"What does he mean, 'You and Henry'?" she asked in disbelief.

"He thinks you love Henry. And that you'll be better off married to him."

Abby shot to her feet. "Why would he think that? I don't care about the money. I've said in no uncertain terms, often, that I don't love Henry." She stared down at the paper in disbelief. "I love Caleb."

Nathaniel's brow furrowed. "Does he know that you love him?"

"Of course he…" Her words trailed off. They'd not had a chance to be alone since Nash had grabbed her. *She'd never actually said the words.*

"He thinks he's doing what's best for you," Nathaniel added.

She shook her head and tried to speak, but couldn't.

"I wish he wouldn't have been so stubbornly set on leaving," Nathaniel said. "I hate to see people give up on love over a misunderstanding."

Abby scrubbed the tears from her face. "He might have given up, but I haven't. I'm going after him. Where exactly did he go?"

Nathaniel grinned at her and then turned to his desk. He wrote the address on a piece of paper and handed it to her. "Hopefully, when I see you again, I'll call you Sis."

Tears welled again as she hugged him. "Thank you, Nathaniel."

Before leaving, Abby crossed over to the examining table. Henry had fallen asleep again. She pressed a kiss to his forehead. "Take good care of him," she said over her shoulder.

"I will," Nathaniel promised.

At the boarding house she paused long enough to enjoy the sight of her mother and father working side-by-side in the kitchen, while her brother and grandmother fluttered around getting in the way. They were all laughing and talking. It was beautiful, and something that Abby knew would live in her heart and mind forever.

Upstairs, Jenna lay face-down on the cot. Fully dressed, but sound asleep. As quietly as possible, Abby pulled an old carpet bag from the wardrobe and began packing.

Jenna sat up and peered at her through puffy eyes. "Going somewhere?"

"Sorry to wake you."

Abby explained what had happened as she folded her second best dress and placed it in the bag—she would wear her best dress.

"I'm glad you're going after him," Jenna said. "And believe it or not, I'm happy for you."

"Thank you, Jenna."

While Abby gathered her hairbrush, ribbons and pins, Jenna rose and opened one of her trunks. Returning to the bedside, she pressed a wad of cash into Abby's hand. "Take this. Find that man before he does something impulsive and foolish."

Abby's mouth dropped open. "I thought you said you were broke."

Jenna shrugged. "I thought you knew I was lying."

"So why were you here?" Abby asked. "Once you knew that

Caleb wouldn't marry you, why didn't you move on somewhere better?"

Jenna glanced away. "I came here because of Caleb, but I stayed because of everyone else."

Abby hugged her, remembering what Preacher said about Jenna being "eat-up with loneliness." *The old man had been right about so many things.*

"I'm glad you did," Abby said. "And thank you for the loan. I'll pay you back as soon as I can. Now, go see Henry. He's asking for you."

"The money's a gift, and I'm on my way to Henry now." Hands on hips, Jenna added, "That doctor had better get used to me being there."

Abby laughed, and then sobered. "Please be good to Henry. He's one of the finest people I know."

Jenna's expression softened. "I will. Somehow that rube has managed to wrap me around his finger. Believe me, only true love could entice me into being a farmer's wife."

Jenna helped her finish packing, insisting that Abby take a couple of her dresses along. "Caleb's never seen these, if you're concerned about that," Jenna said. "He won't know that they're second-hand, nor will anyone else you encounter."

Abby glanced at the colorful garments and took a deep breath. "Do you have something a little more...subdued?"

Thankfully, Jenna wasn't insulted, and the less extravagant garments she returned with were lovely. "Thank you, Jenna. I can't tell you what your generosity means to me."

Jenna shrugged. "You're welcome. And I appreciate your generosity to me."

"What did I do for you?"

Jenna grinned. "You're going to lend me your bed while you're gone."

"Enjoy," Abby laughed as she fastened the bag.

Once downstairs, it took a bit of convincing before her parents would let her leave alone. "I'll go with you," her father said several times.

Her mother echoed his statement, although the way she gripped his arm suggested that without even realizing it, Irene Horton wasn't ready for her husband to leave again. And that was all right. Abby truly wanted to do this on her own. After all, Jenna had traveled all the way from Colorado by herself.

"No, I'll be fine," she assured them. "I'm only going to Austin." Her grandmother was outside with Robby, or she'd probably have had to convince her, too.

Her father cleared his throat. "I've got a few dollars I can send with you," he said. "I wish it could be more. I've already heard from the publisher and they're excited about the Latham gang story. If you can wait a few weeks, I'll have enough to finance your trip."

"As it turns out, I don't need it," Abby said. "I had a little money, and Jenna loaned me some more. I'll pay her back. I have plenty to get me to Austin."

"Okay," her father said. "But if Caleb Calhoun's already gone from there, please contact us before you head off somewhere else."

Abby agreed, and was already down the back steps when she stopped, raced back inside, past her startled parents and into the bathing room. The cherished travel case—with its pristine grooming aids—was tucked inside the carpet bag in a matter of moments.

She made her way to the train station, bought a ticket and boarded while her father's words echoed in her mind. "If Caleb Calhoun's already gone from there…"

Please, Lord. If this is Your will for my life, let me find him.

Chapter Thirty

CALEB STEPPED INTO his rented room in Austin and grappled with a curious sense of displacement. Everything had seemed perfectly normal only a few days before. He'd cleaned the place thoroughly, and bought a couple of things to brighten it up in anticipation of bringing Abby here. He'd planned on finding them a bigger place to live as soon as they returned from their honeymoon.

He had also arranged for a leave of absence from the Rangers, and had even gone so far as to tell Captain Parnell he'd be coming back with a wife.

He'd been completely wrong, and now nothing felt right.

Leaving the room, Caleb headed to the same café he always dined at while in Austin, but even the familiar food didn't taste right. He didn't finish his meal, although he left a generous tip for the harried server.

Afterwards he wandered around town. Without even making a decision to do it, he found himself standing in front of Captain Parnell's desk at Ranger headquarters.

The captain looked up, brows raised. "I thought you were in Moccasin Rock."

Caleb shrugged. "Things didn't work out like I'd hoped."

"I'm sorry to hear that," Captain said.

"Thank you."

"So what are your plans now?"

"I'd like to go ahead and take the time off, although I've decided to leave the area entirely."

Captain's brows rose. "When do you plan on coming back?"

"To be honest, I'm not sure I'm coming back."

"I hate to lose a good man," Captain said. There was sincerity in his voice. "Things got out of control with Bob Horton, yet you stuck with it, and never even showed signs of wanting to quit. I know I've given you a hard time about your method and maturity—both of which needed work—but I've never doubted your motivation. You're the kind of man the Rangers need. You'll be welcome back anytime."

Caleb was so stunned he couldn't say anything. When a tap sounded at the door, he sidestepped so the Captain could see the visitor. And he could sort his thoughts.

However, the visitor was for him. "Caleb?"

He spun around. "Abby, what are you doing here?"

Captain Parnell stood and rounded the desk. "Ah, you must be Miss Horton."

Since Caleb was already off balance, the sight of Captain with a smile on his face wasn't quite as shocking as it might have been otherwise, but it was still unnerving.

"I've got some matters that need tending to," Captain Parnell said as he grabbed his hat from a rack near the door. "Feel free to use my office for your discussion."

After he'd gone, Caleb turned to Abby. "Is Henry okay?"

"Yes, he's fine."

He let out a sigh of relief. "So why are you here?"

Abby took a deep breath, and began speaking in a rush. "I love you. I know you think I need to marry someone with money, but I don't. I know how to work hard. I'll make you a good wife."

He stared at her in astonishment. "You're proposing to me?"

She turned a lovely shade of pink, but she didn't back down. "Yes, I suppose I am."

"What about Henry?"

She gave a little groan. "What about him?"

Caleb wanted no misunderstandings. "I thought you loved him, and I thought you and he were going to travel. He has the means to do that now."

Abby sighed in frustration. "For the last time, I am not in love with Henry. I will always care for him, but I do not have romantic feelings for him. And did you honestly think money would make a difference to me?"

"No, not really."

She put a hand on each side of his face. "Caleb, please listen. I can live on practically nothing, and I can make a meal out of nearly anything. I know twelve different ways to make potatoes."

Caleb pulled her close, finally letting himself believe that it was all really happening. "I don't think it'll come to that," he laughed. "Now let me ask you a couple of questions."

"All right."

"First, are you really wanting to marry me?"

"Yes."

His heart rejoiced at the speed of that reply. No hesitation, no long discussions about details. He loved her a little more with each passing second. He kissed her.

"Now, for the second question."

She laid her head on his chest. "What's that?"

"Do you still want to see New York?"

She straightened. "Oh, I'd love to travel someday. We can do that when we're older, maybe even after our children are older."

He chuckled, and she darted a quick look at him. "Don't you want children?"

"I do, for sure. Although you're running way ahead of me.

Let's get through the wedding first. Now, do you still want to travel or not?"

"When the time is right, yes, I do."

"How about on our honeymoon?"

Her brow furrowed. "Do you mean it? I don't have my savings anymore. Can you afford to do that?"

"Definitely. I'll explain more about that later. Now tell me how Henry was doing when you left."

"Nathaniel's taking good care of him. He said Henry will make a full recovery. And I'm sure Jenna's hovering nearby, fussing over him, and making sure he has everything he needs."

"Jenna? Does that mean what I think it does?"

"Yes, those two are in love and plan to be married, probably as soon as Henry is up and around. I think they'll be good for each other."

"Me too," he murmured, letting the idea sink in. "I'm happy for them."

"And what about us?" she whispered. "Are you happy for us?"

He grinned at her. "Oh, yeah." He pulled her even closer and kissed her. "I love you, Abby."

"I love you, too."

They returned to Moccasin Rock, briefly, where their marriage ceremony was performed by Pastor Wilkie Brown. They were surrounded by friends and family, and one scruffy mutt that slipped in through the open church house doors.

Elijah and Nathaniel both stood by Caleb's side. Mrs. Horton and Miss Culpepper, both crying—happy tears they assured him—sat in the first pew with a distinctly uncomfortable looking Robby sitting between them. Caleb grinned and winked at the boy, and got a huge smile in return.

Jenna was also present, sitting with the Barnett family. Caleb laughed at the way Henry and Jenna were eyeing each other. Good to know there weren't any torches being carried for past loves. He had a feeling theirs' would be the next wedding ceremony here.

The rest of the church was packed with town folk, including Deputy Bliss Walker. Caleb chuckled as he listened to Bliss telling those around him all about the shootout on Main Street. The old man hadn't even been there. That didn't stop him from telling a good story though.

Caleb promptly forgot about everyone else, when Abby entered the church on her father's arm. Beautiful didn't quite cover the way she looked. Radiant was closer.

Bob Horton had tears in his eyes when he paused in front of Caleb. "Cherish her," was all he said.

"I will, Sir," Caleb assured him.

The next few minutes passed in a blur, but when all was said and done, Caleb and Abby were man and wife.

As they exited the church, well-wishers surrounded them. After a few minutes of back-slapping and tearful hugs, Caleb lost sight of Abby. While the others continued to visit, he searched for her, eventually finding her in the little cemetery out back.

She'd bent down to place her bouquet on Preacher's grave.

At the sound of his footsteps, she straightened and turned, a smile lighting her face at his approach.

Caleb's throat tightened as he recalled one of the conversations he'd had with the old man about finding a virtuous wife.

"I've found one, Preacher," he whispered.

Epilogue

CALEB HURRIED DOWN the crowded New York City street, head down against the chilly October wind. He reached for Abby's hand as he quickened his pace...and came up empty. He looked back to see that his bride had halted in front of a large store window.

Retracing his steps, Caleb stood beside her, curious to see what had captured her attention. Even though she'd adapted to being a wealthy woman, she'd not let him lavish her with gifts—despite his best efforts—saying she was a simple girl at heart.

Yet now, her eyes were wide as she stared at something. Leaning in to peer through the glass, he saw only a mundane assortment of household goods. It took a moment for him to realize that Abby was mesmerized by her own reflection. Caleb smiled as she tilted her head, eyes sparkling as she fingered the brim of her elegant new hat.

She lowered her hand when she noticed his reflection in the window next to her. Color filled her face as she turned that sparkling blue gaze his way. "I'm being a bit vain this morning, aren't I, Mr. Calhoun?"

"Not at all, Mrs. Calhoun. Such breath-taking sights are to be enjoyed." But he was looking at her face instead of the hat.

She slapped playfully at his arm. "Would you stop that? You'll have me so full of conceit that I won't even be able to stand myself." She glanced in the window once more. "Seriously though, isn't this the most beautiful hat you've ever seen?"

Caleb nodded, although he was positive that he could place that same hat on any number of other women and it wouldn't look remarkable at all.

Abby turned from the window and linked her arm with his as they walked the remaining two blocks to the Liberty Restaurant, her expression rapt as she studied the throng of people around them. While Caleb studied her.

They'd been married for two months, and had traveled to several of her dream destinations. She'd seen something that amazed her in every place. And now, in New York City, every single thing seemed to amaze her.

After sightseeing earlier in the day, they'd joined the throng of patrons trekking through a stretch of stores known as the Ladies' Mile. Abby had purchased toys for Robby, as well as his friend, Jamie Wilson, and all Jamie's siblings.

She'd also bought gifts for everybody at the boarding house. And she'd finally selected some clothing for herself, including a new coat and hat. Somehow, she'd managed to talk Caleb into buying a new suit. She said he looked dashing, but he felt plain awkward in his new duds and couldn't wait to change back into his denim.

Despite that, he was happier than he'd ever imagined being.

The charitable foundation had been established, and Abby was running it. After years of living a life where every penny counted, she took the responsibility seriously, and was remarkably good at it. Aunt Victoria had loved his new bride, as he'd known she would, and hadn't wanted to see them leave.

Caleb smiled down at Abby now as he ushered her inside the elegant eatery they'd selected for their midday meal. They shared a few minutes of conversation before being presented with menus. Abby opened hers, glanced at the choices, and then her lower lip began to quiver. She placed her hand over her mouth. Her fingers were trembling, too.

He dropped his own menu. "Abby, what's wrong?"

She peered at him over her fingers, big tears filling her eyes, and shook her head.

"Now, darlin' I know you're upset about something. Tell me."

She pointed to the menu. He took it from her, searching for something sob-worthy, but saw only the same items that were listed in his. Some of the dishes sounded foreign, though. Was she embarrassed that she didn't know what they were? No, that hadn't stopped her before. She'd enthusiastically sampled any number of unfamiliar foods as they'd explored their way up and down the east coast.

The tears were flowing freely now, and his chest tightened. "You're gonna have to help me here, sweetheart. I'm starting to panic."

She finally moved her hand from her mouth and murmured, "Potatoes."

He glanced down at the menu, her trembling fingers pointing to several spots where potato dishes—including Chartreuse Potatoes—were listed.

"What about them?"

She drew in an unsteady breath, and continued to stare at the menu without saying anything.

Caleb scooted his chair around the table, and leaned in close, ignoring the curious diners and wait staff. "Let me get this straight, the potatoes are making you cry?"

Abby nodded. "I can't believe I'm saying this, but I m…miss the boarding house."

Relief rushed through him. "Oh." He patted her back. "Then let's go home."

She drew back with a gasp. "You mean it?"

He nodded. "I do. I only wanted to travel because you wanted to. I've seen all this. If you're done, so am I. If you want to return to Moccasin Rock and stay there the rest of our lives, then I'm fine with that."

She stared at him, eyes wide. "What about your job? Can you work for the Rangers from there?"

"I think something could be worked out. Though to be honest, even if it can't, I'll be fine. Maybe I'll see if Eli needs another deputy. If not, I've been thinking for a while about trying my hand at ranching anyway."

"Ranching?"

"Yep. Eli bought some property just to the west of Moccasin Rock, and he's building a house out there. He works on it every chance he gets. There's more land available, and I wouldn't mind building out there, too." He looked at her, worried about her reaction. "Do you think you could learn to love ranch life?"

She gave him a hug. "I think I'll love any kind of life, as long as it's with you."

Grinning, he returned his chair to the original position. "Good, then it's settled. You need to be near your folks, and I'll get a chance to become better acquainted with Eli and Nathaniel. I know their lives haven't been easy, however I get the feeling there's something more there. Something happened that still haunts them. I want to help them if I can."

Abby squeezed his hand. "I think that's a wonderful idea. Plus, I bet they're going to want us near when the baby comes."

He nodded, and gestured to the menus. "Let's order and eat, and then I'll make all the arr…" He stopped. "What did you say?"

She smiled. "I think they'll want us around when our baby is born. They're going to make wonderful uncles, I just know it."

Caleb cleared his throat, his heartbeat picking up speed. "And how soon do you think that'll be?"

"About seven months from now, if the hotel's doctor is correct."

A grin spread across his face, followed by a whoop of joy. The startled waiter headed their way.

"Can I be of assistance, sir?"

Caleb nodded. "Yes, my good man, please bring us some of your finest potatoes."

The man was well-trained. Only a quirk of one brow indicated the request might be an odd one. "Certainly, sir. Any particular way you'd like them prepared?"

Caleb looked at Abby, one brow raised. "What do you say?"

"Any way at all is fine," Abby said with a heartfelt sigh. "As long as I don't have to peel them."

Caleb grinned as the waiter retreated. "What if I decide I want potatoes with every meal once we get home?"

Abby batted her eyelashes and gave him a coy smile. "I happen to know for a fact you can peel a potato."

He laughed and nodded. "That I can."

She suddenly sobered. Grasping his hand, she gave it a squeeze. "But I will be glad to do it," she said. "I will consider it a labor of love."

AUTHOR BIO

A seventh-generation Texan, Laura Conner Kestner spent 25 years in community journalism before deciding to pursue a career in fiction. She's a member of the American Christian Fiction Writers and Romance Writers of America. Laura's won several writing awards, including the 2016 ACFW Genesis Award for contemporary romance, the 2017 Daphne du Maurier award for excellence in mystery/suspense, and the 2016 RWA SARA Emma Merritt award for inspirational romance (for Remember Texas). She was a 2017 RWA GOLDEN HEART® finalist, and a double GOLDEN HEART® finalist in 2018. For more information, or to contact Laura, please visit http://lauraconnerkestner.com